The room was small. On
No furniture or cameras or
identity of her captors. Th
tion window set too high f
of ceiling.

She heard voices in the hall, soft, and then footsteps.
Closer and closer until the doorknob rattled. Jean closed her
eyes. She heard someone enter.

"He still out?" said a man. He had a rough voice, gritty
like a hard smoker.

"Probably pretending," said another. Jean heard shoes
scuff the floor. She peered through her lashes and saw black
shoes and dark blue pants. Cologne tickled her nostrils.

"Hey," said the first man, nudging her ribs with his toe.
"Hey, Jeff. You out?"

Quiet laughter. "Idiot. You actually expect him to say
yes?"

The two men stood close together, relaxed and unafraid.
Perfect. Jean shot out her legs and slammed her socked
heels into a knee. She heard a very satisfying crunch, a sharp
howl, and then she rolled left as the second man tried to
subdue her. He was slow—but then, so was Jean. Her body
felt clumsy, unfamiliar; she barely managed to gather
enough momentum to stand, and by that point, the man—
large, muscular, with a flat square face—was too close for
her to maneuver. She saw his fist speed toward her face—
was able to turn just slightly—and got clipped hard enough
to slam her into the wall. A low *whuff* of air escaped her
throat, and the sound of that partial cry made her forget
pain, capture—everything but her voice.

A man's voice, slipped free from her throat. Deep,
hoarse, and horrifying. . . .

X-MEN®
DARK
MIRROR

a novel by
Marjorie M. Liu

based on the
Marvel Comic Book

POCKET STAR BOOKS
New York   London   Toronto   Sydney

An *Original* Publication of POCKET BOOKS

 A Pocket Star Book published by
POCKET BOOKS, a division of Simon & Schuster, Inc.
1230 Avenue of the Americas, New York, NY 10020

This book is a work of fiction. Names, characters, places and incidents are products of the author's imagination or are used fictitiously. Any resemblance to actual events or locales or persons living or dead is entirely coincidental.

ISBN-13: 978-1-4165-1063-5
ISBN-10:   1-4165-1063-X

This Pocket Star Books paperback edition January 2006

10 9 8 7 6 5 4 3 2 1

Cover design by John Vairo Jr.
Cover illustration by Ashley Wood

Manufactured in the United States of America

For information regarding special discounts for bulk purchases, please contact Simon & Schuster Special Sales at 1-800-456-6798 or business@simonandschuster.com.

To Kielle, who is missed by so many—
and to Amaranth, who will smile when she sees this

1

IN HER FIRST MOMENT OF CONSCIOUSNESS, BEFORE opening her eyes to the world and discovering such things as floors and walls and straitjackets, Jean Grey imagined she had died; that for all she had suffered in her life, all her terrible sacrifices, the final end would offer nothing but an eternity of suffocation, an unending crushing darkness spent in utter isolation.

Her mind was blind. She felt nothing. Heard nothing. Not even Scott. Cut off, like a blade had been dropped on her neck, separating life from thought, life from sensation, life from—*Scott?*—life.

The remembrance of flesh came to her slowly. She became aware of her legs, curled on a flat hard surface; her hands, tucked close and warm against a hard body. *Her* body, though it felt odd, unfamiliar. Not right.

Jean opened her eyes. She saw a cracked white wall decorated by the shadows of chicken wire. She smelled bleach, and beneath that scent, urine. She felt something sticky beneath her cheek. Her head was strange—not just her mind, but her actual head—and her hair rasped against her cheek. No silken strands, but rough, like stub-

ble. Her mouth felt different, too; her teeth grated un-
evenly. Her jaw popped.

Jean could not move her arms. This concerned her
until she realized she was not paralyzed. Her arms were
simply restrained against her chest, bound tight within
white sleeves that crisscrossed her body like an arcane
corset. Again, she tried to reach out with her mind beyond the isolation of silent mental darkness—*Scott, where
are you, what has happened*—to find some trace of that
living golden thread that was a thought, a presence, a—*I
am not alone*—

As a child, alone was all Jean wanted to be. Alone in
her head, alone in her heart, alone with no voices whispering incessantly of their fears and dreams and sins.
Funny, how things could change. Her wishes had grown
up.

Jean tried to roll into a sitting position. Slow, so slow—
her head throbbed, a wicked pain like she had been
struck—and she fought down nausea, swallowing hard.
She had to get her feet back, get free and away, away to
find the others. It did not matter where she was or who
had done this—*results, results are all that matter*—only
that it could not be allowed to continue.

Scott will be looking for me.

Yes, if he could. Jean's last memory of her husband
was his strong profile as he gazed up at the dilapidated
brick façade of an old mental hospital, sagging on its
foundations in a quiet neighborhood located beside the
industrial hinterland between Tacoma and Seattle. Disturbing reports of rising mutant and human tensions had

trickled in from the Northwest for weeks, but without anything specific enough to warrant a full investigation—or interference—from the X-Men.

Until two days ago. Logan had learned through an old contact that mutants were being arrested on false charges and incarcerated in state mental hospitals. Serious accusations, with no real hard evidence—except a name.

Belldonne. An institute for the mentally ill, and a place—according to Logan's contact—where the X-Men would find incontrovertible evidence that mutants were being held against their will.

"And if it's true, then it ain't no holiday they're having," Logan had said. Because prison was bad enough—but add doctors, the ominous specter of science, experimentation, and the scenario became much worse. Mutants, despite the law protecting them, were still easy fodder for overeager scientists who wanted nothing more than to see, in the flesh, the why and how of extreme mutation. Jean understood the fascination. She simply did not think it was an excuse for unscrupulous behavior.

The room was small. One window, covered in fine mesh. No furniture or cameras or anything at all that revealed the identity of her captors. The door had a small glass observation window set too high for Jean to see much but a snatch of ceiling.

She heard voices in the hall, soft, and then footsteps. Closer and closer until the doorknob rattled. Jean closed her eyes. She heard someone enter.

"He still out?" said a man. He had a rough voice, gritty like a hard smoker.

"Probably pretending," said another. Jean heard shoes scuff the floor. She peered through her lashes and saw black shoes and dark blue pants. Cologne tickled her nostrils.

"Hey," said the first man, nudging her ribs with his toe. "Hey, Jeff. You out?"

Quiet laughter. "Idiot. You actually expect him to say yes?"

The two men stood close together, relaxed and unafraid. Perfect. Jean shot out her legs and slammed her socked heels into a knee. She heard a very satisfying crunch, a sharp howl, and then she rolled left as the second man tried to subdue her. He was slow—but then, so was Jean. Her body felt clumsy, unfamiliar; she barely managed to gather enough momentum to stand, and by that point, the man—large, muscular, with a flat square face—was too close for her to maneuver. She saw his fist speed toward her face—was able to turn just slightly—and got clipped hard enough to slam her into the wall. A low *whuff* of air escaped her throat, and the sound of that partial cry made her forget pain, capture—everything but her voice.

A man's voice, slipped free from her throat. Deep, hoarse, and horrifying. It had to be wrong, her imagination: The man with the broken kneecap howled, screaming so loud her own voice must have been drowned out, swallowed up, and yes, that was right, that had to be it—

A strong hand grabbed her hair and crashed her forehead against the wall. Her skull rattled; sound passed her lips, and still it was the same, an impossible rumbling baritone that was not her voice, not feminine in the slightest.

"Hold still," muttered the man, pinning her against the wall. "Jesus, Jeff."

"Who are you?" she asked, listening to herself speak. Chills rushed through her arms and she glanced down, seeing what she had taken for granted upon waking, never noticing, never paying any serious attention to the changes she felt in her body.

Not my body. Not my body.

No breasts, a thick waist, strong broad legs. The ends of black dreadlocks, hanging over her left shoulder.

Her captor did not answer. He was breathing too hard. His companion lay on the floor, muffled screams puffing from between his clenched teeth. Jean heard footsteps outside the room: people running, drawn by the sounds of violence.

"Please," Jean said, listening to herself speak in a stranger's voice. She wanted to vomit. "Where am I?"

The man shook his head. "I thought you were getting better. No wonder Maguire wanted you restrained."

The door banged open. Three men entered; one of them held a nightstick, another had a syringe. She recognized their uniforms.

"Don't," Jean said, staring at the syringe. "I'm calm now. I'm better."

"Sorry." The man pushed her harder against the wall. "No one's going to take a risk on you now."

Jean struggled. Without her powers, she lived in a state of semi-unconsciousness. To take that one step fur-

ther—again—without knowing where the others were—
Scott—or what had happened to put her in another person's body, was more than she could bear.

She was outnumbered and in a straitjacket. Perhaps the men showed surprise that the person they were accustomed to dealing with displayed sophisticated tricks in fighting them off, but they were tough and used to unruly patients. They subdued Jean. They subdued the man they called Jeff. And as Jean felt the sharp prick of the syringe in the side of her neck, she silently called out to her husband, to her friends, to anyone who might be listening, and then, still fighting, felt herself borne down to the hard floor like a slippery fish, slipping swiftly through the curtain of darkness into a deeper unconscious.

2

SCOTT SUMMERS WAS ACCUSTOMED TO DARKNESS. Voluntarily blind, he had long ago learned to curb any and all desire to open his eyes without the protection of his ruby quartz glasses. His was a killing strength—that fire, that sun-fed light in his eyes. People got hurt when he looked at them. People died.

A bad way to live for a man with a conscience. Easier to live life through ruby-quartz glasses and accept the darkness when required. Like now. He was not wearing his visor. Nothing at all covered his eyes. Bad. Very bad.

Scott touched his face, pressing fingertips against his eyelids, afraid to trust himself without that lingering pressure. He listened to the world around him. At first, silence. An unfamiliar quiet, without the kinds of noises one grew accustomed to in certain situations and locales. At home in Westchester, the insects sang like bells all through the dry summer, a constant clipped symphony outside his window through the day and night. Somewhere, too, there was always a familiar voice talking; laughter, maybe, or the distant rumble of a movie. Comfortable sounds, like family. Like Jean, breathing quietly beside him, her body warm.

Not here, though. Not now. He was cold and alone.

Scott mentally reached for his wife. She did not reach back. There was no golden thread flaring bright hot, no soft touch upon his heart. A complete disconnect, as though all those years spent linked together were nothing but fantasy, a fairy tale for a lonely man. It felt like Jean was dead.

Scott sat up. His head hurt. His heart hurt worse. As he moved, he noticed something strange about his body, something very disturbing. Something that he should have noticed right away, because such was the nature of his loss.

He was missing certain . . . parts. He also had some new ones. He touched them. His hands moved lower, still probing.

"Oh, God," Scott said, and his voice was high and sweet. He took a chance and opened his eyes. Nothing happened. He could see like a normal man, with normal colors, without explosions and beams of cutting light. He looked down and saw small white hands resting in a cotton pajama lap, hands that were attached to slender arms that rose, rose to a body that had . . .

Scott stood up. He was in a small white room. No lights on, just nighttime shadows. There was a cot behind him, a spindly table on his right. No other furniture. One tall window, chicken wire hugging the glass. Very industrial. It reminded him of the orphanage where he had spent much of his youth.

Again, he forced himself to look down at his body.

No. This is not my body at all.

Not unless he had developed the ability to shape-shift into a woman. Which, considering everything he knew about himself, was highly unlikely.

So. Someone had done this to him, a separation of his physical and mental identities. And if him, then what about the others? The last thing he remembered was standing in front of the Belldonne mental hospital with his team—Jean, Logan, Rogue, and Kurt—all of them looking to him for the final word on their approach, their handling of intelligence that said mutants were being un-fairly imprisoned in the building in front of them.

Yes, well.

Scott walked to the door. He had to stand on his toes to peer through the observation window. He could see only a small portion of the hall, which was empty, devoid of any decoration or color. Dimly lit, white and sterile. He tried the doorknob but it would not turn. Scott glanced around the room, looking for something he could turn into a lock pick. He came up empty, until he realized what he was wearing.

Scott took off his bra. He tried not to look at his breasts—or rather, the breasts of the strange woman he seemed to be inhabiting—because that was wrong and impolite and . . . God. So bizarre.

The bra had wires. He pried them both out, tucking one in the waistband of his underwear—*no looking, no looking, you will get your own body back*—twisting the other into something resembling an actual tool. Scott was suddenly very grateful for all those long training sessions with Gambit, in which learning to pick a lock, to survive on nothing but a piece of wire and will, was essential to winning.

The lock was easy. Scott cracked open the door and held his breath, listening. Nothing but quiet. He slipped from the room into the empty hall, devoid of anything but doors. White floors, white cracked walls, cold and easy to clean. No security cameras. For a moment, the flickering fluorescent lighting hurt Scott's eyes. He rubbed at them, trying to cope with his new ability to see in color. What little there was, anyway.

Scott did not know where to go, only that he had to move, had to learn why he was here, how, what had happened to the rest of his team—*Jean*—then get out, run, make things right. Scott was good at making things right. You had to be, when you led the X-Men.

Somewhere distant, a man screamed. Startled, a cry of pain. Scott heard shouting. Careful, his feet small and covered only in thin white socks, he loped down the hall after those sounds—and oh, it was strange moving in that body, that unfamiliar shell with its foreign muscles and rhythms and parts. He could not reconcile his mind to the loss of its physical home, had trouble staying focused on the now, when everything about him was strange and new.

Despite the turmoil ahead of him, the hall remained empty. It was a familiar emptiness, one he associated with his youth. In places where the inhabitants lacked control over their own lives, nighttime meant lockdown, enforced rest. Easier for the graveyard shift, few in number and too underpaid to care about bathroom trips or nightmares.

You are not a child anymore. You are not in the orphanage.

No. He was in a mental hospital. Belldonne, if he was not mistaken. He had studied the blueprints of the place during the short flight to Seattle and it was easy for his mind to translate the two-dimensional lines, the pictures of halls and rooms and stairs, into something concrete, physical. When one had a power like his—creating light that could ricochet, bounce, reflect—one learned very quickly how to visualize the reality of things.

And the reality of this institution was exactly how he had envisioned the physical promise of the blueprint design. Which meant, except for not knowing what floor he was on, that he could easily get in and out of Belldonne. The bigger problem was that he did not know if the rest of his team was in here with him. Until he found out more, he could not afford to take the chance of leaving them behind.

And if you are the only one here? What if there is another person—this woman—looking out through your eyes? Using your powers? Interacting with the others?

That would be bad. He wondered where his body was. He wondered where Jean was, if she was still herself and had noticed the change in his mind. If anyone could fix this, it would be her.

The hospital was not very big. Scott, still following the rumble of concerned voices, those cries of pain, finally drew near enough to hear actual words, like: "careful," and "get ready." A doorknob rattled and Scott peered around a corner in the hall to watch as three men entered a room.

He heard sounds of a struggle—more shouting—and then, after several minutes, a deep quiet broken only by the sobs of a hurting man. Scott remained very still.

The door opened. Two men emerged, carrying another between them. Scott thought his leg might be broken: The injured man could not stop whimpering. Scott got ready to run, but the hospital employees moved down the hall in the opposite direction. The door opened again. Two more men emerged, one of them saying, "He's never been this violent. I thought Maguire was kidding us when he said to straitjacket him."

"He said the same thing to me about Mindy, that I should take precautions, that she might go wacko. Can you believe that?"

"Mindy?" He sounded shocked. "What the hell?"

"Exactly. I didn't do it, either. Maguire doesn't know everything."

"He predicted Jeff. You should have heard him, too. He even talked different."

"Whatever. That shot'll keep him down until tomorrow. Let the day shift handle the rest of his shit."

"Yeah," said the man, though he did not sound happy about it.

They left. Scott listened to the quiet footfalls fade into silence. The old hospital ticked and creaked around him; somewhere distant, another person cried out. A woman, this time. She sounded like she was having a nightmare. Maybe she would wake up on her own, maybe not. Scott knew what that was like.

He peered around the corner at the door. The lights

were off in this section of the hall; a money saver, to only light every other corridor. Hoping no one else would return, Scott left his hiding place. Exploring the hospital no longer seemed as important as the troublesome patient inside that room, because if he had been body-snatched, then why not the rest of his team?

You're drawing too many conclusions. You need facts.

And he had one: The hospital employees had been surprised by the patient's behavior. Something about this "Jeff" was different, and though it might be nothing more than a chemical imbalance, Scott had to check it out. He could not take the chance that he might be passing up a friend—or his wife. He desperately hoped Jean was okay.

The door was locked, but he still had his little wire. He worked fast.

The room he entered was far bleaker than the one he had awakened in. There was no furniture, no comforts of any kind. In the middle of the cracked dirty floor lay a large man. Dark skin, dreadlocks. Straitjacket pulled tight. There was some blood at the corner of his mouth.

Scott crouched beside the limp figure, studying that face, wondering if this was stupid, how it could be possible that anyone he knew was trapped inside that body.

You're inside a woman, he reminded himself. *It's possible.*

Cautious, listening for any movement outside in the hall, Scott crouched beside the man. "Hey" he said, shaking that thick shoulder. "Hey . . . Logan?"

Hey, nothing. Scott sighed. This was a dead end, at least until the man—Jeff—woke up. Until then, he had to keep moving, try to figure out why and how he was here. Maybe even fulfill the intent of his mission and discover if there were mutants being kept against their will.

Ha, ha. Funny.

Scott left the room with its sleeping man. He did not look back.

The thing about institutions of any kind—orphanage, nursing home, mental hospital—was that the staff always gossiped about the individuals in their care. It was inevitable, the best catharsis available, and even though such discussions were discouraged so as to prevent any potential mean-spiritedness, Scott knew all too well that it was impossible to curb a tongue in need of wagging. As a child, he himself had been the focus of adult gossip, sometimes pleasant—sometimes not. He knew how the game was played.

Which meant that just before dawn he returned to his room and waited for the staff to come check on him. It was difficult, but Scott was good at being patient, at waiting on moments. He had excellent control.

There was sunlight streaming through his window when the door finally rattled and a woman entered. She was short and plump, with a round dark face and squinting eyes. She gave the impression of being difficult, rough, but she smiled when she saw Scott and her voice was loud and cheerful as she said, "Good morning, Mindy. How did you sleep?"

Mindy. Scott remembered that name. He said, "I slept fine, thank you."

The woman's smile disappeared and she stared at him, unblinking. Scott thought, *Oh no*, and tried to look dumb.

"You talked," she said.

Scott said nothing. He looked down at his hands, folded primly in his lap. He wished he knew how Mindy usually sat, her expressions and behavior. He did not want any special attention, no trouble. He did not want to be the focus of the gossip he so desperately wanted to hear.

The woman drew near. "Mindy," she said, and placed her hands under Scott's chin to force his head up. He refused to look into her eyes. *Shy*, he thought. *Maybe this Mindy is shy.*

"Mindy," she said again. "Say something else." Scott stayed silent, and after a long moment the woman sighed, releasing him with a shove. "Yeah, you be stupid for another day. Suits you fine, I guess."

It did suit him, just fine. Scott glanced at the tag on her uniform. PALMER, it said, in big letters. Nurse Palmer.

"Come on." She stepped back from the bed. "Dr. Maguire wants you supervised while he's on vacation, but I don't have time for that. You just follow your routine, Mindy, and we won't have a problem. Right? Go on, now. Get washed up and then head down to the recreation room. They've got music there today."

Scott did not need to be told twice, though he was circumspect in his movements, trying to take on an air of quiet timidity that he hoped was like the real Mindy. He had a feeling he was doing a lousy job. Though he did not look at Nurse Palmer, he felt her studying him, and her scrutiny made him uncomfortable.

She did not say anything, though, and when Scott shuffled down the hall toward the women's bathroom—a door he had passed, and almost entered, during his nighttime excursion—Nurse Palmer turned and strode away in the other direction. She unlocked the door next to Scott's room, and entered with much the same greeting.

At least you know more than you did before. Even if it was not much, although if Nurse Palmer's reaction was any indication, Mindy had a completely nonthreatening reputation that meant he could run circles around the hospital and its staff and not get into very much trouble.

The bathroom felt more like a locker room, complete with open showers and toilet stalls. The air smelled warm, moist. Scott looked at himself in the long mirror above the sinks.

His first reaction was to shout, to close his eyes—and indeed, some strangled sound did pass his lips, though his gaze never wavered from the fine feminine features staring back at him from the mirror. Pale skin, high cheekbones framed by short black hair. Brown eyes. Mindy's face looked Asian; Chinese, perhaps. She was . . . pretty.

He shuddered, finally looking away. He could not stand to see himself, to gaze through those strange eyes and know who he was, trapped inside a stranger's body. It was too surreal, too disturbing. He felt lost. Mortal, even, in a way he never had before. It was the ultimate violation, a stripping away of the illusion that he had any control over his life, his body.

He turned and walked to the toilets. His bladder hurt. It was not easy, relieving himself, but he managed.

He washed his hands, his face—trying so hard not to look at himself again—and then left the bathroom. He followed his memories of the blueprints, walking down the long corridor until he found a wide set of stairs. Scott heard voices; the hospital was waking up. Indeed, by the time he reached the first floor, the halls were already filled with shuffling, talking, weeping, staring, bodies. Nurses and security guards mingled among the patients, but many of the staff gathered at various stations located throughout the corridor. Most looked tired; they clutched mugs of coffee and watched the patients with dull eyes.

The most alert employees seemed to be located at the nurses' station across from the recreation room, which also doubled as the dining hall. A small line of patients stood before a utilitarian service line, holding trays and taking food from several women who stood behind a low stainless-steel wall. Scott's stomach growled. He got in line.

"Yo, yo, yo," muttered the short man in front of him. He had wild hair and bulging eyes, hollow cheeks covered in a light beard peppered with silver. "Yo, Mindy. You got a pencil on you?"

Scott said nothing and the man whispered, "Yo, shit. Shit, shit, shit. Mindy, you got some shit on you?" He began laughing, loud, with a hint of hysteria.

"Shut the hell up," someone said. A woman. Scott turned, and had to look up to see the tanned face, the hard green eyes and unforgiving mouth. He felt very short.

The woman smiled, tight-lipped, and looked over

Scott's head at the—now silent—heckler. He clutched his tray to his chest and swallowed hard.

"Yeah," she said softly. "Yeah, you be quiet now. Got that?"

He nodded. Scott would have nodded, too, if he was that man. This woman looked like she could break him in half and smoke on his bones for breakfast. Which made him wonder.

"Logan?" he asked. The woman gave him a strange look.

"When did *you* start talking? And no, I'm no Logan." She shoved her finger into Scott's shoulder. "Do I look like a man?"

Scott shook his head and turned quickly away. He picked up a tray and took the plastic-wrapped egg and biscuit sandwich handed to him by one of the cooks. She also gave him an apple and a box of orange juice. Finger foods only, apparently. No silverware, no sharp pointy objects.

"Hey!" The woman held up her sandwich and stared at the cook. "Thought I told you girls I'm a vegetarian."

She received no response. Scott got the feeling this was something they heard on a regular basis. The woman muttered and nudged Scott with her elbow. "Come on. Freaks are animal murderers. One of these days I'll make *them* into chop suey and see how they like eating it."

Which might be difficult, seeing as how they would presumably be *dead* when she was through with them. Scott did not point that out. He dutifully followed the taller woman as she led him to an empty plastic table by

the window. The chairs were also plastic, covered in vi-
brant colors that distracted Scott. His eyes hurt, looking at
those chairs, but he felt hunger, too, for the rich variety of
blue and green and yellow. Jean sometimes let him see
the world through her eyes, but this was better. He had
forgotten how clear and sharp the color yellow could be,
that snap of green shine in the apple.

The woman snagged the only red chair—a red that
was better, richer, with more variance and warmth than
he remembered—and went to another table to grab a
second of the same color for Scott. She pushed away all
the other chairs until they clogged the walking space
around their table. Some of the patients gave her dirty
looks; the rest did not seem to care or notice.

"Red's best," she said, turning her chair around so that
she straddled it. "Red is hot. It's like fire."

Scott nodded, unwrapping his breakfast. Red was
good, except when it was the only color you could count
on seeing for the rest of your life.

He glanced around the dining room. He would have
preferred to sit closer to the nurses' station; all the good
gossip would be there, every little complaint and nu-
anced praise. If any of the patients were acting unusual,
that was the best place to find out. Still, he did not want
to upset the woman, and she seemed to like . . . Mindy. A
couple minutes, then. Surely she would get bored with
him before long.

But she did not get bored, and over the next half hour
proceeded to tell Scott everything about herself, smoothly,
and with enough practice that she sounded rehearsed, like

the words spilling out of her were tradition, some game she played, like—*last night they made me go around in the circle and say my name is Rachel, like I'm a Gemini, which means I'm nuts, and yeah, I showed them my scars, said "see these scars, these scars on my arm," and no that's not from drugs, stupid, not from anything like that, because it was done to me here, you know, like they give you all this medicine in your ass, just go JABBING it in when they want you to calm down, but I ask nice so they give it to me in the arm or with pills, you know, to help me think better, which is such shit because I think just fine, really just fine, and they're a bunch of meat-eating Nazis in this place and why the hell are you eating that egg, Holy Crap, they turned you into one of them, Mindy, give me that trash, don't put that in your body*—which meant that all Scott got was a scrap of biscuit and an apple, and that was enough to make him irritated.

He was just getting ready to give up and switch tables, when Rachel looked behind him, frowned, and said, "That's weird."

Scott, at this point uncaring about how the real Mindy would and would not act, turned in his chair to look. He did not see anything out of the ordinary, and said, "Who?"

Rachel stared at him. "You *are* talking."

Scott ignored that. "Who is acting weird?"

Rachel, still looking like the Antichrist was speaking out of Mindy's mouth, said, "Renny. He's like you. Doesn't talk worth shit. But he's over there now, chatting up a love storm with little blond Betty."

Scott looked, and sure enough he saw a slender dark-skinned man leaning over the shoulder of an older blond woman. She was smiling, he was smiling, and Scott thought they both looked like they were having far too much fun to be one of his X-Men. Surely, if one of his team had been kidnapped, they would not be using this as an excuse to flirt.

Yeah, right. He stood up. Rachel said, "What the hell?"

Scott said, "I'll be back," and he walked over to the man called Renny. He was peripherally aware of the nurses watching from their station, and remembered the conversation he had overheard the previous night. The doctor had asked that Mindy be carefully observed, something the graveyard shift had scoffed at. Maybe the day shift scoffed, too, but Scott still felt their hard gazes. He was most likely giving them something to talk about now. Mindy was acting out of character.

Scott got close enough to hear Betty giggle and say, "I love your new accent," and then he was right up against Renny's side, and the man looked down into Scott's eyes and there was a gleam there, this hint of a smile that was so familiar it made him wonder about souls and personalities and too many other existential matters that he had no time for, and Scott said, "Kurt?"

Teeth flashed. A slender hand reached up to touch the tip of a brown round ear. "*Ja*, it's a miracle. . . . Scott?"

"How did you know?" He grinned, unable to stop himself from looking so happy. He *was* happy, thrilled to finally know he was not alone in this place.

"The face is different, but something else remains."

Kurt smiled, clapping his hand on Scott's shoulder. He drew him away from Betty, who watched them leave with a pout. "It is good to see you."

"We need to find the others," Scott said, quieter. "Assuming, of course, that we're all here."

"It would make no sense to take only two of us, especially *us* two. We are strong, Scott, but not quite as threatening as Jean, Rogue, or Logan. No, no. The others must be somewhere near."

"Any idea how this happened?"

Kurt shook his head. It was disconcerting to see this stranger speak and act with Kurt's mannerisms, but Scott pretended it was the work of an image inducer, that their new bodies were a hologram, some odd camouflage hiding their true selves. It was easier that way, though not terribly honest.

Kurt's gaze flickered, which gave Scott enough warning to turn. Rachel was approaching fast. She looked intense.

"A friend?" Kurt asked mildly. Scott did not have time to answer. Rachel stopped in front of him with her fists planted on her hips and an ugly tilt to her hard mouth.

"You've been holding out on me," she said. "Bitch."

"I don't understand," Scott said.

"All this time you could talk and you never said anything to me? And now, with this lowlife, you're all coochy-coo? After all I've done to help your ass? Screw that. I'm sorry, but that's frickin' rude."

"Wait," Scott said. "Rachel—"

She took a swing at him. Scott blocked the blow, instinct pouring through foreign muscles, making them work in ways they were not accustomed. Mindy was not a physically strong woman; Scott had to readjust, but he was too slow—Rachel got in one good blow, straight to his gut. He heard shouting, Kurt's accent in an unfamiliar voice, and then white—white uniforms gathering, pushing, and Rachel screaming obscenities as she was carried to the ground, slammed on her stomach with her face pressed into linoleum and the back of her jammies yanked down so that some woman could stick a needle into her pasty backside.

And then Kurt was there, helping Scott to his feet. Behind them, a woman laughed. Low, soft, and sweetly sensual. Familiar.

"Sugah, sugah," said a raspy voice, which was not as recognizable. "I knew if I looked for a fight, I'd find you boys."

Scott and Kurt turned. Rogue smiled.

3

ROGUE, OF COURSE, LOOKED LIKE A STRANGER. SHE was tall and sinewy, with a weather-beaten face that was all hard wrinkles and light scars. A fighter's face, with gray eyes and short-cropped silver hair. Her body was lean— no soft curves, no youthful figure, just some breasts and narrow hips. But her laugh, that smile . . .

It was eerie, how much of Rogue came through on the stranger, as though the woman he knew and valued as a friend had become a ghost pressed to flesh; insubstantial, but with enough presence to be seen by a keen eye. Scott did not think the same could be said of him. At least, he hoped not.

"Kurt," Rogue said, staring at the man who had been Renny. "I know that accent anywhere."

"I'm Scott," Scott said, unsure she would recognize the person behind Mindy's face. His stomach hurt like hell. Rachel packed a hard punch. He wondered if he felt the pain more intensely because of his new body; he never remembered his old scuffles hurting quite this much.

Rogue smiled, revealing yellow teeth. "I knew that. Logan would never have let that gal get in a punch, and if it was Jean, there wouldn't have been a fight. Odds were for it being you."

Kurt laughed. Scott shot him a glare.

One of the nurses approached Scott; the leg of his blue uniform was flecked with blood and his face looked drawn, tired. His tag said PENN. "Are you hurt, Mindy?"

"No," Scott said, and kicked himself for once again opening his big mouth. Still, it was inevitable—he had been seen speaking to several different individuals over the past few minutes, and if Mindy was as quiet as everyone seemed to believe, then someone was going to start asking questions sooner rather than later. Better to get it over with now.

Nurse Penn gave him an odd look, but did not comment on Mindy's newfound propensity to talk. He studied the other two patients standing beside Scott, moving only slightly when his colleagues brushed past with Rachel hanging limp in their arms. His gaze never wavered.

"Now this is interesting," he said. "Mindy, Renny, and Crazy Jane, all together, holding an actual conversation. Mindy's no trouble, but you other two? Gotta say this combo has me scratching my head."

"Maybe we're getting better," Rogue said, still sounding like a Southern chain-smoking biker queen.

"Yeah." Penn laughed, rubbing his jaw. "Thing is, just last week you tried to strangle Renny with your bra, and the week before that you had someone run interference while you cornered him in the men's bathroom and made to rip off his balls. Man usually cries when he sees you now."

"Ah," Kurt said. "I cried earlier."

"And then I made him stop," Rogue said. "We're friends now."

"Practically siblings," Kurt said, slinging an arm over her shoulders. Scott coughed. Penn frowned.

"Something's not right here," he said. "Really not right. Doc Maguire told us to watch out for you guys. Said we should lock you up in the quiet rooms. Now, I don't like doing that unless there's good call for it, but you mess up—you even blink at each other wrong—and I'll have your asses hauled off so fast you won't know what hit you."

"Dr. Maguire," Scott said slowly, recalling that name from the night before. "Is he here for us to see?" Because he found it very curious that one man could have singled them out. Very curious, considering what had happened to each and every one of them.

Again, Penn frowned. "He's on vacation. Thought you knew that, Mindy. Course, you never talk much so it's hard to tell just what goes through your head."

Scott said nothing, just tucked his chin in a close approximation of shyness. He fussed with the hem of his shirt with small pale hands. Shy and nervous, small and sick, nonthreatening as a little kitten.

Penn sighed. "Sorry. I'm glad you're making progress. Really. If you need to see someone, there's a doc coming in this afternoon. Okay?"

" 'Kay," Scott mumbled, well aware of the suspicious twitch around Kurt's mouth. In his smallest voice—which he discovered was quite small and very timid—he said, "Dr. Maguire knew I was going to get better? Did he . . . did he say who else?"

"Oh," said the man, uncomfortable. "He didn't actually say you were going to get better. Remember? Quiet rooms, Mindy."

Scott nodded, still looking down at the ground. Meek, ever so meek. "But I'm not alone?"

"No, kid. You're not alone." He looked sorry he had said anything, and began backing away. Scott could not let him leave. He needed those names.

"Who else?" he asked softly, finally looking him in the eyes. "*Please.*"

It was like catching a deer in headlights. Scott would never have been able to get away with this in his own body, but Mindy had a history here, a presence, and Penn slowly said, "He put out the call on you three and Jeff. Jeff and Patty. So far those two have lived up to the warning. We've got our eyes on the rest of you. Doc is almost never wrong."

Your "doc" sounds like suspect number one, Scott thought, lowering his gaze. Nurse Penn walked away, but not far. He stopped at the station where some other employees waited, still holding coffee mugs, still with keen gazes as they surveyed the room and its milling patients. Rachel's outburst had been an unmemorable ripple in their morning; nothing more, nothing less.

Scott turned so that his back was to the nurses and security guards. "I know where Jeff is. We need to find this Patty."

"Jean and Logan," Rogue murmured. "What the heck happened to us, Scott? Where are our real bodies?"

Kurt made a deep sound, low in his throat. "*Meine*

freunde, until we find our old selves, these *are* our real bodies."

"Thanks for the reminder," Scott said, still trying to ignore his breasts. "Okay, then. Kurt, I want you to find out as much as you can about Dr. Maguire. Rogue, look for this Patty. Be discreet. You've already got a reputation and we don't want you locked up. I'm going to see if I can get in to see Jeff."

Rogue frowned. "What if they're the wrong people? Might be a coincidence that doctor named us."

"I don't believe in coincidence," Scott said. "We'll meet back here in an hour."

Interesting, living in a stranger's skin. Rogue, much to her surprise, found that she did not like it. An old fantasy, to be sure: being another person for a day, someone normal. No mutant powers, no burdens. Just a regular life and an ordinary body covered in delightful, touchable, skin.

She was a good daydreamer. Fantasies full with the thrill of titillation, acting upon the forbidden. Touch me, touch you. One warm palm sliding against a cheek, a throat, and oh, some kiss, something sweet on the lips. Heaven. Heart's desire.

And now she had it—or at least, the possibility—and she found that the flesh was not so forgiving, that her dreams frightened her.

Ah, Remy. I wish you were here.

She was also quite grateful that he was not. Too many complications. She was not even certain he would want her, looking as she did. Old, rough, the product of a hard life. The irony being, of course, that this body with its scars and aging aches, was probably a better reflection of her heart than the real thing.

Stop feeling sorry for yourself. You got no time for pity.

Right. She had work to do. One thing the Brotherhood of Evil Mutants had taught her, long before she ever joined the X-Men, was that you did your work or you died. Only the strong survived. Life never favored whiners.

And at least she was still a woman. Poor Scott. He and Kurt had already slipped out of the dining room, and it was funny watching them; Rogue did not know who Mindy and Renny had been before, but now they looked like trouble—the cartoon kind, little rascally animals that tiptoed about with mischief on their minds. Scott could not help himself; there probably wasn't a lick of humor in him right now, certainly no mischief—but in that body, with that delicate face reflecting his stubborn frowns, there was an aura of the surreal, the ridiculous, that Rogue simply could not shake.

Kurt did not make it any easier. She could tell he was enjoying himself. But that was Kurt, always able to take the best out of any situation. Rogue wished she had that talent. Despite wanting to laugh at her friends, she did not have the same sense of humor about her own predicament.

At the far end of the dining room was an area filled with shabby orange couches and battered faux-wood tables. Games littered the floor and scratched surfaces: chess, checkers, playing cards, even a shabby version of Monopoly. Bodies, too. Some of the men and women looked like tattered versions of the games, old and plastic, so heavily medicated as to be near death. They smelled like urine and sweat and despair. Rogue hated it.

This could have been you, if you had never learned how to control all the voices in your head.

Friends, enemies, strangers—men and women who had been sucked into her soul over the long years, thanks to her powers. Some of them still spoke to her, still whispered schemes in her dreams. Yes, she could have ended up in a loony bin. Still might, if she wasn't careful.

Actually, forget that. She was already here.

There were patients in the recreation area who looked like they were having actual conversations. Rogue wandered over to them. She needed to find this Patty, and those folks seemed like a good place to start. If she got desperate, she might try the nurses and security guards. She hoped it did not come to that. Based on what she had already heard, "Crazy Jane" had a reputation, and asking for the whereabouts of another patient might look suspicious. The less contact she had with the authorities in this place, the better.

She chose her targets carefully; she did not want to be seen with people who might not normally associate with someone like Crazy Jane. Too many questions, and in this place, she had no power—nothing to protect herself with except brains and caution.

Not that she could complain. The alternative, after all, was death—and considering how easily she and her friends had been taken over, she was surprised to still be breathing. Why anyone would go to the trouble of stealing their bodies—and then keep their minds intact—was beyond her.

Rogue found what she was looking for in the far corner of the recreation area, sitting at a small table. A young man and older woman, both of whom looked capable of handling someone like Jane—but sane enough to actually know something. She moseyed over. Their voices carried.

"My mom is coming today. God, is she a nightmare." The young man tapped his fingers along the edge of the table. Up close, he looked and sounded so youthful, Rogue revised her opinion and downgraded him to "boy." Scraggly hair, pointy chin, shiny forehead.

"Love, Kyle," said the woman across from him. She was eating an apple, holding it tight in a pudgy fist. "You can't complain about that."

"The hell I can't, Suzy. Did you know—" He stopped, finally noticing Rogue. She cast a shadow on their table. "The hell *you* want, C.J.?"

C.J. Huh, cute. Rogue said, "Just company. Anything wrong with that?"

"This is a *private* conversation." He gave her the finger, but it was halfhearted, like an old habit.

Rogue grabbed the nearest chair and sat down. "If it was so private, sugah, you shouldn't have been talking so loud. Ain't just the walls that have ears in this place."

"Funny way you're talking. You been taking lessons in redneck?" Suzy's small eyes could have been blue or brown; every time she blinked, they seemed to change.

"Don't know," Rogue said, making a stronger attempt to dull her accent. "You been taking lessons in how to get your face punched in?"

That earned her a thin smile. "Good old Jane. Always so predictable. I love getting a rise out of you."

"That's not all you like getting," muttered the man. Rogue shot him a sharp look, wondering what *that* meant. The woman laughed.

"Bad, you're so bad!" She set down her apple and began shuffling cards. Instead of passing them out, however, she cut the deck in half and then fanned the stack with her palm. She looked at Rogue and her eyes shifted from blue to brown. "Choose one, Jane. Come on. I dare you."

Rogue did not want to choose a card. She had come here to ask questions, not participate in games. Nor did she like the peculiarity of the woman's shifting gaze, her intensity. Rogue, faced with that scrutiny, was reminded again of her precarious situation; she felt exposed, weak, utterly and miserably human. For all her fantasies to the contrary, Rogue wanted her powers back. She wanted to be a mutant and feel safe again. Safer, at any rate. She could not escape the irony of that.

"Well?" said Suzy, sly. She tapped the cards with one hard fingernail. "Let's see what fate has in store for you."

If Rogue had her way, fate would provide both of her missing friends, as well as a swift escape from this place and a safe return to their bodies so they could begin the ass-kicking that someone so royally deserved.

Rogue chose a card. She had a job to do, and that came first. If she humored this woman, played along with her crazy games, then maybe she would be more willing to answer Rogue's questions.

A nine of spades. Rogue did not know what that

meant. She looked at Suzy, and was not comforted by the flush creeping up her sagging neck.

"That's a bad card," she said.

"Of course," Rogue said. "Those are the only kind I get."

"It means you've cast yourself in an illusion," said the woman, leaning close. Her eyes shifted, dark to light: unmistakable and eerie and utterly unnatural. "You don't know the difference between dream and waking."

"I know enough," Rogue said smoothly, though on the inside a chill settled deep in her gut. Her eyes might belong to a different woman, but they did not lie. Suzy was a mutant. Probably low-level, perhaps only a physical permutation, but with enough kick in her genes to set her apart. Rogue wondered why she was in the hospital, if her incarceration had anything to do with her mutation. She wondered if this woman, because she was a mutant, might know something about why the X-Men were trapped here. It was no accident that Rogue and her friends were living in the bodies of strangers. Wasn't any machine she knew of that could accomplish that, which meant a person had done the deed. Another mutant.

Rogue shifted in her chair. She should have just stuck with a simple interrogation instead of an attempt to fit in.

You never could do anything simple.

"Why are you here?" Rogue asked Suzy. Another bad question, but she might as well go for broke. She wanted to know if the woman was here against her will.

Suzy said nothing. Kyle's gaze darted to both women, back and forth, back and forth. His fingers drummed the air. He looked worried.

"I want to talk about my mom," he said.

"I tried to kill someone," said Suzy softly, ignoring him. She stared into Rogue's eyes. "Bang, bang, you're dead. But you already know that, C.J. Or you should."

"Yeah?" Rogue said. "My memory's bad. Remind me of something else, Suzy. Did you enjoy the killing?"

"Suzy," said Kyle, imploring.

Suzy bared her teeth in a smile. "I was crazy at the time. I didn't know what I was doing. Something *you* should be familiar with."

Rogue shrugged, holding Suzy's gaze. The mutant woman was here for a good reason, and if her, then maybe others—if there were other mutants in Belldonne. Rogue had the feeling that Logan's contact was full of it—or else had deliberately misled them. If so, it was the best trap that had ever caught her.

"C.J.," Suzy said. "You're not acting like yourself."

"That's because I'm crazy," Rogue said, and shoved the nine of spades back into the lineup of cards. "Did you hear about Patty?"

Kyle looked relieved by the change of subject. He shook his head, still playing air drums with his fingers. "Dumb girl. She screwed over the wrong guard."

"What'd they do to her?"

"Quiet room," Suzy said, still staring, eyes narrowing into pins of shifting color. Pain prickled the spot between Rogue's eyes; watching Suzy's face was enough to give her a headache.

Kyle slid forward on his chair. "You thinking of busting her while she's down, C.J.?"

"Only if I can find her," Rogue said, allowing the rough gravel of her voice to pack the menace she needed. "Which quiet room is she in?"

"Third floor, near the west-wing station." Suzy picked up Rogue's discarded card. She ran the edges over her fingers and palm, and then pressed it to her lips. "You'll need a distraction."

"You offering one?"

Again, she smiled. "Interesting that you need to ask."

Rogue frowned, and glanced around. No one but the nurses and security guards were paying attention to them; most of the other patients slumped in chairs or shuffled across the floor, radiating a dull discontent that seemed borne of boredom, confinement. There were some areas of dynamism—nervous anxiety, scattered bursts of laughter—but beneath even that was an undercurrent of unease and fear. No one wanted to be here. If you did, Rogue thought, then you really were sick.

She stretched and kicked back her chair. This body still felt strange; an ill-fitting glove, one that had unfamiliar aches, an odd rolling looseness in her joints. She stood and Kyle grabbed her arm. It was startling, for a moment horrifying, to feel his hand on her bare skin.

Not my skin. Not mine. You're nothing but human here, sugah. Remember that.

Still, it did not matter that her skin was safe. Touch was unnatural, wrong. Dangerous. Rogue gave him a look that felt as unfriendly as her thoughts, and his hand flew off her arm. Kyle cowered, like he expected to be hit.

"It's all right," Rogue said, ashamed that he was so

afraid of her, of the woman who had once inhabited this skin. Suzy laughed.

"You need to learn some things, Kyle," she said, still playing with the nine of spades: the illusion, the dream. "Some bitches you just don't touch."

Truer words were never spoken. Rogue left to find Patty.

The hospital surprised her. It was, quite clearly, an asylum of some kind, but none of the hospital employees stopped Rogue as she climbed the stairs to the third floor. No one questioned her movements, or tried to restrain her. So much for having a bad reputation.

Not that there was much point to restricting anyone's movements; there was no place for the patients to wander other than the halls and other public areas. The facility felt more like a prison than a place of healing.

Chicken wire—and, occasionally, bars—covered all the window glass, which was often too cloudy and distorted to allow any kind of outside view. The only exits—and Rogue had found them both, first thing that morning—were secured by locked metal doors guarded by security personnel. No security cameras, either, except by those doors. Rogue thought that was poor planning, but the hospital was clearly old and probably underfunded. Good for her and the others, but it did not speak well of the care real patients received, or the kinds of protection the staff had against those same patients. Rogue could not imagine being forced to live here, day after day, perhaps for years at a time.

The third-floor west-wing station was located right off the stairs. Unlike the station across from the recreation room and dining hall, this one was enclosed in glass and resembled an office space rather than a medical treatment area. The desk had room for only one nurse, but there was a door behind her, and Rogue could not tell if more people might be sitting on the other side. She doubted it; the hospital had too few staff for anyone to be idle for long.

"Can I help you, Jane?" asked the nurse. A thick brown braid covered her name tag. She made no move to leave the protection of her station.

"No," Rogue said, fighting her southern accent. "I'm just walking. Doctor . . . Dr. Maguire's been teaching me some techniques, stuff to calm me. I'm just trying it out."

The nurse gave her a thin smile. "That's nice. The doctor has made such progress with you and the others. Really, he's a miracle worker. We're so lucky he decided to come here."

Yes, terribly lucky. Rogue thought he might be working more than just miracles. So far, he seemed to be the only connection between the X-Men and their new bodies. Scott was right not to believe in coincidence.

"I heard Patty went crazy on someone," Rogue said. "I guess those techniques didn't work for her."

The nurse sighed, glancing at the first closed door outside the station. Rogue glanced at it, too. The lock looked standard; easy enough to break, with the right tool.

"It's such a shame," said the nurse. "Patty has been so calm lately. We thought for sure it would last after Dr. Maguire left. He did warn us, though. We should have listened more carefully."

Rogue said nothing, simply stepped up to the door and

peered through the glass observation window. She saw a tiny plump body wrapped in a straitjacket, blond hair spreading wild over the white tile. If that was Patty, then she was either unconscious or pretending. Rogue did not feel lucky enough to place a bet.

"Please move away from there," said the nurse. She looked wary now, and Rogue did not miss the way her hand crept beneath the desk. Call button, no doubt. Rogue thought it strange that simply looking at Patty would be enough to make the nurse concerned, but she was not familiar with Jane's history. Could be she and this Patty had a fighting past, much like the one she supposedly had with "Renny."

Rogue shuffled backward toward the stairs. The nurse said, "Have you taken your meds today, Jane?"

"Yes," Rogue said, and then left, fast. The last thing she wanted was to get into a protracted conversation about medication, especially when she did not plan on taking any. The pills offered to her early that morning had met a quick end after being cheeked, then spit into her palm and tucked beneath her mattress. When that first nurse had unlocked her door, Rogue had not yet figured out what was happening, but she knew enough to recognize that her body was remarkably different—and that pills of any kind had to be a bad thing.

She heard shouts before she reached the dining hall, the crash of something large. She ran, dodging other patients who hovered in her way, trying to move fast in a body where her knee ached and her lungs labored for air.

What she found was a fight. None of the participants

were familiar, though it was somewhat difficult to tell, given that a nurse was facedown on the floor with blood spreading around him, and the three laughing people kicking him had their backs to her. There was a terrible smell, like feces had been spread on the walls, and sure enough she saw dark stains—not on the walls, but on the floor, on the white uniforms of the nurses trying to reach their fallen colleague.

She forgot she did not have superpowers, or maybe it did not matter. She was closer to the fight than the nurses and she slammed her way through the crowd until she reached the smallest of the attackers. He did not see her coming and Rogue grabbed both his ears, twisting them, yanking backward with all her strength. The man screamed in pain, but Rogue did not let go. She twisted harder, and when his knees buckled, kicked the weakest one out from under him and rode him hard to the ground. Hit his head once against the floor, not holding back as she was accustomed to doing, because she was weak now, just human, and she needed all the strength these muscles could give her. She heard a satisfying crack, and the man went very still.

Rogue stood, muscles unaccustomedly sore. She never hurt this bad when fighting Magneto. She turned to go after another of the nurse's attackers and got slammed in the gut with a nightstick.

"Get down!" screamed a security guard, two words which Rogue dimly realized she had been hearing a lot of for the past minute or so. He hit her again and Rogue fell to her knees, trying to protect her head as he landed a third blow across her shoulders. Everyone near the fight, participant or not, was getting slugged into submission. The people in charge were too upset to differentiate between good and bad. Rogue huddled in a tight ball, waiting for another blow. It never came; the security guard had already moved on to someone else. The fight was dying down; the nurse's attackers were all on the ground, and several people cared for the injured employee.

A not-so-gentle hand touched Rogue's back. She peered up into Suzy's face.

"Bad cards," she muttered, the colors of her gaze twirling like a pinwheel. Blood flecked her chin. "You're in a lot of trouble."

No kidding. She hurt bad. Stifling a groan, Rogue tried to stand. Her knee popped. If this was what getting old felt like, then she knew why people fought it, kicking and screaming.

She saw Scott and Kurt—or rather, their new bodies— edging close. They appeared concerned. She waggled her fingers at them and mouthed, "I'm okay."

"No," Suzy said, gazing down at the man lying so still at their feet. "You're not."

Rogue stared at her, and then studied that quiet body, the unmoving chest. A deep chill spread through her, accompanied by dread, horror.

"No," she murmured, bending down to feel the man's throat.

No, it's not possible, I'm not strong enough, I'm only human.

Human, maybe. But still strong enough to kill.

4

SECURITY TOOK ROGUE AWAY. SCOTT WATCHED, UN-
able to do a thing to stop them. He and Kurt tried; they
went to the supervising nurse, who happened to be Nurse
Penn, to argue on her behalf. All they got for their trouble
was a strange look and a simple, "I know what happened,
I saw it all."

Scott was not comforted.

"Now what?" Kurt asked. "What will they do to her?"

Penn shrugged. "Jane will be locked up until the administrator has time to review the case. If they find she
murdered that kid with deliberate intent, she'll probably
be shipped off to the psychiatric ward of the state prison
facility. Even if she's not found guilty, she'll probably be
sent there. That woman is too dangerous for this place.
Something you know all about, huh, Renny?"

Penn did not wait for an answer. He left them, walking
quickly after the small group hauling away Rogue. The
men who had started the fight lay on the ground in a
drugged heap. A security guard prodded their ribs with
his nightstick.

Scott and Kurt followed Nurse Penn. He never turned
around to see if anyone watched him, which was good,

because Scott did not want to explain why he and Renny, two of the most unlikely people to be interested in Jane's welfare, seemed so concerned.

He was glad Rogue did not fight them, and watched her straight back, her careful easy walk. They took her to the third floor, to a nurses' station where the woman at the desk looked at Rogue without much surprise. Scott and Kurt hung back in the stairwell, trying to listen as the hospital employees argued about where to put her. The station nurse wanted Rogue locked up in her own room, but the security guards—and Penn—thought there was too much furniture, too many resources to make a weapon, especially in her "current state."

The current state being that of a murderer. Never mind that she had acted to defend their colleague. Never mind that she was not fighting them now, but instead waited, unemotional and calm. A good act; Scott could not imagine what Rogue was feeling at the moment.

The security guards won the argument. The desk nurse said something muffled, and then Scott heard keys, the rattle of a door. Velcro ripping.

"Let's go," Scott said to Kurt. "At least we know where she is now."

"Temporarily. I do not trust that she will be there for long."

"Then we need to find everyone fast and get the hell out of here." Once they escaped this place it was only a short run to the Blackbird, which they had left close by in a local park. Calling the Mansion from the jet would hopefully convince the people back home that they were not mere impostors.

Assuming, of course, that the jet was still there. If someone had their bodies, they also had access. The Blackbird opened its doors on spoken command of certain passwords, or if the internal sensors confirmed the physical identity of a permitted flyer. The idea of strangers in his jet made Scott sick. He did not want to think about it.

He and Kurt walked downstairs and sat at a table in the far corner of the recreation room, where they watched nurses continue to soothe the patients, who stared wide-eyed and groaning at the corpse still lying on the ground. Scott wanted to groan, too, but for a different reason.

"What did you discover about Maguire?" he asked Kurt.

"Not much. I found his office, but it was locked and I had nothing to open it with. The nurses, though, were quite helpful. According to them I have been in treatment with the doctor for quite some time, and am, er, less crazy now. Even, perhaps, functional. Though I cannot be all that functional, or else Rogue's former inhabitant would not be able to beat me so thoroughly."

"Former inhabitant," Scott mused. "So you think we're alone in these bodies?"

"What?"

"It's possible the original owners are still here inside us, suppressed by our own minds."

"I would rather not consider that," Kurt said. "I prefer to be solely responsible for my actions, rather than take the risk that there might be someone else with me, directing what I do."

"I did say suppressed."

"And I say that everything rises to the surface eventually."

He could not argue with that, nor did he want to. He, too, preferred the idea of being this body's sole occupant, but that raised the uncomfortable possibility that someone might be inhabiting *his* body, as well. A stranger, gazing out from his eyes, using his powers.

He mentioned this to Kurt, who turned so very solemn that Scott wished he had said nothing at all.

"I have thought of this," Kurt confessed, rubbing his chin against his clasped hands. "And I find that it disturbs me greatly. Strangers—especially the strangers we now reside in—using our powers and living our lives? I cannot imagine the trouble."

"I can," Scott said, "and it scares the hell out of me. Everything Professor Xavier built and that we supported could end in an instant given the wrong act, especially one that is done in our name."

"Ah, but we are jumping to conclusions. Without more information, we cannot know if this was an accident or deliberate, Maguire or someone else, if the switch was localized to us, or widespread. We are trying to walk on clouds right now, *mein freund*, and nothing good ever comes of that."

"Pessimist."

Kurt smiled. "Come, let us go and see if we can learn something new about this place."

So they walked, peering out windows where they saw barbed wire and chain-link fences; sliding doors with security checks and metal detectors; more nurses' stations surrounded in glass, where the walls were soft blue and cream.

The nurses and security guards put their backs to the

walls when they passed; they did it subtly, without overt gestures of fear, but Scott felt it. Even little Mindy, who seemed to have a reputation of good behavior, fell under the same hospital safety procedure.

Don't turn your back, don't let down your guard.

They found the window where the patients got their meds, and some of those men and women were already lined up, waiting: trembling, shaking, muttering obscenities under their breath while rubbing their arms so hard, so fast, skin turned red. When the nurse at the window appeared with plastic cups of medicine and water, the entire line pressed forward, hungry.

Scott and Kurt walked away, fast, before anyone noticed them just standing there and forced something down their throats. Their fears were not unfounded; they passed men tied down in wheelchairs, struggling as nurses roughly pushed pills into their mouths.

"They do not separate the sexes here," Kurt pointed out. "I find that odd, and I must admit, dangerous."

"Maybe they only mix during the day. Or perhaps the patients don't have a record for sexual violence. That, or the men have been chemically castrated."

"Scott."

"Oh, um. Sorry."

Kurt coughed, glancing down at himself. "And Jeff? You said you were going to check on him. I forgot to ask you."

"There were too many people around his room for me to break in. I looked through the window, though. He's still unconscious."

"Still?"

"I was in there last night. I picked the lock on my door and took a look around. Our Jeff, whoever he is, got in a fight with the nurses."

"Could it be Logan?"

"Maybe." Hopefully not Jean. He was not sure he could handle his wife looking like a man. A chemically castrated man, at that. Logan, on the other hand . . .

"You're smiling," Kurt said. "Care to share?"

"Not particularly," Scott said. "Take me to Maguire's office."

Kurt led Scott down narrow halls into the most distant part of the first-floor wing. They passed only one nurse, and she had a familiar face.

"Well, isn't this cute." Nurse Palmer placed her back against the wall. "What are the two of you doing down here?"

"Going to see if the doctor is back," Kurt said, while Scott stared at the floor, demure as a little doll. "We miss him."

"He's not there, honey," she said.

"We miss him," Kurt said, with a wonderful whine in his voice that made him sound like a twelve-year-old boy. "Can we at least go wait by his door?"

She hesitated, and then sighed. "Sure, Renny. You and Mindy go wait for him. Stay out of trouble, though. I don't want to hear any stories."

"Of course," he murmured, and she shot him a hard look. Scott held his breath, but all she did was stand beside them, waiting, and he realized that she was not willing to turn her back on them.

Scott nudged Kurt and they shuffled down the hall, listening hard to the quiet as Nurse Palmer watched them leave. Only when they neared the end of the corridor did Scott hear footsteps. He glanced over his shoulder and saw Nurse Palmer disappear around a bend in the hall.

"Why do I feel as though that was a close call?" Kurt murmured.

"Because it was," Scott said, resisting the urge to run. He thought about Rogue and Jean and Logan, and knew they did not have much time at all, not if they wanted to remain together.

Maguire's office was at the end of the hall. There were two other offices besides his, but Scott and Kurt listened at the doors and heard nothing. Either everyone was on vacation, or the doctors only came in on certain days of the week.

Scott pulled the lock pick from his underwear, which made Kurt laugh. He unlocked the door and the two of them entered a small dark room where the air smelled like paper, coffee grounds, and the hint of something floral, like roses.

The desk faced the door. It had a neat surface, with small piles of files in one corner, and a tiny lamp in the other. The walls were bare—no books, no paintings, nothing at all that was personal. An antiquated computer sat on a small table; a close examination showed dust on the keyboard.

Kurt thumbed through the files. "There are only five people here. Guess who?"

Scott grunted. He was too short to peer over Kurt's

shoulder, so he scooted the man aside and grabbed some paperwork.

"Mindy Chan," he read out loud. "Suffers from a debilitating social disorder, which manifests as . . ."

"As what?" Kurt asked absently, reading his own chart.

"I can't function in normal society and I don't talk. Ever. But I think I already knew that."

"How terrifying for her to be in this place, then." He flipped some pages. "My full name is Renfield Brooks, and according to this, I suffer from high anxiety brought on by acute agoraphobia."

"Being here must have been a nightmare for him."

Kurt shook his head. "I cannot imagine anyone voluntarily checking themselves into this institute."

"It doesn't have to be voluntary." Scott read through the rest of his file. "This makes mention of some improvements during private therapy sessions, but it doesn't say anything that would help us. No indication that Maguire was prepping Mindy for . . . I don't know what."

"Stealing souls, maybe?"

"That's a little dramatic."

"Really? And what about waking up naked in a body that is not your own, in a mental hospital where you are occasionally strangled by women and their bras?"

"That's just strange and unusual," Scott said. "Do we have an address and phone number for Maguire? Do we even have a phone?"

He searched the desk and found a wire leading to a partially closed drawer. Bingo. If he could contact the Mansion and only convince someone to listen to him . . .

He dialed one first, which was a mistake because even as he began punching the rest of the number he heard a voice on the other end say, "Hello, this is the nursing station. Hello, who is this? Is this—wait—is there someone in—"

Scott hung up the phone, cursing himself. "We better get out of here. Right now."

"I've got his address," Kurt said, tearing off a page from the top file. He patted the folders back into a presentable pile, and then the two of them left the office at a fast walk. Moments later, Scott heard voices. There was no place to hide.

Scott grabbed Kurt's arm and pulled him back down the hall to the office next to Maguire's. His fingers slipped on the lock pick, but then the wire went in and the door clicked open. He shoved Kurt into the room and followed close behind, shutting the door just as he heard men round the bend at the end of the hall. Quiet, holding his breath, he looked the door.

"Sheila said the call came from Maguire's office." A deep voice, loud and irritated. Kurt sat on the floor behind the desk. Scott joined him. They listened to wood rattle.

"The door's locked."

"Open it up, anyway. Sheila usually doesn't make mistakes."

Scott listened to keys jangle, the harsh sound of heavy breathing. The insulation was so poor he could hear the men shuffling around through the walls.

"There's no one here."

"Yeah, I can see that. Bonnie said she talked to two of

his patients on her way upstairs. They came down here to wait on him."

"Heh. How long did you say the doctor was going to be gone?"

"Don't know. Maybe a couple weeks. I can't remember if he really said. He left yesterday, though."

"That's a long wait. Those sad asses must have gotten tired or something. Hey, you think he would miss that lamp?"

"Right, you're funny."

The men left and did not stop to check the other offices. Scott sighed. His stomach hurt and he had sweat rolling from the creases beneath his breasts. Every movement acted as a reminder of what he was missing.

They crept back into the hall, listening for anyone else who might have the inclination or power to lock them up for trespassing. Everything was quiet, except for some distant screams that seemed more like pleas to God than angry statements of defiance.

As they left the office corridor, Scott heard the soft hiss of rubbing cloth, the crinkle of paper. It was too late to hide. They rounded the corner and came face-to-face with a short slim man wearing a white lab coat. He had black thinning hair and a pair of spectacles perched on the end of his nose. He gave Scott and Kurt the once-over and smiled coldly.

"Can't get enough of your resident genius, huh?"

Scott, quite certain that the man was a doctor and that Mindy should not talk in front of him, stayed silent. Kurt, after a moment of confusion, adopted a pathetic whine and said, "We were just waiting for him to come back."

The doctor, astonishingly enough, mimicked him and sneered. "I can't imagine what he saw in you five, spending all his time trying to make you better. Like some god requiring sacrifice, and the hospital let him get away with it. Can you imagine? All it did was increase the workload on the rest of us while miserable discontents like yourself pandered to him like little virgin sacrifices." He stopped to catch his breath and looked at Scott. "I heard from the nurses that you talked today. Congratulations."

And then he pushed passed them and disappeared around the bend in the hall.

"Did any of that make sense to you?" Scott wiped stray MD spittle from his cheeks.

"Only the last. I sense much anger in his heart."

"I sense the need for some of that medication he's prescribing."

Kurt smiled. "We learned something, though. Or at least, he affirmed what has been implied. The five of us— or rather, our bodies—were Maguire's pets."

"And pets," Scott mused out loud, "are sometimes trained for a specific purpose."

"What is ours?" Kurt asked.

"I don't know," Scott said, "but I hope it's a good one."

They put Rogue in the quiet room with Patty, which would have been a luckier break than it was, had her cellmate actually been awake and not drooling. Rogue did not know why they would risk putting someone potentially unstable—a woman who had just killed a man with her fists—inside the same room as another unconscious patient, but apparently Patty was a sacrifice they were willing to make in the interests of not giving Crazy Jane access to weapon-making materials such as dresser drawers and bed frames and sheets. Oh, the danger.

They put her in a straitjacket, though, which was bad enough. Then again, they probably would have left her in a straitjacket in her own room, which made her wonder if Jane had very talented feet, the way they'd gone on about her making things to terrorize them with.

"We'd knock you out, but the administrator is going to want a word with you. We need you lucid enough for that conversation. After that? Lights out, baby." The security guard seemed especially cheerful. Rogue thought about giving in to the temptation to bite his ankles, but decided that was one more mark against her that she really did not need. She thought his socks looked dirty, too.

Which was all a fine distraction, because when they finally left her and closed the door, she did not have any excuse but to think about the man she had just killed. Rogue had taken lives before, but it never got easier and this time was worse because it was so useless, such an accident, with no real purpose. Yes, she had been trying to save a man's life, but the man who had been doing the killing was sick, insane. He might not have had true control over his actions. And she . . . she had slammed his head into the floor under the misguided and arrogant belief that as a human woman she would not be strong enough to kill him with a blow.

Self-important, conceited, overconfident . . . maybe that was the real Rogue, the woman who could fly and bench press two tons, whose invulnerable skin could steal the powers and memories of any living thing on the planet. Yeah, that might be her.

It's not so easy being normal.

What a joke.

She looked at Patty, who lay on her side, facing Rogue. She appeared short and was definitely soft, with a round face, freckles, and fine golden hair that fell around her chin. Young, cute as a button, and wrapped up so tight in her straitjacket, Rogue thought she resembled an over-stuffed marshmallow.

Jean, Rogue thought. *Jean has to be in there.*

Awkward in her straitjacket, she scooted closer to Patty, studying the slack face for anything familiar, some ghost of her friend. With Scott and Kurt it had been easy; their mannerisms and odd little idiosyncrasies were just as clearly identifiable as the faces they had been born with.

But there was nothing special about Patty. Unconsciousness could be blamed, perhaps, but what if it was more than that? Perhaps not all of them had been transferred to new bodies. If their team had been attacked—and it certainly seemed that way, with a clearly definable loser—was it possible that Jean and Logan had escaped?

If anyone could, it would be those two. Rogue hoped so. She leaned a little closer for a better look.

Without warning. Patty transformed from a marshmallow to a viper, flinging herself at Rogue with teeth flashing: a little doll gone rabid. Rogue gasped, rolling backward, barely snatching her foot away before Patty latched on to it with her mouth.

Right. Not Jean.

"Logan!" Rogue hissed, clipping the side of Patty's face with her heel. It had to be him. No matter what he looked like, no one else in the world could pull off that combination of animal crazy, hateful rage. Logan was one of a kind.

Patty went very still. She lay on her stomach, chin pressed against the floor, blue eyes keen and sharp on Rogue's face.

"Who are you?" she asked, and the voice was low, rough. Not the kind of voice a woman like Patty would have. No.

"Two guesses, sugah," Rogue said.

Patty blinked, and in that moment Rogue stopped thinking of her as a "she." It was Logan, breasts and all.

"Rogue?" he said, and when she smiled, he closed his eyes. "What the hell is going on?"

"Jean got tired of your PMS jokes."

"*Rogue.*"

"I don't know. Really, Logan. I found Scott and Kurt, but Jean is still missing. Although, now that I know who you're supposed to be, I have a good idea where . . . or, um, who . . . she's in. Our bodies are gone. I don't know where or why."

"We're in that mental hospital, right? Jesus Christ. I can't smell anything."

"We're human now," Rogue said quietly, remembering the feel of that man's head in her hands.

"Try not act so happy about it, darlin'. And why are you in here with me?"

"Oh, Logan. I . . . I killed a man."

"Great," he said. "You're screwed."

5

THE NEXT TIME JEAN OPENED HER EYES, SHE FOUND
that nothing had changed. She was still restrained, still in
the white room, and still mind-dead. She was almost glad
for everything but the latter.

She tried to move and pain soared through her head.
Just more of the same. She was right back where she had
started, with nothing to show but an even worse headache and the certain knowledge that breaking people's
kneecaps in this place was not going to get her anywhere.
Time to gather information and strategize.

Her first instinct—basic, like breathing—was to reach
out with her mind and simply steal the information she
needed. She suffered a quick reminder of how impossible
that was, and had to bite down on her tongue to keep
from swearing. She was not going to rest here helpless.
She refused. There were other ways to use her mind and
not all of them relied on being a mutant. It was something Jean was beginning to realize she had forgotten.

She pressed her face into the floor to give herself better leverage as she rolled to her knees. Dreadlocks fell
around her face, and she remembered she was a man.
Which might have been more distressing if she was free,

but at the moment, she did not have time to indulge herself in thinking about it. Much.

Fighting the urge to vomit, Jean carefully stood. She had to lean against the wall for several minutes; she desperately wanted to lie down again, but was afraid if she did, there would be no getting up. Despair and fatigue were a dangerous combination, and she teetered close to suffering from both.

She heard someone out in the hall and steeled herself for another bad encounter. The lock turned, the door opened, and an unfamiliar man in a white nursing uniform peered into the room. He had brown eyes, brown hair, and an unmemorable chin.

"Hey, Jeff. How you feeling?"

"Fine," Jean said, still amazed at her new voice. "I'm very sorry about last night. I don't know what came over me. I woke up frightened. Is that man . . . will he be all right?"

"Just peachy." The nurse gave her a strange look. "Has Maguire been doing a Henry Higgins on you?"

"Excuse me?" Her head hurt so badly she wanted to scream.

"Your voice. You're talking different."

"Oh," she said. "Well . . . Maguire tries to do a lot of things to . . . help."

"I guess so." The young man entered the room, glancing over his shoulder at the hall behind him. "Just between you and me, Jeff, this time you really fucked up. Maguire had the administrator all convinced that you shouldn't be transferred—and boy, was the doc pissed when they suggested it—but after last night . . ." He moved a little closer, smiling. "Well, you know. Easy come, easy go. I think they're going to do it fast, in the next couple of days before Maguire comes back. Easier on him if he's not here to see it."

Easier on the administrator, who would not have to deal with any immediate protests. Jean studied the young man's uniform, recalling her previous night's encounter. She most certainly was inside the mental hospital. Why was another matter entirely—but if she was here then the others might be, too. The problem was finding them.

"Why are you telling me all this?" she asked, not liking the smile on his face.

"Because I want to see you squirm." His smile widened.

The long hall felt like an extension of her room, a prison nightmare of doors and barred windows. The air smelled like disinfectant: stale, chemical.

The nurse did not turn his back on her. He kept his distance, walking several steps behind with a rolling gait that felt like he was winding up to hit something. She glanced over her shoulder.

"I'm having trouble this morning," she said. "I keep forgetting things. How long have I been here? Why was I seeing the doctor?"

He laughed. "They must have cracked your shit up last night. Damn. What do I tell you, Jeff? That you're a junkie? That you almost beat a man to death for not giving you the time of day, because that's how much you needed to know if you were late for meeting your dealer? Yeah, you're a real angel. I don't know why Maguire wasted his time on trying to iron you out, but he had his favorites, and man, when he latched on, there was no changing his mind."

"Who else were his favorites?" Jean asked.

He gave her a strange look and said, "Here's the bath- room."

The bathroom was a large space, with stalls on one side, a row of urinals on the other, and an open cattle shower between them.

"You need to crap?" he asked.

"No." She wondered if that was a mistake. Perhaps he would take his guard down if she sat on the toilet. She could try to subdue him—

Too late. He pushed her to the urinals.

"I'll try to be gentle." He grinned and unzipped her pants. It was a horrible sensation, feeling his hands down there, and even though this was not her body she felt in- dignant for herself, for the man she was, and stared at the wall as he shook her loose.

"Well, come on." He looked down, and then up at her face. "We don't have all day, Jeff."

Her bladder ached but this did not feel natural. She had trouble relaxing that part of her body.

"Don't mess with me," said the nurse. "I'll take you back to your room."

"Wait," Jean said. "Please. Just . . . turn your back. I need a minute. I need some privacy."

"Right," said the nurse. "You just want to kick my ass. Oh, but wait—your hands are tied. Tough, man. Real tough."

Jean grit her teeth. "Fine, don't turn around. But step back a little. I can't go with you watching me."

"Aw, you're shy like a little girl. Okay, Jeffy. If it makes you feel better, I'll ease back a little. Just so." He moved. She turned back to the urinal and stared at herself, trying to overcome the desire to scream in frustration. There was also just the simple need to scream—for no good reason, other than the fact she had a penis attached to her body and there was currently no way to escape from it.

She did finally manage to urinate, but it took time and she could hear the nurse grow more and more impatient. She was actually surprised he lasted as long as he did, until finally he stalked over and slipped her back inside those hospital pants. He went to the sink and washed his hands.

Another man entered the bathroom. Slender and dark, with a narrow face and bright eyes. He wore the loose garb of a hospital patient.

"Well, now," said the nurse. "Fancy this. Jeff, meet one of those people you so conveniently forgot. Renny, can you believe it? She doesn't remember you."

"Ah," said the man, with an odd smile. "You do not remember me, *mein freund*? Truly? If it helps, my favorite color is blue."

Jean's breath caught. After a moment, she said, "Mine is red."

"What a lovely color, too," said Renny. Jean thought, *Kurt, that is Kurt,* and he said, "We have all been wondering how you are. I cannot believe you forgot us."

"Hey," said the nurse. "What's with the German accent? The hell is Maguire giving you guys?"

Jean ignored him. "How are the others?"

"Fine," Kurt said, and then the nurse grabbed Jean's shoulder and shoved her to the door.

"Playtime is over. Renny? Don't hang out here too long, man."

"Bye," Jean said, and then, fast, "This might be the last time you see me. I'm being transferred."

"What?" Kurt looked startled. Jean tried to say more, but the nurse pushed her out of the bathroom and Kurt did not follow. She did not blame him. Best not to attract attention in this place. It was enough that the others were here. Selfish, yes—but better than wondering if her friends and husband were alive or dead.

She and the nurse passed a slender Chinese woman, leaning against the wall beside a poorly lit stairwell. She seemed very pretty, though it was hard to tell with her gaze so shy on the floor. She sneaked a peek at Jean and winked.

Jean stumbled. The nurse pushed her. "All your little friends are here, huh? You got a girlfriend, Jeff?" And then, to the woman, "You better get moving, Mindy. You make eyes at Jeff, I might just ask you to do the same for me."

Something hard flashed through the woman's gaze— for a moment, Jean thought there would be a fight—but then she looked away and shuffled down the stairs. The nurse laughed.

Jean glanced over her shoulder. Behind the nurse's back, the woman—Mindy—peered around the stairwell.

She met Jean's gaze and pointed at her eyes. Mouthed, "Scott."

Jean took a deep breath and looked away. If she stared any longer she would say or do something stupid. Scott. Thank God. He was okay. Kind of. Her husband was a woman.

Wow. Someone was probably laughing about this.

And when she found that person, he was in big trouble.

Kurt left the bathroom after Jeff and the nurse disappeared from sight. He ran to Scott and said, "That was Jean."

"What?"

"Truly, I am sure of it."

Scott stared down the hall, trying to recall that masculine face, the dark eyes. A part of him was not entirely surprised. There was one moment—brief, startling—when he looked into Jeff's face and felt that trickle of connection that he always had with Jean: comfort, a sense of coming home.

But that immediately seemed wrong, and the reason was superficial: Jeff was a man. Scott, enlightened politically correct mutant that he was, felt strange having those kinds of feelings for a man. But if Jean was in there . . .

You love her. You love her and it doesn't matter.

"It is lucky we decided to come and check her room, *ja?* If we had not seen her in the hall . . ." Kurt hesitated. "Jean believes she will be transferred soon, perhaps tonight. She managed to tell me this."

"Perfect," Scott said. The hall was empty; most of the patients seemed to be downstairs in the recreation room. The nurses' station on this floor was at the other end of the wing. He began walking after Jeff. Kurt followed.

"Scott," he said.

Scott ignored the tension in his friend's voice and said, "How athletic are you now, Kurt?"

Kurt shook his head. "If you are asking me what I think—"

"I am."

"—then yes, *mein freund*. I am strong enough."

Scott began to run. He turned the bend in the hall and saw the nurse pushing Jeff—*Jean*—into her cell. Scott did not slow down. Silent, fast, he raced toward the nurse and the man looked up at the last moment, saw it was Mindy—sweet quiet little woman—and brought his hands up too slow. Scott slammed his tiny fist into the man's throat, Jean kicked out the back of his knees—and then as the nurse went down hard, choking, Kurt arrived and hit the fallen man hard in the face, again and again, until he went very still. Scott checked his pulse.

"We are still clear," Kurt said, breathing hard as he looked up and down the hall. Scott stood and reached for Jean. He gazed into her unfamiliar face and said, "Are you okay?"

"I am now," she said, and turned around. "Get me out of this thing."

Scott ripped away the Velcro ties and helped Jean slither out of the straitjacket. Kurt attempted to drag the nurse into Jean's cell.

"I could use some help," he muttered. Scott and Jean grabbed arms and legs and hauled the nurse out of the hall, stowing him right up against the wall where he would be out of sight from someone looking in through the observation window. Kurt wrestled him into the straitjacket.

"That won't keep him quiet," Jean said, but Kurt removed the nurse's tennis shoes and stripped off his socks. He stuffed them both in the man's slack mouth. Scott searched his pockets and pulled out a set of keys.

"We need to get Logan and Rogue," he said.

"That is not going to be easy." Kurt stepped back from the nurse and peered through the observation window.

"My life stopped being easy the day I hit puberty," Jean said, nudging him aside to carefully open the door. Scott pressed up against her back, listening hard. He heard nothing but the distant echo of voices, the sounds of men and women in motion.

The three X-Men left the cell and hurried back down the hall to the stairs. Logan and Rogue were being held one floor above them, but in a different wing. According to Scott's memories of the hospital blueprints, the only way to reach them required going down to the first floor and past the recreation room to another flight of stairs in the adjoining wing. It was a crowded area; Scott did not like their odds.

"If someone sees me . . ." Jean whispered.

"I know," Scott said. "But the only surveillance cameras are near the exits and there are more patients than staff in this place. If we're careful—"

"That might not be enough," Kurt said. "Someone is coming."

There was no time to retreat; they were trapped on the stairs. Taking a deep breath and hoping for the best, Scott pushed forward. Up until now, he and Kurt had relied upon no one paying attention to them. With Jean, that would change. Scott imagined that most of the staff knew that she—or rather, Jeff—had been locked up for violence. If anyone questioned why she now walked free—

It was Nurse Palmer who appeared in front of them. She carried a stack of files and her steps were slow, heavy. The light from the window behind her no longer seemed quite so bright; Scott wondered what time it was. Night would be a better time for escape.

You should have left Jean in her cell until you were ready to leave this place. You just worsened your odds.

But then, Scott preferred to take his chances with Jean at his side, rather than risk a transfer or some other harm to her. The X-Men had no control over their lives in this place.

Scott did not stop walking nor slow his pace; for a moment he thought Nurse Palmer would let them pass, but at the last possible instant she stepped in front of him. Scott teetered on his heels to keep from running into her. Jean brushed up against his back.

He glanced at Nurse Palmer from under his lashes and found her staring at Jeff. Her forehead creased into a thick frown. "Now, this can't be right. Who let you out of lockup, Jeff?"

"I don't know," Jean said. "One of the nurses. He said

he didn't want to take time to feed me, so I should do it myself."

"Of all the . . ." Nurse Palmer shook her head, shifting backward. Scott wondered if she was getting ready to run. He did not blame her; she was one solitary woman, outnumbered by three mentally unstable individuals. Scott was surprised she had even bothered confronting them.

"He's hungry," Kurt said. "Can't he have dinner with us?"

Nurse Palmer narrowed her eyes. "No, he cannot. And why do you care so much, Renny? Jeff has always terrified you, and now, suddenly, you're acting like friends? You're spending time with Mindy and looking for Dr. Maguire? Something is wrong here. You're acting out of character." She gave Scott a searching look. "All of you are."

She backed down the stairs and Scott knew they had only moments before she began calling for help. He said, "Wait," but this time Nurse Palmer did not respond or act surprised by his willingness to talk.

And then another woman appeared, running lightly up the stairs from the first floor. She looked vaguely familiar. Her eyes were odd, and she wore the loose uniform of a patient.

"Suzy," said Nurse Palmer, and the woman smiled, stepping so close that Scott felt sure the nurse would say something—a shout, a warning—but colors shifted in the patient's gaze, whorls of gold and green, and Nurse Palmer shut her mouth.

"Those are real heavy files," said the woman, Suzy.

"And it's been a hell of a long day. I think you better move on now and find a place to rest your feet."

Nurse Palmer shook her head, though her gaze never wavered from Suzy's eyes. The woman swayed close, her hips round and soft like her voice, and she said, "Go on now. These people aren't important at all."

"But—"

"No." One word, dropped into the air like stone. "Now *go*."

Nurse Palmer turned and walked up the stairs. She did not look at Scott or the others as she passed. She did not seem to see much of anything at all.

No one else moved. They looked at Suzy, whose smile widened.

"You're so screwed," she said.

"Have we met?" Scott asked.

"No," she said. "You're usually not much of a talker."

Right. He kept forgetting that part.

"Thank you for your help," Kurt said politely. "But forgive me if I question why."

Suzy smiled, nasty. "Renny, Renny, Renny . . . that's your name and don't wear it out, right? You're not shaking in your boots, *Renny*. You don't act worried at all. You act like a man with balls."

"And that surprises you?"

Her smile widened. "Bras and toilets, Renny. Remember that nice diversion I created for the nurses?"

"Ah," he said. "Yes."

She folded her arms over her chest "You're a terrible liar. You were then, and you are now. Whoever you are."

Scott frowned. "What do you mean by that?"

She merely looked at him, and again he cursed his big mouth. Her eyes swirled like the sun shining through water, light to dark, pupils expanding and contracting like the beating of a heart, subtle and hypnotic. He looked away, concerned about staring too long into that gaze.

"Smart," she said. "Some are more susceptible than others, but they don't always realize it. I'm a bitch, so I warn them."

"You're a mutant," Jean said, and Scott thought about the mission that had brought them here. "Are you being kept at the hospital against your will?"

Suzy laughed out loud. "Shit, Jeff. I liked you better when you were a thug. No, I'm not being kept here against my will. I say I deserve it. I'm just a little crazy sometimes. Just a little."

"Just a little?"

"Just a little song, just a little dance, nothing at all special. Crazy, I'm just a little crazy." She showed some teeth. "And you all are impostors. You and Renny and Crazy Jane and God knows who else. Impostors, illusion, wrapped up in shadows. You're all screwed."

"Are you a telepath?"

"That's too big a word for a girl like me," she said, sly. "Use smaller talk, *Mister* Mindy."

Scott went very still. "How do you know?"

She tapped her head. "I just do. Instinct, maybe. Or the cards." She pulled a stack of them from her pocket, a regular playing deck, well used and rough at the edges. "It took me a while with Crazy Jane, but when I figured her out, the rest of you were easy. I saw you all talking. That shouldn't be, no matter what Dr. Maguire has been doing with you."

"Do you know anything about that?" Scott stepped close—too close, maybe, those eyes might be danger-ous—but he needed to know, and if this woman had the answers—

"No," she said, and he could not tell if she was lying. "I never got a chance to talk to the doctor. Not many did. He came and started seeing only certain patients. And then he narrowed those patients, and then again, again, until he had you five. You special dirty little five."

"Does that make you angry?" Kurt asked.

"Everything makes me angry, *Renny*. That's why I'm here. Partly, anyway. But you shouldn't be here. You shouldn't at all."

Scott studied her face, that smile, those cold eyes. "Are you offering to help us?"

"I'm offering something," she said. "I got a feeling I should. Crazy Jane pulled a bad card and I been pulling more. Five of hearts, Five of diamonds, Five of spades and clubs. Five seems to be the magic number and after seeing you love children all together, all friendly when you've never been friends at all, I got my message loud and clear."

"Which is what?" Scott asked cautiously.

She picked her teeth with a fingernail. "To set you free, little red bird. I'm going to set you free."

6

AFTER SEVERAL HOURS OF WAITING IN THAT DISMAL little room, with an equally foul-tempered Logan, Rogue was somewhat relieved when the nurses came to fetch her for a meeting with the administrator. They did not remove the straitjacket.

Mr. Beckett was a small man, with a shiny bald scalp surrounded by a thinning ring of brown hair that looked far more youthful than his wrinkled drooping face. He reminded her of a bored hound dog and he sounded like one when he talked, all slow vowels and questions that felt like proclamations.

"Are you a troublemaker?" he said, when she sat down. "I think you are a troublemaker."

"Okay," Rogue said. Mr. Beckett frowned, tapping the file in front of him with a pencil.

"Frankly, I expected more. You made remarkable progress with Dr. Maguire, but several incidents over the past month have demonstrated that your road to recovery is . . . challenged. This latest episode is a vile example of that."

"I was trying to defend that nurse."

"Several of my staff have said that. I was not there, so I

cannot verify the veracity of their stories. Either way, it matters little. A patient is dead, which is a kind of permanence that I do not appreciate inside my hospital."

Rogue did not appreciate it, either. She mourned that death. Her heart hurt. Her hands felt dirty.

"*But not that dirty,*" Logan had said, during their brief conversation. "*Because your intentions were good. You were trying to help someone. Hell, darlin', that happens to me all the time. You want to see a screwup when it comes to keeping people alive, just take a good hard look at me. That's the picture they're using in the dictionary.*"

Which was enough to make her smile—a good sign—though as far as pep talks went, it was not enough to wash away the guilt. In Rogue's experience, not much could do that except for time.

"What was his name?" she asked, because she had to know, she had to remember this man's death in a personal way and not just as a face, an incident, a mystery.

It was the wrong question. Mr. Beckett snapped his pencil and threw the pieces down on his desk. They bounced; one of them hit Rogue's chest.

"This amuses you, doesn't it?" He leaned back in his chair and placed his hands palm down on the desk.

"No," Rogue protested, but he shook his head.

"I don't want to hear another word out of your mouth. I am transferring you to the mental health ward at the women's correctional facility. You should have been sent there a long time ago, but Dr. Maguire insisted that you remain under his care."

"You must have had a good reason for listening,"

Rogue said, watching his expression harden. She had nothing left to lose; she did not care that her accent crept in. Even if she sounded nothing like Jane, the man in front of her would never imagine the truth.

"Dr. Maguire is highly respected," Mr. Beckett said slowly. "Very."

"So he used his influence to bully you," Rogue said.

Beckett's face flushed an even deeper red. "The nurses will take you back to the quiet room now. If nothing else, you can spend more time with your . . . therapy mate, before you leave."

"That's very kind of you," Rogue said, thinking, *You stinky little weasel.*

"I thought so," he said, and gestured at the door.

Logan was propped up against the wall when Rogue returned. He grinned and said to the nurses, "You guys planning on feeding us? I could use some grub."

"Shut up," said the man. "I'm not getting close enough to those teeth to feed you. Chew on each other if you get that hungry."

"Heh," said the other, leering. "I'd like to see that."

"I bet," Logan said. The nurses left, laughing. Rogue gave him a dirty look and slid down the wall, rubbing up against his shoulder.

"They're sending me to prison," she told him. "I'm going to be jail bait."

"I always knew it would happen. You're such a rough rider. Always asking for trouble."

"Well, I got it in spades. I just hope the others can find a way out of here before they take me away. Otherwise,

I'll be sitting behind bars until you guys figure how to switch me back into my real body."

"Good vacation. Lots of time for self-reflection."

"Make new friends?"

"Prison friends are the best kind."

"They got your back?"

"Sometimes literally."

Rogue laughed. Logan nudged her with his shoulder. "See? It'll be okay, darlin'. Remember that time we were in Genosha together? No powers then, either, and they strung us up like a couple sides of meat. Worked out okay, though."

"Yeah." She remembered the terror of waking up naked and alone in a small cement cell. That had been infinitely worse than this. Here, at least, there were rules. In that other place, all she'd had was the tender mercy of soldiers—and they weren't all that merciful. Then, as with now, not having access to her mutant abilities felt more like punishment than a gift, and she wondered if that was not the way it would always be. If perhaps that wasn't what she preferred.

Of course, continuing to think like that was just a waste of energy when she had far more pressing matters at hand. Like not going to jail and being separated from her friends.

Somewhere distant Rogue heard a man scream, and she thought, *I'm right with you.*

Rogue listened a little longer, but the sound was too heartrending, broken. Trying to distract herself, she said, "How are we going to get out of here, Logan?"

"Easy," he said, his voice low, gruff. "We're going to run."

"And how do you know that?"

He smiled and pointed with his chin at the door. "Because there's our ticket out."

And Rogue looked and saw Kurt peering through the observation glass, and thought that Logan might be on to something.

Kurt, knowing himself to be a natural charmer and quick-escape artist of fabulous ability, was quite accustomed to entering—on purpose—situations that some might consider volatile and dangerous. Whether it was the high trapeze or a bloody brawl with the Friends of Humanity, he was always ready to meet difficulty with a smile. Easy as a breeze, for a man with a light heart.

Until now. Kurt still smiled—even as he and Scott and Jean prepared to enter the most crowded part of the institute—but it was a struggle, a cheer he had to force upon himself in order to stave off despair.

Kurt missed himself. He had, since awakening in this place, fought a continuous battle against his instincts, those basic primal desires to use what came so naturally: teleportation, agility; his tail, even. He missed those parts of him, felt the ache of their loss, and though he was a man who did not dwell on things that could not be changed, this struck him at the core of his heart.

He thought he knew who he was without his gifts. Maybe. He hoped the others had a stronger sense of their identities. Ahead of them lay a hard road; he could not imagine what would happen if they found themselves incapable of separating personality from power, if they lost their resolve simply because the easy way was not open to them.

You worry too much. The X-Men have suffered and endured worse than this, and have survived. You do not need to fear for them. Or yourself.

Except, he could not shake the feeling that this was different, the loss so deeply personal, so sharp, that the cut would go deeper than any bullet or knife, go deeper than anything they had yet encountered.

Or maybe he was just being dramatic. He got like that, sometimes.

"Are you ready?" Scott asked. The three X-Men stood inside a tiny broom closet filled with cleaning supplies that Suzy assured them were never used in the early evening hours. The janitor, according to her, went home early—and the nurses did not like to clean. The closet was located beneath the stairs and was within hearing distance of the recreation room. Even now, Kurt heard the loud scrape of pushed-back chairs, the heated rumble of voices.

"Are you sure you trust her?" Jean asked. "She seems unbalanced."

"Yes," Scott agreed, "but right now we need all the help we can get."

"And you really think I can just . . . slip past those nurses and security guards in there?" Jean pointed at herself. "In case you hadn't noticed, I'm not the woman I used to be."

"We need to rescue Logan and Rogue. I could leave you here and go retrieve them, but you would still have to cross the recreation room in order to access our best escape route."

Jean sighed. "Better to get it over with now. I just wish . . ."

She did not finish telling them what she wished, but Kurt thought he knew. Jean wished she had her body back. Kurt had a similar wish for himself. Living as a mutant—with all the powers granted him—was easier than existing as a human.

You have become so very spoiled by the incredible things you can do. Your only saving grace is that you have not known any other kind of life.

Kurt heard a commotion out in the hall; a man screaming obscenities, howling like his heart was being torn from his chest. Something large crashed; a table, perhaps. Or a body.

"It's time," Scott said. He cracked open the closet door and peered into the hall, then slipped out, gesturing for Kurt and Jean to follow. They did, and followed the sounds of chaos until they reached the recreation room. Not one person paid attention to them. Everyone— nurses, security guards, patients—stared at the scrawny young man writhing on the floor, contorting so wildly, with such abandon, that Kurt feared he would break his spine in half. From his mouth poured sounds of horror. Kurt wanted to clap his hands over his ears. Suzy had promised a distraction; her friend Kyle was certainly giving one.

Scott grabbed Jean's hand and tugged her across the room, pushing through the thin crowds of patients who stood in their way. Kurt ran after them. Not one paid attention to their passage; the nurses surged toward the young man, shouting orders to one another as they grabbed his heaving body and struggled to hold him down. Kurt glimpsed Suzy; she winked at him and followed.

Past the recreation room the halls were almost empty of people, though several security guards raced past as Scott, Jean, and Kurt reached the stairs. No one looked twice; the three of them could not compete with screams that sounded like murder.

They ran up the stairs and at the top saw a nurses' station encased in glass. A woman sat inside, playing with the end of her braid, and when she saw the three X-Men she stiffened. Kurt approached first, but before he could say anything he felt a hand on his shoulder, a push, and Suzy slid past him. She placed her palms on the glass and stared at the nurse. Simply stared, and the woman went very still, her gaze open and glassy. Suzy said, "Go to sleep," and the nurse closed her eyes. Her face went slack.

Kurt heard voices, sounds of movement on the stairs. Suzy said nothing, simply ran off in that direction without a backward glance.

"I found them," Scott said, gesturing at the door nearest the office. The stolen keys rattled in his hand. Kurt pushed past and peered through the observation window. He saw Rogue, and beside her a small plump golden-haired woman who looked like the idyllic American country sweetheart. And then she gave him a nasty smile and it was all Logan.

Scott unlocked the door. Logan and Rogue were already on their feet and Kurt and Jean quickly freed them from their restraints.

"Are you both okay?" Scott asked, glancing out into hall.

"Peachy," Logan said. "Is that you, Jeannie?"

"No," said Jean, standing behind him. "That would be me."

Logan turned and stared. "Whoa. I wish I could have been there for that first meeting."

Jean narrowed her eyes. Logan held up his hands and backed off.

"Come on," Scott said, holding open the door. "We need to get out of here."

"You got a plan?" Logan asked. He rubbed his knuckles—a familiar gesture, one that pained Kurt to watch. Logan, like the rest of them, relied on his mutant gifts as a natural extension of flesh: arms, eyes, legs. Metal claws.

"I'll tell you after we start moving." Scott entered the hall. Kurt followed close behind; his heart jumped when he saw a shadow in the stairwell, but it was only Suzy.

"You're moving too slow," she said, as dappled green and gold whirled lazy pinwheels around her pupils.

"Are you sure you can't get us past the front doors?" Scott asked.

"Hell, no, little red. My eyes can only work their magic on one person at a time, and the hospital's got multiple watchdogs on each exit. Unless you want to fight your way out, the back way is best."

"I could use a good fight," Logan muttered.

Scott led them down the long corridor to a set of locked steel doors. The metal showed off dents, chipped paint; the hinges were rusty. Scott abandoned the keys and took out his lock pick.

"What is this supposed to be?" Logan asked, glancing over his shoulder. Kurt followed his gaze. At the very opposite end of the hall he saw some of the facility's patients watching them.

"This wing of the hospital is almost seventy years old. According to the blueprints, there's a set of old service stairs behind this door. They lead down to the original laundry room."

"Ah, the laundry room," Logan said, as the doors clicked open. "You can always count on a laundry room for a great escape."

The stairwell was unlit and smelled like wet concrete and mold. Jean and Logan entered the darkness; Kurt began to follow them until he realized that Rogue, Scott, and Suzy were standing quite still, staring at each other.

"This is as far as I go," Suzy said. "I'll watch the doors, cause a ruckus if anyone tries to go down for a spot check."

"Why are you doing this?" Scott asked. "And why haven't you already escaped? No matter what you say, I know you could leave here any time you want."

Suzy glanced sideways at Rogue. A small smile touched her lips. "I stay here because I should. Everyone has their proper place. You should understand. These bodies aren't yours, after all. Just dreams and illusions."

A card appeared in her hand: a battered nine of spades. Suzy gave it to Rogue, who held it gingerly between two fingers.

"I'm crazy," Suzy said. "But Jane is crazier. I miss that."

"Maybe you'll get her back," Rogue said quietly.

"No," Suzy said. "She's gone. But at least now I don't have to look at a stranger wearing her face."

Kurt, Scott, and Rogue entered the stairwell. Suzy, still smiling, closed the doors after them.

He went blind in the darkness and pressed his back against the wall. Careful, they made their way down the stairs one tiny step at a time. Kurt brushed up against a soft arm.

"Hey," Logan said. "Jeannie and I waited for you."

"Thank you," Kurt said. "But please, ladies first."

"Funny."

"Do you hear anything ahead of us?" Scott whispered.

"No," Jean said. "How long do you think it will take them to find out we're missing?"

Logan snorted. "More than the five minutes we've been gone. These aren't exactly agents of SHIELD we're dealing with here."

"Maybe not, but they hog-tied *you* just fine, now didn't they, sugah?"

The stairs curved, but at the bottom they found a door. A thin line of light cut the air below it and they carefully watched for any flicker, any distortion that would signify movement on the other side. Nothing changed. Logan got down on his hands and knees and after a moment patted Kurt's ankle.

The door was not locked from the inside. Holding his breath, Kurt carefully opened it. He saw a bare wall, with thick pipes hanging from the ceiling. The room was empty except for canvas sacks heaped in a pile on the floor. Large metal push bins lined the far wall beneath a small dingy window, where the only view was the underground portion of a cement holding wall. The weak light of dusk trickled through the glass.

The room had no door, only a narrow hall that led deep into shadow. Logan followed it until he disappeared from sight; he returned less than a minute later and said, "This place is a maze. About twenty yards out I started to hear machines running, maybe even people talking. Is all of this locked off or do we have to worry about wanderers?"

Scott shrugged. "It should be locked, but I can't say for certain."

"Someone may check this area after they find out we're gone. It would be stupid not to."

Jean peered into the darkness. "Did you see places to hide beyond this room?"

Kurt saw Scott glance at Jean, and then look quickly away. Too quickly, it seemed. Kurt thought she noticed, and it hurt him to see that flicker of uncertainty pass through her eyes.

"Some crawl spaces that'll get mouse droppings up your nose. They don't go back very far, so a flashlight would be enough to catch us."

"Then let's get out of here before anyone comes looking." Scott peered up at the window. Kurt followed his gaze and studied the late evening sky.

"*Mein freund,* if you wait only fifteen minutes, it will be full dark."

"We're sitting ducks," Rogue said. "Though I prefer my chances when it's not still light out."

"But they'll have tightened security by then," Logan said. "Assuming, of course, that anyone notices we're gone."

"Security is heaviest inside the building. They've got double entry checkpoints, metal detectors, and all the windows but these are covered in wire. It's not easy getting out of here, at least for a regular person. I don't think the hospital will spend much man power looking for us outside the building. At least, not initially. By the time they do, we should be far and away from here. The Blackbird is parked only ten minutes away."

Assuming it was still in the overgrown playing field where they had left it.

"You're forgetting the fence," Rogue reminded him. "I've seen the barbed wire."

"Suzy said there's a place where the chain link is loose."

"Suzy," Logan said. "That's the woman who helped us?"

"A mutant," Scott said. "And listen, Logan, I think we were fed false information to lead us here. This place was a trap."

"You don't say." Logan crouched against the wall, resting his hands on his knees. "Problem is, I trust my source,

Cyke, and he promised me some illegal antimutant activity. Besides, a body-snatching trap? Wouldn't there be easier ways to take us down, other than drag us all the way out here on some false lead? *Especially* for the person strong enough to do this?" He pointed at his breasts.

"I don't have all the answers, Logan, but this," and he pointed at his own breasts, "is an indication that something went horribly wrong when we came here, and I *don't think it was an accident.* The one thing all of our new bodies have in common is that they shared the same doctor, a man named Jonas Maguire. He took quite an interest in us."

"And the false imprisonment of mutants?" Jean asked.

"I haven't seen anything to support that," Scott said. "The one mutant we have met seems to believe she *should* be here, and I don't think anyone is compelling her to feel that way. I don't think anyone *could*."

"I agree." Rogue shook her head. "Suzy is crazy."

"Crazy enough to know we were impostors," Scott said. "And crazy enough to help us."

"I trust my source," Logan said again. "Besides, you seem to be implying that this Maguire had something to do with our situation. I'll buy that. He might be a mutant, or he could have orchestrated hiring one to gun us out of our bodies. *But,* how could some doctor arrange to set up the kinds of rumors that got us out here in the first place?"

"He didn't have to make up the general stuff," Rogue said. "We did find pockets of mutant and human tension inside the city."

"And he's a doctor. All he has to do is talk long enough, and someone will eventually spread the story."

"I still don't like it," Logan said.

"You never like anything," Scott said. "And right now, I'm less concerned with details. We need to get out of here."

"Stage one of that plan has been completed," Kurt said. "Now we must make a run for it."

Not something he looked forward to, but at the moment, it was all they could do. Stuck inside the bodies of strangers, without any real rights or resources . . .

Kurt sighed, wondering once again if he had gone soft. So many in the world, mutant and human alike, suffered indignities at the hands of others. His situation was no worse, and at least he had friends with him. At least he still knew who he was, even if the flesh was different.

It was a very small comfort.

7

Fifteen minutes until full dark. They decided to wait. Logan, unable to sit still, immediately crept back up the stairs to listen at the second-floor door. He did not hear anything. Did not smell anything. He had no idea if that mutant woman had kept her promise and still watched this door. He felt like someone had plugged up his nose and ears, and while he missed his claws—that fine ability to slice and dice—it was those two lost senses that bothered him the most.

Ain't no use moping over things you can't change. Just be glad you're still alive and make the best of it.

Because the alternative meant a long slow rot in this godforsaken hole and he would rather die trying to escape than stay here one more minute. The hospital stirred up memories, what few he had, and none of them were pleasant.

He did not hear an alarm, but as he stood with his ear pressed to the door and pretended he was still a whole man—without breasts—he heard the distant slam of a door and the sound of running. A muffled shout, more pounding feet, bangs and thumps—a very loud "damn"— and then, finally, a shuffling noise just beyond his door and the sense that, yes, someone had been standing there all along. Logan wished he had something to make a barricade with. His thick skull would probably do the trick.

He crept back down the stairs. The old laundry room was so dark by this time he had trouble seeing. He ran into a tall solid body and said, "Jeannie?"

"Yes, Logan." Her voice was quiet, solemn. The others were gathered below the window. Scott had his fist wrapped in one of the canvas sacks.

"Game's up," he told her, and everyone stopped and looked at him.

"They've begun looking for us?" Scott asked.

"Yup."

"Lovely," Jean said.

Logan frowned and gestured at the window. "You going to fit through there, darlin'?"

"I'll make it. It's better than staying here."

"Yeah," he said, wondering what her new body smelled like. "How do you like being a man?"

"I'm discovering that it's the same as being a woman, except for certain anatomical differences."

"You'll have to get Scott to educate you on the finer points."

"I suppose," she said, but her voice was dull. Logan fumbled in the dark for her hand. Her new skin was rough, the touch masculine, but he forced himself to think of the woman inside and found it was not so difficult.

"Hey," he said. "Any tips for me?"

That brought a moment of soft laughter. "Have you tried going to the bathroom yet?"

"No."

"Ask me that question after you do." She stepped toward the others and Logan was forced to let go of her hand. He watched Jean touch Scott's slender shoulder—the blackmail opportunity of a lifetime—and she said, "Let me break the window."

"No," Scott said. Logan grinned. The X-Men's team leader barely cleared five feet and his hands were small and delicate.

"Go on, Cyke," he said. "Be the woman in the relationship."

Rogue coughed. Jean shot him a venomous glare. "You don't have a healing factor, mister. Watch what you say."

"Sure thing," he said.

"Jean," Scott began, but she blew out her breath and snatched a sheet of canvas from the floor. Wrapping up her hand, she pushed Scott out of the way with a not-so-gentle nudge and slammed her fist through the glass. Logan bit back another smile. He loved a woman who knew how to use her hands.

Jean cleared the glass away, shoving canvas out the window and covering the broken glass so that it was safe to climb out into the hospital's yard. She tried to be quiet, but it bothered Logan that her work was all he could hear, that there was nothing else, no layered sensations like he usually encountered: sounds upon sounds, blanketed upon one another so that his mind had to peel back and taste each individual mark of man or beast or object.

His hearing, however, was still good enough to catch a muffled angry shout.

"What was that?" Rogue asked, and Logan cracked open the door to peer into the darkness of the stairwell. Far above him he heard hinges creak, and then Suzy began raising hell with her voice.

Logan shut the door and leaned against it. "We need to go. *Now*."

"They shouldn't have found us this fast," Scott muttered.

"They haven't found us yet," Jean said, and grabbed Scott's arm. "Up you go, sweetheart."

"No," he said, but Jean grabbed her husband under his arms and lifted him up to the window. Scott did not fight her, but Logan saw the conflict on his scrunched-up face: embarrassment, anger, worry. He scrabbled through the window and Logan heard glass crunch beneath the canvas.

Jean gestured at Logan. "Come on. Smallest ones go first."

Logan heard a scuffling sound behind the door, followed by a quick attempt to push it open. Logan threw himself backward, digging his heels into the ground, bracing the door shut. Fists banged against metal, and he felt the vibrations through his body.

"I could use some help here," he growled.

Rogue slammed her shoulder against the door and said, "Go on now. I'll hold this."

"You and what army?"

"Logan!" Jean barked. She already had Kurt pushed

halfway through the window. Rogue gasped as the door slammed hard against her body, opening; Logan stumbled. He turned and saw flashlight beams streak the darkness; the outline of a hand and head—

—and then the door opened even farther and three men pushed through. Logan threw himself amongst them, fists out, kicking and punching. He bit an ear, tasted blood. Someone grabbed his waist and pulled hard; he heard shouting, Jean's deep voice, the high yell of the man bleeding into Logan's mouth.

Rogue grabbed the man holding Logan and threw herself backward. Logan was carried with them both, but the nurse released him before they hit the ground and he rolled right up against another nurse, who grappled with Jean. Logan slammed his heels against the man's knees. He cried out, falling, and Jean moved with his head in her hands and she slammed him into the floor. Above her, Kurt scrambled down from the window, Scott hanging after him.

There was one man left. Logan felt air move against his neck and he turned just in time to see the nurse swing a flashlight at his knees. Kurt pushed him out of the way but moved too slow; he took the blow and his gasp seemed like the clearest most ringing sound Logan had heard since waking up in this place.

Logan threw himself on the nurse, wresting away the flashlight with a cool catch of his wrist. Several blows later—fast and brutal and infinitely satisfying—the man went still. Logan stared down at that slack face, breathing so hard he thought his lungs might burst.

"Kurt," he growled. "You okay?"

"*Ja*," he whispered, but his voice was strained. Logan stood up. The rest of the team, seen in the reflection of the flashlights, looked unharmed.

"Jean," Scott said, hoarse. The upper half of his body hung precariously through the window.

"I'm fine," she said, taking two long strides to the doors and shutting them. She grabbed Logan's wrist as she returned to the window, dragging him with her. She gave him no time to protest, simply grabbed him under his arms and pushed him up to the window. It was a weird sensation, being hauled off his feet that way. Scott pulled him past the edge of the concrete holding wall into the grass.

Kurt was next, hissing only once as he passed through the window. Logan and Scott helped him crawl onto the grass. Rogue appeared behind him, though she had a harder time squeezing through. Breathing hard, casting nervous glances around the darkened yard, they waited for Jean. She did not come through the window.

"Jean!" Scott whispered. She did not say anything, but Logan heard large objects moving, along with some thumping sounds. He imagined her barricading the door with bodies.

Her dark hands finally appeared, grappling for a hold on the cement. Everyone reached down and pulled, struggling to get her through the window.

"Come on," Logan muttered, grunting as he searched for a better hold on Jean's body. She gasped, wriggling hard. Behind her, distant, Logan thought he heard shouting.

"They're coming," she gasped, and then screwed up her face as she writhed her way through the small opening and threw herself onto the grass. Logan and Scott grabbed her wrists and began running even before she completely had her feet under her. Logan heard a muffled shout from behind them.

Trying to keep to the darkest parts of the yard, Scott led them toward the fence. Kurt did the best he could to keep up, but it was clear that the pain in his knee was near crippling. Logan stayed with him, pulling his arm over his shoulders and hauling him faster. He heard more shouting, distant but in transit, and then they were at the fence at a spot next to a tree and Scott fell to his knees, scrabbling.

"She said it was here," Scott muttered, wrenching at the chain link. "By the tree."

Logan looked up and down the line, but he did not see another tree. The yard was barren of anything but grass. He saw beams of light bobbing.

"No time left," he said. "*Scott.*"

But Scott made a low noise and suddenly there was a gap, tiny, and Logan shoved Kurt down on his stomach and pushed him through. He grabbed Rogue next, and then Jean, pushing on her feet to help her slither under. The flashlights were closer now, so close, and Logan dove through, scraping his body and face. Rogue and Jean grabbed his hands, pulling him the rest of the way, and then they did the same for Scott so that his small woman's body looked like it was flying beneath the fence.

They ran. The nursing staff and security were so close

Logan could make out the expressions on their faces, and somewhere near he heard sirens. The area around the hospital was residential; they disappeared into the shadows of a tree-lined street and then Logan whistled and made them follow him down a back alley behind a row of houses, running, running, the sirens getting louder, and there were lights on in the houses, all of them, people awake and doing things, and that was good because it served as sharp contrast to the quiet places, the still and silent, like one small home at the end of the block that was dark and had no car in the narrow driveway.

The owner was a gardener, with a particular fondness for big bushy flowering plants that provided wonderful cover when one lay amongst them. Ferns tickled Logan's nose; he inhaled deeply, savoring what little he could of the scent. It was like smelling freedom.

"What next?" Rogue whispered. Sirens blasted the air and then passed, two cars in succession.

"We need to get back to the jet," Scott said. "That's our first priority."

Logan grunted. "Sorry, Cyke, but I disagree. There's no guarantee the jet's still there. We need to go prepared. Different clothes, at the very least. We also need to lay low for a couple hours. Once the excitement has died down, it'll be safer to go to the park."

"It's close," Scott argued. "One of us could go alone."

"No," Jean said. "I think Logan is right. If whoever is responsible for this went so far as to take our bodies, we have to assume he took everything else as well. If not, then the jet will still be there when we're ready to find it."

"The jet is our only way home," Scott said.

"That doesn't matter if we lose each other," Jean said, and then, softer, "Don't do this."

He sighed, and looked sideways at Logan. "Are you thinking about that house? They might have a security system."

"Maybe," Logan said, though he did not think the neighborhood looked wealthy enough for that kind of advanced precaution. The hyperparanoid, the ones who had the money to spare on installing alarm systems, usually lived in more glamorous places. "Looks empty. It may be our best bet."

Logan did not wait for approval. He slithered out of the bushes, keeping low to the ground as he ran the short distance across the garden to the back door. He felt someone behind him. Scott.

"You'll need this," he said, handing Logan a little wire that had already been twisted up and primed. Logan grunted his thanks and used the pick to jimmy the lock until it clicked. Careful, holding his breath, he turned the knob and opened the door only enough to feel along the edge of the door frame. He found a loose chain, an extra dead bolt. It was a good sign that neither lock was in use.

Logan crept into the house, testing the stillness with his senses, listening as hard as he ever had in his life. He moved from the kitchen to the living room, and from there to the stairs; slowly, painstakingly traveling up to the second floor. Scott did not join him.

The rooms upstairs were empty. Three bedrooms, one of which had been converted to an office. Another evidently belonged to a teenage girl and the third was a master suite with its own bathroom. Logan returned downstairs. Scott stood by the front door, sorting mail that had been pushed through the slot.

"There's quite a bit here," he said quietly. "At least three days old. Vacation?"

"I hope they don't come back tonight," Logan said. "I'll get the others."

Careful, watchful for witnesses, the rest of the team entered the house. Kurt immediately found a soft chair and sank into it with a sigh.

"Take nothing but clothes," Scott told them. "Anything you think won't be missed."

Logan's first inclination was to go for the husband's belongings, but Jean quickly steered him and Scott into the wife's messy pile, as well as the daughter's room.

"I don't want to wear this bra anymore," Logan complained to Rogue, who pulled a long sleeved crew neck and some jeans from the closet.

"You better wear it," Rogue said. "Girl like you needs one."

He decided not to respond to that. He grabbed a blouse from the mother's wardrobe, but had to go to the teen's room for jeans and underwear that fit. He hated trying things on. It was miserable.

They dressed quickly, and were soon presentable enough to go into any public place and not immediately be associated with a mental hospital. Or a hospital of any kind. They looked normal, like average people of middle income. Not rich by any means, but unthreatening in their lack of money. The kind no one paid attention to.

They took turns using the bathroom. Logan did not enjoy the experience, nor did he care much for looking into the mirror. He could not avoid his face: the golden hair, the soft cheeks and full lips.

When he left the bathroom he walked across the room to the window. He saw a police cruiser roll slowly down the street with its lights off. Past the house, the cop snapped on a floodlight, sweeping the lawn and bushes.

Rogue joined Logan at the window and he felt her stop breathing for a moment.

"This is going to be a hard night," she said.

"Yeah," he said. "You got all the uniforms?"

Rogue held them up for him to see. "Jean has the rest. We need to find a place to stash them."

"Let me check out the basement," he said. The cruiser turned left at the end of the street, but Logan thought it would be back.

He found the basement door by the living room and felt his way down into darkness. Cobwebs brushed his face. A lightbulb chain banged against his forehead, but Logan did not turn on the light. He could not be sure that the basement was fully enclosed; he did not see any light coming in from outside, but the risk was not worth it. He used his feet and hands to feel around the damp room and finally found some boxes beneath the stairs. There were clothes inside. Logan picked up the box and, stumbling, made his way back to the kitchen.

Quickly, silently, the X-Men packed their hospital clothing at the bottom of the box. The clothes inside smelled like the basement and seemed particularly old. Logan hoped that would be enough to keep the family from digging too deep into the box. One day, maybe, someone would find these uniforms. Hopefully by then they would have their bodies back.

When Logan returned from the basement, he found everyone seated in the living room but Scott. Logan went into the kitchen and found him leaning against the counter. He stared at the phone hanging on the wall. Logan said, "Not here. The number will show up on their bill."

"I know, but the longer I wait, the worse I feel. Like I'm not going to get another chance."

"You'll get one, Cyke. I want to contact them as much as you, but it's going to have to be a pay phone—and not one in this neighborhood. We'll have to go farther out." That, or risk being picked up by the police.

Scott shook his head. "Someone went to a lot of trouble, Logan. I don't know where our bodies are, but if we're not in them, I don't want to know who is."

"The people we're inhabiting, I'd guess."

"But why put mentally unstable individuals inside us?"

Logan had an immediate answer to that question, but it was too disturbing to speak out loud. Instead he said, "It might make them easier to control."

"By Maguire?"

"I don't know as much about this guy as you do, but sure. Why not?"

"I don't know what a mental health specialist would have against us."

"Hell, man. Even our mailman doesn't like us. It could be any reason."

"Thanks for your help."

Logan snorted. "You know where this guy lives? We should go to his house and see if he's there. Even if he's not, I bet he'll have stuff around that can tell us what he's up to."

"We broke into his office at the hospital. Kurt stole his address. He lives in a neighborhood called Old Victoria."

"Ritzy," Logan said. "The man must have money."

"You familiar enough to get us there?"

Logan wanted to laugh. "Cyke, I'm familiar enough with the Seattle area to run some of these streets blind-folded."

"How's that?"

He shrugged, not particularly inclined to spill his guts about some of the work he'd done for Nick Fury. The jobs had been long and drawn out, requiring a native's understanding of the city.

And Logan was always good at going native.

Scott and Logan rummaged through the cupboards and found boxes of cookies, pretzels, and Ritz crackers. Careful with crumbs—and mindful they should not finish every-thing—they sat in the dark living room and munched on snacks. Several times the police car drove slowly past, but the cop never stopped. After several hours of taking turns sleeping and watching, Logan said, "He hasn't been back for two hours. I think it may be safe to move."

"Let's wait one more hour." Scott studied Jean, who

lay curled beside him in a heavy sleep. Rogue and Kurt had their eyes closed, too. Logan was not entirely sure how deep into la-la land they were, but any bit of rest would help them when they started moving.

Logan slept for a time, with images of wolves and straitjackets and a long sharp fence filling his head—and then stayed awake while Scott stole several minutes of his own rest. The cop never returned.

"It's time," he finally said, shaking Scott awake. "We stay here any longer and we'll be walking with the rising sun." An exaggeration; it wasn't even two in the morning, but time would move fast once they left the house.

They used the bathrooms one last time, and then left the house through the back door. Logan led them down the backstreet until they came to the main road. He did not see many parked vehicles; none of them looked like a police cruiser. Logan did not have the time or patience to check for unmarked vehicles.

They cut across backstreets and took shortcuts across lawns, always watching, always listening. Only once did they hear a car and they hid out behind a detached garage. It was nothing more than a little Jetta, but it made Logan more cautious as they emerged from the shadows.

When they reached the park—a multiacre spread of sandboxes, soccer fields, and grassy picnic mounds— Logan made them wait inside the tree line as he studied the open field for movement. Everything was still except for the light brush of wind across his face, lulling leaves into a soft music.

"I'll go alone," Scott said. "It's safer that way."

Logan did not disagree. Jean also said nothing. They watched him leave the cover of shadow into a lighter dark, a small figure walking quickly across the grass to a spot in the center of a field. Scott stood there for several minutes, staring at nothing.

"Crap," Logan said.

"I'm not surprised," Jean said. "We'll just have to be more resourceful."

"It's one of the things I do best, darlin'."

"I know," she said, and her smile was small and wry.

Scott did not say anything when he returned from the field. He examined his hands and then their faces, looking each of them in the eyes. He saved Jean for last, and if Logan had been at all sentimental, he would have felt a twinge of sympathy for the sorrow and apology in that man's gaze.

"No one knows us," Scott said, quiet. "We don't have our powers, we're wanted by the police, and we're dead broke."

"Right," Logan said. "Survival time."

8

THEY WALKED QUICKLY, KEEPING TO ALLEYS AND SIDE streets as they crossed from residential neighborhoods into industrial parks. Night in the dead zone between Tacoma and Seattle was quiet, filled only with the occasional rumble of a car engine or the shout of some drunk making friends with a bottle.

"It's a good ten miles between here and downtown Seattle," Logan said. It was difficult for Jean to listen to him when he sounded like a woman. Or maybe a better word was "eerie." If she did not look at him, if she pretended hard enough, she could almost convince herself that Logan was still a man and that his voice, with its same gruff growl, was the product of some terrible helium accident.

With Scott it was different. She could not yet pretend with him.

"That will take us all night," Kurt said. Rogue walked close beside him; Jean thought it was in case his leg gave out. He was trying not to limp, but she remembered that blow to his knee, his high cry.

"Yeah," Logan said, and Jean knew there would be no discussion about whether Kurt could handle the distance.

They had to keep moving; first, to locate Jonas Maguire, and if that proved unfruitful, then somehow to find a way home, and fast.

Scott brushed up against her side. She glanced down at him—and oh, that was strange, being taller than her husband—and said, "Hey."

"Hey," Scott said softly. "How are you feeling?"

"Okay," she said, sensing his discomfort. Her voice sounded loud in the quiet of night, and she slowed her pace, creating some distance between themselves and the others. "How about you?"

He smiled, grim, and ran his fingers through his hair. A familiar gesture, one that made her heart jump, her stomach twist. She reached out and touched his face. Just a slip of her fingers against his cheek. Her hand was large and dark against his pale skin, but it was becoming her hand, her body, and though startling, she could breathe now when she looked at herself. She could accept her new form, even if she desperately wanted her old one back.

Scott's breath caught. Jean said, "Close your eyes," and he did. She brushed her fingers against his lips, running them across his throat, and he swallowed hard.

"It's still me," she whispered, aware they were falling even farther behind the others. She did not care. She had to make sure he understood, that whatever else happened, he could live with the changes between them. She hoped it was not permanent, but if it was . . . oh, God, if . . .

Scott opened his eyes. Brown eyes, rich dark eyes. Not

his eyes, though. Jean wished they were. He grabbed her hand, held it against his face, and said, "I know."

Do you, really? Jean wondered, aching for her powers, that sweet comfort of knowing his thoughts. A burden, too, but now that she was without the ability, she knew better than to take it for granted. She was appalled, too, at how vulnerable she felt without her gifts. Surely, she was stronger than this. She had to be.

A smile flickered across Scott's mouth. Jean said, "What?"

He shrugged, and tucked her much larger arm against his side. "It's . . . funny. There's no way in the world anyone could mistake you for my wife—"

"Oh, really," Jean drawled.

"—but there is something of you in this man you're wearing. I can see it. I can see it so clearly when you look at me."

Jean smiled, and this time it was genuine: a first, since waking up in her new body. Scott gazed up at her and quietly said, "There. There it is. My Jean."

She did not know how much she needed to hear those words; she took a deep breath, savoring the unexpected looseness in her chest, her gut, and held on to the look in his eyes, trying to memorize the moment so it would always stay fresh inside her heart.

"Scott," she said. "What if I stay like this? What if we're both . . . stuck?"

He did not look away. "Do you know who *I* am, Jean?"

She smiled. "Is that a trick question?"

Scott stopped walking. He reached up and touched

her cheek, brushing his thumb over her lips. Jean wanted to close her eyes, to pretend he wore a different face, but that would be a disservice, and Scott's eyes were open. He was not pretending.

He drew close, and this time it was Scott who fit into her body, Scott who was small and lithe and feminine, and his small hand touched the back of her neck. They both hesitated, staring at each other: those strange faces housing familiar hearts.

"You don't have to," Jean finally said, when the silence stretched too long.

"I know," he said, "but I want to. You're still my wife, Jean."

He stood on his toes, and Jean bent down and closed her eyes. He kissed her, soft, on the lips. His mouth felt odd, but the passion was still there, and after a moment she gave herself over to the comfort of being touched by the person she loved.

It did not last. She heard footsteps, a low sigh.

"We don't have time for this," Logan muttered.

"Shut up," Scott said. "We're having a moment here."

"You can take a whole year for all I care, but not until we're someplace safe. Come on, Cyke. Don't make me be the voice of reason in this outfit. We're already screwed up enough."

"He's got a point," Jean said. "Cyke."

Scott gave her a dirty look. Logan, showing a remarkable degree of restraint, said nothing at all. He turned and walked back to Kurt and Rogue, who waited quietly beneath a scraggly tree, one of many that lined the broken sidewalk; no doubt part of an old project meant to greenify a section of the city that was, even at night, extraordinarily dour. Kurt leaned against the narrow tree trunk, rubbing his leg. He stopped when the others got close.

"How are you doing?" Scott asked him.

Kurt straightened, throwing Rogue a wry smile. "We were just discussing that, *mein freund*. I will be fine."

"Right," Rogue muttered. "His knee is popping every time he straightens his leg."

Scott frowned. "You've made it this far. Can you keep going?"

"I must," Kurt said, and then waved his hands in the air. "*Ach*, don't look so concerned. I am not crippled. It could be worse."

Could be, and probably would be, after this night. They had no money, no transportation other than what their feet could provide them. Jean said nothing, though. She did not imagine hitchhiking was an option, not in this part of town and not at night.

"Screw it," Logan muttered, and stalked off down the street.

"Logan?" Jean said. She ran after him. "Logan, what are you doing?"

"What I should have done earlier," he said. "But I was trying to be decent. Forget that."

He stopped beside an old Chevy van parked at the side of the street and began looking at the ground, which was littered with debris.

"Go get the others, Jeannie," he said, picking up a rock.

No need. Everyone was already close behind, looking puzzled but not terribly surprised by Logan's outburst.

"Logan," Scott said slowly, looking at the rock in his hand. Logan flashed them a quick grin and then in one smooth motion smashed the rock through the driver's-side window of the van. The glass shattered.

"So much for being subtle." Scott watched the street around them. Jean listened, but heard no one stirring inside the nearby buildings. She doubted that would last.

"Don't get your panties in a twist." Logan reached through the broken window to unlock the door. He climbed in and leaned over to open the passenger side. "Everyone, move it."

"You know," Scott said, remaining still, "hot-wiring cars only works in the movies."

"Then you must be really bad at it." Logan grabbed a large piece of broken glass and used it to pry off the old plastic dash beside the wheel. Jean grabbed Scott's arm and steered him to the other side of the van, where Rogue and Kurt were already buckling into the large backseat. Scott grabbed the front; Jean joined the others, sliding the door shut behind her. The interior smelled like beer and cigarettes.

Logan found two wires and stripped them with a sharp edge of glass. Scott rummaged through the glove compartment. Jean, too, cast around the back of the van, looking for anything useful. All she found were some worn *Playboys* and a pair of very dirty underwear. Jean nudged the soiled boxers with her foot. Rogue shook her head.

She heard popping sounds accompanied by colorful

language. The van's engine roared to life and Logan shifted gears, pulling away from the curb. He blew on his fingers.

"I feel so guilty," Kurt said. "What if stealing this car ruins some man's life?" He glanced out the back window. Jean looked, too. The street was dark and empty.

"Say some prayers for him," Logan replied. The wind rushing through the broken window whipped blond hair across his chubby face. He brushed it away impatiently. A *hard-nosed little brat*, Jean thought fondly. Logan looked like the kind of girl who could nurse a kitten back to health and then rip the face off a trucker, all in one breath. Which was entirely accurate, considering what Jean knew of the man inside that woman's body.

"Where does Jonas Maguire live?" Jean asked.

"Old Victoria Hill," Scott said.

"Like I said, I know the area," Logan said. "It's on the north end of downtown. Real ritzy. We're gonna stand out, looking like we do."

"This is Seattle," Jean said. "Besides, we don't look that bad."

Logan said nothing, though she sensed he disagreed. He pulled onto the freeway. Jean saw the first flicker of downtown lights, the edge of the ocean pushing up against the city shore. Boats, headlights shining, trawled slowly through the waters. The air rushing into the van suddenly felt colder; it smelled like salt, the chemicals of hard industry.

"I still don't get how this Doc Maguire could have had anything to do with our situation." Rogue drummed her fingers against the faux-leather seat. "What kind of beef would some psychologist in a mental hospital have with the X-Men?"

"The better question is why some psychologist who's rich enough to be living in Old Victoria would be working at a dump like Belldonne."

"A good conscience?" Kurt suggested.

Logan grunted. "A good conscience doesn't pay the mortgage, Elf. Not in this town, anyway."

"He was there for at least a year," Scott said. "Working full-time, with a concentrated focus on the most troublesome patients in the ward. Namely, us. Our bodies. Based on what I overheard, the doctor practically made us well. That's why not many of the nurses took him seriously when he told them to restrain us."

Rogue shook her head. "He obviously didn't do so great by me, or did I imagine all those stories?"

"What stories?" Logan asked.

"The previous occupant of Rogue's body became very creative with the use of her undergarments," Kurt said, dodging Rogue's fist. "Particularly with me."

"Right," Logan said.

They drove in silence until Logan pulled off the freeway, and then followed the road into a quiet business district shadowed by the tall towers of downtown Seattle. Jean guessed it must be near four in the morning; the sidewalks were empty except for a few lumpy bodies curled on cardboard flats. Jean imagined herself as one of those people, forced to sleep on the street, and swallowed hard.

"That looks like Japanese," Scott said, pointing out a large sign plastered against an old brick building. Jean looked closer and noticed quite a few billboards written in Asian languages; there were restaurants, too, neon signs spicing up windows with names like HONEY COURT PALACE and DRAGON PEARL. Jean's stomach growled. Rogue glanced at her, and the two women shared a knowing look. Their snacking at the house had not gone far, but until they had money, it would be longer yet until they saw food.

"We're in Chinatown," Logan said. "Or the International District, however politically correct you want to get."

"Why are we here?" Scott asked.

"Gotta change cars, Cyke. At least our plates, but a car would be better. Something a little nicer for when we go into Old Victoria."

"It's four in the morning," Jean protested. "Surely no one will pay attention."

"The cops will, and excuse me for saying so, darlin', but none of us have ID, and the car we're driving screams 'poor.' I don't care how progressive this city is supposed to be, we go marching up like that, in one big group, and someone is going to ask questions. If nothing else, they'll look twice, and we don't want that."

Jean blew out her breath. "You're paranoid, Logan."

"No, I'm realistic. I've been in the gutter and I've been on top, and let me tell you, Jeannie, it ain't no picnic being on the bottom. When you got nothing, some people feel like they can treat you like nothing. We've got too much at stake to take a risk on something like that."

"*Ach*," Kurt said softly. "Just leave us behind, then. If we are such a burden, then let us off in some safe place and we will wait for you to go check out this Jonas Maguire's home. That would be easier, *ja?* But no more stealing cars, Logan. Even that has risk."

For a moment, Jean thought Logan looked sorry. Scott, glancing at him, said, "I don't like the idea of us being separated. We have no way of communicating with each other—"

Rogue jumped in. "And all we have right now is each other."

"*But*," Scott continued, as Jean knew he would, "Logan has a point. As a group, we attract attention."

"And I sure as hell don't want to break into a man's home with a crowd," Logan added.

"So, what? You leave us behind in some back alley, twiddling our thumbs while you run out and save the day? Logan—"

"This is not about Logan, and this is not about saving the day," Scott interrupted. "This is about survival, Rogue. We are in deep trouble, and this Dr. Maguire may know why. Anything that improves our odds of getting in and out of his house without detection, and *anything* that gets us home in one piece we will do, no matter how much it hurts our pride."

"Scott," Jean said. He ignored her, turning around in his seat to look out the window. A breathless silence filled the van, a waiting silence, and if Jean still had her powers, Scott's head would be full of words instead of this speechless isolation.

But that was the problem. Jean wondered if she and her husband even knew how to communicate with the spoken word; for so long they had relied on her telepathy to know every nuance of the other's soul, and now—now—

It hurt and she could not make it better, because now was not the time for fighting, nor would she ever fight in public with Scott. Not when they were on a mission and the others needed to have confidence in his decisions. Her anger never trumped her loyalty.

"Logan," Scott said quietly. "Find a safe place to park the van."

"Yeah," he said, glancing over his shoulder at Jean. "I got that."

Logan drove through narrow side streets that emptied into the heart of downtown; a landscape of artful steel and glass, towering over elegant facades of stone and brick, all of which pushed upward along impossibly steep hills that had their stolen van gasping for breath. Jean feared she would have to jump out and push.

"Gotta love these old engines," Logan said, patting the dashboard. "Come on, baby."

He drove them out of downtown, passing through quiet neighborhoods; gently rolling streets lined with small comfortable homes and tiny yards, all of which ended abruptly on the edge of a large thoroughfare that took them on a winding path past the Seattle Space Needle, the park, and up yet more hills, up and up, until Logan pulled off the road into a small empty U-Park located beside some local shops, and stopped the car in the darkest corner farthest from the street.

Jean saw two people huddled together in the nearby bushes. They lay on top of a blanket. She could not clearly see their faces, but she thought they watched the van.

Logan unbuckled his seat belt. "We're in lower Old Victoria. Maguire's house is on Highland Avenue, which is about a mile from here at the top of the hill."

"I can't imagine what you were doing on your last visit to know all these things," Rogue said. "I think you've got this entire city memorized."

Logan shrugged. "I did some jobs. This and that. Point is, if I leave now, I should be back before it gets too light out."

"I'm going with you," Scott said. "No arguments."

"Fine." He did not look happy; Jean was surprised he did not put up more of a fight. Rogue, given the look on her face, was equally shocked.

"So it's all right to bring *him* along?"

Logan shrugged. "We're both chicks, Rogue. The only trouble we're going to attract is a drunk or a pervert. We look too innocent for anything else."

"Oh, God help us all," Jean said.

Rogue narrowed her eyes. "You're a sexist pig, Logan."

"Oink." He climbed out of the car, but leaned back in before shutting the door. "You kids be good. No fighting."

Scott turned and gave Jean such a grave look, she opened the back door and jumped out after him as he slid from the car. He had a tiny figure, his slender legs dangling over the pavement as he dropped from his seat to the ground. Jean towered over him.

"What is it now?" she asked.

Scott frowned and drew her away from the van. "There are a lot of unknowns about all this," he said in a low voice. "Our plan is solid, but you know how it is, Jean. Nothing is safe. If we're not back by midmorning— earlier, even—get out of here. Don't take the van. Clean it for prints, then walk away. Find a pay phone and keep calling the school until you get someone to listen to you."

"I love it when you patronize me."

"It's such a turn-on, right?"

"Only for you," Jean said. "I don't like this."

"Neither do I," Scott said, "but what do you want me to do? I won't risk all of us on something so chancy as breaking and entering. If anything goes wrong, the worst that happens is that Logan and I will be sent to jail or returned to the hospital. If you three are free, though, at least we still have a fighting chance of finding someone— Xavier, this Maguire—who can fix us."

Jean sighed. Scott touched her hand, her cheek.

"Come on, sweetheart. You know I'm right."

"I don't know anything," Jean said, "but I'm too tired to argue with you. Go on, then. Go with Logan and be a cowboy for the night."

"Cowgirl," Logan said, appearing beside them. It did not matter he no longer had his body or his mutant powers; he still moved silent as a ghost.

"I keep forgetting that part," Scott said.

"I can't imagine how," Jean said, shifting uncomfortably. Logan grinned, but Scott grabbed his arm and steered him away before he said anything inappropriate. Scott looked back over his shoulder and Jean tried to see her husband in that small feminine face, those large dark eyes.

"Bye," he said. Jean did not respond. She turned around and climbed into the passenger seat of the van.

"I hate this," Rogue said, but so quietly, so forlorn, that Jean could not bring herself to be irritated at her friend. "I don't like being left behind. I want to help."

"Yes," Jean said, tapping her feet on the floor. "Logan made a good point, though. All of us together would draw attention. Two young women, though?" She shrugged. "Less threatening."

"Really. Seems like a bunch of lousy stereotypes to me." Rogue pursed her lips; a familiar expression, much like the way she cracked her knuckles and then rubbed her arms, like she had something unpleasant under her skin. "I think Logan just likes playing it alone, but he's taking Scott along for the ride because he knows our fearless leader won't take no for an answer. We, on the other hand, are like a bunch of puppy dogs, sittin' pretty. Nice and obedient."

Kurt stared. "You are truly angered by this. That . . . surprises me."

"I don't know why," Rogue said. "Seems to me I got a right to be a little miffed. Some . . . jerk . . . steals our bodies, takes our lives, and I can't participate in bringing him down? Not even a little bit?"

"No one is holding you here," Jean said, too tired to talk reason to her, especially when she agreed with everything Rogue said. "You can still catch up with them, if that's what you really want."

Silence. Rogue shifted in her seat and lay back her head, staring at the van ceiling. Kurt patted her hand, saying nothing, but adding to the atmosphere a quiet sympathy that was gentle and comforting. Kurt had that way about him, no matter what he looked like.

Jean thought about her own appearance, staring down at her hands as she leaned against the cold hard window. Dark brown skin covered large fingers and sinewy wrists, thickly muscled forearms that felt strong, and no doubt were; she felt her face, the bristles and thick jaw, the masculine features that were so utterly foreign. How strange, to know she was a woman, to feel like a woman, and yet be trapped in a man's body. She envied Rogue, and wondered just how Scott and Logan were handling their own displacement. Neither one had truly complained—not that they would—but it had to be just as strange and frightening.

Jean listened to the sound of her borrowed heart, beating slow and sure inside the chest she wore. Like a costume made of flesh, one that she could never take off.

Put inside this body because someone has a purpose for your face, your identity, and they cannot risk there being two of you.

None of them talked. They sat and waited, lost in thought, until Jean noticed that the sky was beginning to lighten and that traffic on the street behind them had increased. Worry spiked her gut. She lifted her feet off the dashboard and got ready to leave the van. Maybe walk up the street just a ways, and see if she heard anything unusual. Police sirens, rushing to pick up her husband and his crazy companion.

"Someone is coming," Kurt whispered. Rogue and Jean looked at him and he held up his hand. "Listen. There is a scuffing noise on the concrete."

Jean listened, and after a moment, heard that light brush of footfall, even and unhurried. Only one, though.

Logan would be silent, she told herself, but she did not open the door. A shadow appeared on the other side of her window. A man peered in. He had a nice suit jacket on, and his face was hard and thin.

"Hello," he said.

"Hello," Jean replied, wary of the look in his eye. He smiled, but it was cold, full of teeth. She could not see his hands.

"I've been watching you for a while. There a reason you're parked here this time of morning?" he asked.

"Is there a law that says I can't park here?"

"Maybe. Depends on the why, and those girls you're waiting on."

"Girls?"

The man rubbed his chin. "I got a little something going on down the street. This is a high-class neighborhood, you know? Takes a certain kind of girl, a certain kind of connection and know-how. You're doing it all wrong; the car, the clothes your girls are wearing. Keep this up and you'll bring the cops down on us all."

"We're not here on business," Jean said, finally understanding. "Those . . . girls . . . simply went to visit a friend."

"Friend." The man laughed, low. "Right. We all got friends we have to visit early in the morning, don't we? Thing is, I'm not the kind who likes to share my . . . friends. My girls don't, either. Which is why, right now, I'm gonna ask you real polite to move this ghetto-ass car of yours, and get the hell out of my neighborhood."

"I can't do that," Jean said, not bothering to make any more denials. "I have to wait for my girls to come back. I'm sure you understand. I'll leave when they arrive."

"Not good enough."

"It will have to be." Jean felt Rogue and Kurt shift quietly behind her. She wondered how anyone, even in this altered state, could mistake her for a pimp. She wished she could read this stranger's mind, or take over his body with nothing but a thought. Make him crawl back to the hole he lived in.

Again, that cold smile. The man stepped away from the van and finally Jean could see his hands. He held a gun.

"Oh, darn," she said.

9

It had been almost ten years since Logan walked these streets, and like most old neighborhoods, nothing much had changed. The houses still had their irregular steep-pitched roofs with patterned shingles, the lawns were still immaculate, and the view of Elliot Bay and Lake Union still managed to take his breath away. Or maybe that was just his body. Patty, whoever she was, had terrible endurance, and these hills were the steepest in the city.

"I don't like leaving them," Scott said. His breathing seemed far more regular; Logan envied him for that.

"They'll be fine," Logan said, still trying to grow accustomed to the high squeaky tones of his voice. "You seem to forget that you're dealing with X-Men here."

"Powerless X-Men."

"Gimme a break, Cyke. You think Jean's telepathy or Kurt's teleporting are all that makes them strong?"

"Of course not, but it does give them an advantage."

Logan shrugged. He couldn't argue with that. Then again, there was no use crying over things that might never be changed. You just picked up the pieces and kept moving. Did the best with what you had.

And what he had was the flabby misused body of a

twenty-something woman who looked far too cute for his taste, and who was pierced in several areas that should never know the touch of hard steel. Two of them were rubbing against his shirt.

Kid really was crazy. It had taken a legion of scientists to stick metal in Logan's body. He didn't understand anyone who would do it voluntarily.

They passed only one other person during their walk, a bespectacled older man with a golden retriever, who smiled at them both, but made eyes only at Scott. Logan did not mind in the slightest. Scott give him a hard look and said, "Don't even think about it."

"What?"

"You know very well what."

"Aw, hell. You need to get in touch with your feminine side, Scott. Ain't no time like the present."

Scott grunted. "Doesn't it bother you at all that you're a woman?"

"Would bother me more if I was still in my own body and missing certain . . . parts."

Which had been his first thought upon awakening in the hospital. A bad place to go, if you were a man. *Very* bad. Discovering his young perky breasts, seeing that unfamiliar face reflected in the glass of his window, had made him feel immensely better because this was clearly not his body. And if this was not his body, then somewhere out there he— Logan, Wolverine—was still a whole, healthy man.

"Okay," Scott said. "I see your point."

Logan grunted. "We're getting close."

"Thank God. My thighs are killing me."

"Don't complain too much. You want to stay toned, you know. Keep those legs smokin'."

"Logan—"

"Why do you think Jean gets on that StairMaster every day?"

Scott sighed. "You are totally out of control."

"You say that so much it's practically habit. Gotta find a new line, Scooter."

"Right. Is it possible that becoming a woman has made you even more obnoxious?"

"That's just you. Must be PMS."

"Bad joke," Scott said, but Logan did not give him a chance to say more. He stopped walking, gazing from the numbers on a gray mailbox to the house behind it, perched like a fine diamond, one of many, in the crown of Old Victoria Hill.

Jonas Maguire's house was a large white Victorian set off the street and surrounded by trees. Perfect cover. Logan and Scott walked up the front sidewalk like they owned the place, which in his experience, was the best way to act when you were trying to set up a con. A little confidence went a long way, especially in the city, where no one paid much attention to the private lives of their neighbors, and odd comings and goings at night could be ascribed to some quirk of behavior, rather than any criminal wrongdoing.

"He must have a security system," Scott whispered, as they stepped on the wide front porch. Hanging pots bobbed with the outlines of geraniums and ferns. Rocking chairs sat at the very end of the porch, and over the antique mail slot was a wooden carving of a fat cow. It was all very innocuous and country.

"Yeah, this one's a real mad scientist," Logan said. "Wonder if he knits."

Scott peered around the edge of the porch. "The garage is detached, so no go through there. Do you think he has a house sitter?"

"I could knock and find out."

Scott actually seemed to think about that. "We could always say our car broke down."

"Forget it. I was joking. You do that and someone will be on the phone to the cops. We won't have time to do anything." Logan examined the lock. It was simple; looked like the original, even. "I need something to pick this with. Do you still have that wire?"

Silent, face devoid of expression, Scott reached into his pants. Logan stared. He began to ask, but Scott shook his head. Yeah, he was probably better off not knowing—but it still wasn't easy touching that wire.

While Scott watched the street, Logan bent over to work. It was difficult to see—he missed being a mutant—but he slipped the wire in the lock and jimmied it around until he heard a very satisfying click.

"Security," Scott reminded him again.

"I know," Logan said, but without more time or the tools to do a proper examination of the property, they were going to have to wing it anyway. Alarms or not, that door was coming open.

And when it did, when Logan pushed his way into the house, he heard not a sound. He looked around for a security panel, some blinking red light that would give it away, but there was nothing.

"This Maguire is a real trusting guy," Logan said, stepping sideways so that Scott could enter.

"Maybe he has a reason to be."

"If he's a mutant, you mean."

"The evidence suggests that he is."

"But why us?" Logan sniffed the air; a reflex. He felt only slightly foolish. The house had no discernable odor; perhaps, only, a hint of some flower, perhaps a rose. He listened, and though he heard nothing, wondered if that was only his own weakness, whether there was something he was missing, something escaping his notice, all because he was human now, and weak.

Not weak. Not for one minute, don't you tell yourself that.

Because he was only as weak as his spirit, and he refused to let this—his new body, these circumstances—break him.

"I think this is his office," Scott said, peering into a room off the main entry. The woodwork was old, classic, with fine carved flowers in the dark trim and shining hardwood floors that smelled like lemon. A large desk faced the sole window. Its surface was clean except for a computer, a thin sheaf of paper, and one framed picture of a dark-haired woman with a lovely smile and amazing cheekbones.

"Wife?" Logan asked.

"Could be," Scott said. He glanced around the room. "Check upstairs. I can handle this."

"Yes, ma'am." Logan flashed him a grin and ducked out of the office. He examined the kitchen first, a quick walk through, and then headed up the stairs on light feet, listening for any movement, any sign they were not alone. Everything was quiet. No life here. Nothing except for them.

All the doors stood open. Logan perused the rooms, taking in the complete lack of furniture or personal items. No paintings, no soft chairs; Maguire had a bed, but it was only a twin, covered in a threadbare quilt. One pillow. One closet half-full of dress shirts and suit jackets. One dresser, with only one drawer filled with underwear.

And one drawer for a teddy bear. Very soft, very worn, and missing both its eyes. It had been placed carefully inside the dresser, sitting in the center with its little mournful face turned up. Logan picked up the bear, holding it gingerly in his hands. He sniffed its fur. It smelled clean, like detergent.

He heard footsteps in the hall. Scott entered the room, stopping when he saw what Logan held.

"Does this mean anything to you?" Logan held up the bear.

"It's the only personal item I've seen in the house, other than the photograph downstairs."

"Which means it's important, because this guy doesn't have crap. Looks like he moved into this house with a suitcase and set up shop."

"A temporary living space? Something that gives the appearance of permanence?" Scott pulled a folded piece of paper out of his pocket. "I found this on his desk."

Logan took the paper. "An e-ticket receipt for a flight to New York. The good doctor left last night. That's convenient."

"Very. I'd say the evidence against Maguire is getting stronger."

"I'd say you're right. I'd also say that our bodies went with him, but probably in *our* jet."

"That requires specialized knowledge to fly, Logan."

"Cyke, if the man really did do a mind switch on us, then he's probably strong enough to pull some information out of our heads while he's at it." Logan hesitated, staring at the teddy bear. "Here's what I don't get. This is a man who has no life. Or rather, the life he does have has been built around a specific purpose. My guess? To screw us. I wanna know why."

"You're assuming a lot. We don't really know him. His goals might not be to hurt us, but to *use* us."

"Don't get technical on me, bub. Your wife is a man and the both of us have boobs. I'm not feeling the love."

Scott rolled his eyes. "Fine, I agree that his intentions aren't exactly noble. In fact, I'll even go so far as to say he has it in for us—"

"—thank you—"

"—but that doesn't answer your question. Why?"

Logan gazed around the room. The teddy bear felt soft and warm in his hand; he was reluctant to put it down. "Did you find out who the woman in the photo is?"

"No," Scott said, "but she must have been special."

"Yeah. This isn't a man who owns a lot. Which makes me wonder why he would leave without the picture and the bear. They're easy to pack and they obviously mean something to him."

"He's traveling light."

"Not good enough."

"Because he thinks he's coming back?"

"Or because he knows he's not."

"As in what? He thinks he's going to die? He plans on committing suicide?"

"Maybe. It doesn't seem like he has much of a life, anyway."

Scott shook his head. "If I was going to kill myself, I would want my most precious mementos nearby."

"As a reminder of your misery?" Logan waved the teddy bear in Scott's face. "Does this really say 'why, God, why'?"

"Maybe to Maguire."

"Or maybe he's left the trappings of his life behind, so he can be free to do what needs to be done. He's going out as a man of resolve."

"That still doesn't explain why."

"I don't think we're gonna get that 'why' until we catch up with him, meaning we need to find some way of getting back to New York before he finishes what he started. Whatever that is."

"Infiltrating the X-Men?"

"As a start. He has something bigger in mind, that's for sure." Logan shook the teddy bear. Quiet, almost to himself, he murmured, "What the hell is going on here?"

"That's what we're going to find out." Scott folded up the receipt and stuck it back in his pocket. "Come on, Logan. Let's get out of here."

Two things happened before they left Jonas Maguire's house.

The first was that Scott made a phone call. It was almost 8:30 in the morning on the East Coast. Plenty of time for everyone to be up and about and ready to answer phones.

The school had a 1-800 number for the students in case they ever needed to reach someone at the Mansion and did not have enough money for a pay phone. Just another safety precaution—Jean's idea, even—and Scott had never been happier for it.

He tried Storm's extension first, but that proved to be a dead end. Scott was not sure who else was at the Mansion. The day before he and his team left for Seattle, Bobby and Sam had dragged Piotr off to the woods for a camping trip. Gambit and Jubilee were supposed to be around, but they did not pick up their phones, either.

Scott gave up and called the main line. It rang five times before someone answered. The voice belonged to a girl, young and breathless; one of the students, though Scott did not recognize her.

"Hello?" she said. "Um, Xavier's School for the—"

"Is Ororo there?" Scott interrupted. "Storm?"

"Uh, sorry. She went out early to go shopping. Can I take a message?" Polite, distant, the perfect voice for dealing with strange adults. *But I am not a stranger,* Scott wanted to say. *You know me. I probably taught you geometry last week. Brat!*

Scott grit his teeth. "What about any of the other senior teachers? Gambit? Is Sam or Bobby back?"

"I'm sorry, ma'am, but they're all gone for the day. It's the weekend, you know. If you give me your name . . . ?"

He almost said "Scott," but stopped himself just in

time. Without seeing him face-to-face, listening to everything he and the others had to say, it would be difficult to convince Storm or any of their friends that they were the real X-Men. They all knew secrets about each other that could not be faked, but just finding the chance to get them to listen was going to be an ordeal.

"My name is Mindy," he said carefully. "I'm a very close friend of Scott Summers and Jean Grey, and I have some important information about them for Ororo. *Very* important."

For a moment there was only silence on the other end of the line. Scott said, "Hello?" and the girl made a small sound.

Quiet, tentative, she said, "Are they okay? They've been gone for a couple days."

Scott hesitated. There must have been something in his voice, or maybe the girl was just that perceptive.

"No, they're not okay," he finally said, striving to be calm, to not shout into the phone. "You need to get that message to Ororo as soon as possible. Understand?"

"Yes, ma'am," said the girl, and Scott felt a great deal of pride at the change in her voice, the seriousness of her commitment. Good kids, all of them. Maybe the X-Men weren't doing such a bad job of teaching the next generation.

"Do you have a number where she can reach you?" asked the girl.

"No," Scott said. "Just tell her I'll call back again in a couple of hours."

"Okay," she said, and that was it. The girl hung up.

Scott felt a brief pang in his heart when the connection died. In this body, with his identity stolen, he was nothing but an outsider looking in, some distant unknowable human—a wannabe, a stranger—and it hurt. It hurt that the student had not recognized him, that she would never believe him if he told her the truth.

Crazy. She would think you're crazy. Even your friends are going to think you're crazy, unless you can convince them of the truth.

It would be easier if Xavier was around, but he and Hank were in Geneva for the next two weeks, attending a mutant-rights symposium. Mutants representing mutants, in an effort to stem the tide of world legislation aimed at curbing the use of their powers. Scott did not know how to reach him, and even if he did, calling Geneva collect from a pay phone and actually getting through was highly unlikely. Xavier was keeping the company of world leaders; getting someone to fetch him for a call on some unrecognized line might be as difficult as getting his body back.

Logan entered the study. He carried a plastic shopping bag.

"What have you got in there?" Scott asked, frowning.

"Maguire still had some food in his refrigerator. I also took some of his clothes and underwear. Couldn't find any money, though."

"We need to figure out how to get some," Scott said, rubbing his face. "Okay, let's—"

Logan held up his hand; a sharp gesture, one that made Scott shut his mouth and listen. Logan closed his eyes.

Scott heard it, then. Sirens.

"Are they coming here?" he whispered, already moving out of the office. "Did we trip something on our way in?"

"Maybe someone saw us."

"We've been here almost twenty minutes. The cops would have gotten here sooner if we were seen breaking and entering." Or if they had triggered an alarm.

"Whatever," Logan said. "Let's move it."

They left through the kitchen, which had a back door that opened into a tiny garden filled with roses. The grass had not been mowed in quite some time, a sharp contrast to the front yard. Scott stepped on something squishy. There was enough light in the sky for him to see the remains of a fat slug beneath his shoe. Scott blinked hard; he still had trouble adjusting to the sudden influx of so many different kinds of color.

The sirens sounded closer; Scott and Logan pushed through a gap in the neighbor's bushes and used the cover of chaotically manicured trees and tall decorative grasses to partially hide their movements as they raced from one yard to the next, until half a block down from Maguire's home they made their way to the sidewalk and peered out at the road.

They watched the nearby intersection; two police cruisers sped past Highland Avenue down the hill toward lower Old Victoria. Scott sighed, rubbing his chest. He forgot he had breasts and got a handful before he remembered. Logan smirked at him.

"Shut up," Scott said, even though Logan hadn't said anything. They left Highland, still listening to the sirens. There were more cars on the road, but none slowed as they passed Logan and Scott. They were just two women out for an early-morning stroll.

"Those cop cars seem to be stationary now," Logan said, just as the sirens went dead. He looked at Scott, and there was no mistaking the question in his eyes.

Scott forgot subtlety. He ran down the hill.

At the first sight of flickering red and blue, Logan grabbed Scott's arm and made him slow to a walk. His heart pounded so loud he could barely hear the voices over the radio, the click of car engines cooling. He heard women talk, and thought of Jean when he heard that voice. He had to remind himself that she was a man now, and that the person talking had to be Rogue. Rogue, or some other woman.

"What happened?" Logan murmured, as they crossed into view of the U-Park. Scott forgot to breathe. There was an ambulance and a body on the ground beside their van. Scott could not see the face—too many people surrounded it—but the van doors, back and front, were open and he did not see anyone inside.

"They're gone," Logan said, and then: "Heads up, Cyke."

Scott tore his gaze away from the long legs stretched on the ground—*what was Jean wearing, oh God, what was she wearing, why can't I remember*—and looked up into the blue eyes of a narrow man in a black uniform.

"Ma'am," he said, nodding at Scott, and then Logan. "I don't suppose either one of you saw what happened here?"

"No," Logan said, and his voice was particularly soft, and very much that of a girl. Scott did not think he was that good of an actor, but considering what he had to work with, it probably should not have been such a surprise.

"You should move on, then. This really isn't pleasant to look at."

"What happened?" Scott asked, and then as an afterthought, "This is such a safe neighborhood."

The officer shrugged. "Like I said, this isn't something you want to be around, ladies."

"You're right," Logan said, grabbing Scott's arm. "Thanks."

He steered them away from the crime scene, and when they turned the corner and were out of earshot, hissed, "What were you trying to do, start up a conversation? Don't forget where we escaped from. They probably already have our pictures circulating."

"I wanted to know what happened."

"What happened is that someone got dead. All that matters is that it wasn't one of us."

Scott stopped walking. "Are you sure about that?"

"Jesus, Cyke. Don't you know what your friends look like?" Logan ignored Scott's answering scowl and said, "The dead guy had gray slacks on. All of us are wearing jeans or sweats."

Scott's hand hurt. He looked down and found his nails digging into his palm. He tried to relax and failed miserably. "Where do you think they are?"

"Must be close." Up one street were more residences, but here in this part of the neighborhood Scott saw only small shops and restaurants, most of which were still closed. It was a very upper-middle-class atmosphere, with not too many places for people to hide.

There was, however, a small green space down one block and across the street. Too small to be an actual park, but with enough flowers and greenery to be a pleasant place to sit and talk. Scott saw movement, someone tall and dark.

"Over there," he said, and led Logan across the street. He glanced behind. Shrubbery hid the police cars from sight, though Scott still feared being watched. No one followed them as they walked to the small public garden, and as they neared, Scott once again saw the tall figure of a man, hair large and wild with dreadlocks.

"Scott," Jean said, "we were worried about you."

"Worried about us?" He reached out and grabbed her hands, drawing her close. It was awkward, having to look up into her face, but he drowned his discomfort in the relief of finding her safe and alive.

He found Rogue and Kurt sitting on a bench. Near them were two other people: a heavily wrinkled man with silver hair, and another man, much younger, with bright blue eyes and a wry, twisting, mouth.

"These are the chicks he called whores?" said the young man, looking at Scott and Logan. "Dude. What an idiot."

"Sounds like we missed a lot," Logan said to Kurt.

"*Ja*. A barrel full of fun."

"A smokin' barrel," Rogue added. "Some high-class pimp came up to the car and accused Je—er, Jeff—of sending you two out as hookers."

"In this neighborhood?" Logan frowned. "He must have been high."

"Nah," said the old man, running brown fingers

through his hair. "Over here the girls don't walk the streets. They got cell phones now. Schedules they have to keep. Billy, he used to drop 'em off around here and then they'd go walk to their appointments. Didn't look like hookers, either. Sweet girls. Kind of like you two."

"But with way more flash," added his companion. "Nobody around here would hire you."

"Thanks," Logan said. "But who the hell are you?"

"This is Luke, and the older gentleman is his partner, Ed." Jean gave them both a small smile. "I think they may have saved our lives."

"Jeff is giving us way too much credit." Ed put his hands behind his back and stretched. His clothes were dark and raggedy, and his thick backpack overflowed with odd bits and pieces of material and plastic. There was an emptiness to his eyes that bothered Scott, but his smile seemed genuine enough. "All we did was provide a distraction."

"Yeah, we saw that gun and Ed here came out of the bushes where we were sitting and he was like, 'Hey, dude,' and then Jeff opens the door and steps out and these other two come out of the car, and Billy is all like, 'Stay back, assholes,' and then Jane and Renny do some weird shit and Jeff disarms him with some Jackie Chan move and a kung-fu kick to the nads. Dude fights dirty."

"I bet," Logan said, giving Jean an odd look. "That man back there. He looks dead."

Jean raised her eyebrows. "I didn't shoot him. I did, however, hit him over the head when he was down on the ground."

"Do you still have the gun?" Scott asked. Jean lifted up

the edge of her shirt and revealed a .44 sticking out of her pants.

"That's a good way to castrate yourself," Logan said. "Safety's on, right?"

"Of course," Jean said.

Scott turned to Luke and Ed. "Thanks for your help. We can't offer much in return, though."

Ed shook his head. "Wouldn't ask for nothing, anyhow. I'm sure you folks would do the same."

Scott nodded. The X-Men would do the same, though in the past their interventions had involved only mutants. Violence between humans was something they did not often get involved in, if only because the mutant issues always seemed more pressing. More . . . timely.

Of course, when one considered that mutants were still a minority, and that most reported day-to-day violence was between regular nonpowered humans, Scott wondered what else they could be using their gifts for. Was it enough just to help mutants?

You don't just *help mutants*, he reminded himself. True enough, but it seemed like that was all he *ever* thought about. Other heroes, like the Fantastic Four and Spider-Man, certainly did not "specialize." Or at least, they did not seem to.

"We have to get out of town," Logan said. "Heading east to New York. You guys know if Balmer Yard is still the best jumping station out of Seattle?"

Ed grinned. "You another train runner? Never met a girl so young who rode the rails. It's a dying art."

"Yeah," Logan said. "But it ain't dead yet."

The old man laughed. "Baylor's still good. Watch out for the bulls, though. They're getting more careful about surveying the empty cars."

"Bulls?" Scott murmured.

"Security guards," Logan said. "Old hobo lingo."

They waved good-bye to Luke and Ed, both of whom wanted to sit a while longer in the garden, or maybe—as they said—scrounge up some breakfast from one of the local café owners. It was tempting to stay with them and try to do the same, but the cops were still down the street and it was a miracle that none of them had come over yet to ask any questions.

"Actually, they did," Rogue said, when Scott voiced his concerns.

"You must have told some kind of story," Logan said. "I'm surprised they didn't take you guys in just on principle."

"You are such a pessimist." Kurt said, limping beside him.

"Yes," Logan agreed. "But I'm usually right, too. What gives?"

"We talked real pretty," Rogue said, giving him a sly smile.

Kurt placed a hand over his heart. "I pray thee, good Mercutio, let's retire! The day is hot, the Capulets abroad—"

"And if we meet," Jean interrupted in a deep baritone, "we shall not scape a brawl, for now, these hot days, is the mad blood stirring." She smiled. "I think I like saying those lines in a man's voice. It adds dramatic heft."

"You quoted Shakespeare at the police?" Logan asked disbelievingly.

"No," Rogue said, "but we started spouting it as soon as we saw them coming. Acted like we were some poor actors out for an impromptu morning rehearsal. You should have seen the looks on their faces."

"Right," Scott said slowly, "because what kind of criminals spout the great Bard?"

Jean shrugged, still smiling. "People see what they want. We gave them something different from the outset, and so they were less inclined to believe we were capable of violence. Illusion, sweetheart. Dreams and illusion."

Rogue stumbled. Kurt touched her arm and said something low that made her smile—a smile that did not reach her eyes.

"We're all tired and hungry," Jean said quietly, watching Rogue.

"Logan found some food in Maguire's house."

"Temporary measure," Logan said. "We need money. We also need to get to New York as fast as possible."

"Which is why you asked about the train station?"

"Ain't no station, darlin'. It's the tracks."

"I'm not comforted. There must be a better way."

"Jeannie—" Logan began, but Scott held up his hands.

"Unless you want to keep stealing cars—which I suppose is an option—and unless we can find enough money for bus or plane tickets, I think this is our best choice."

"Have you tried the school?"

"Everyone we needed was gone. Shopping."

Jean blew out her breath. "If we wait here—"

"Personally," Kurt called back, "I would prefer *not* to wait. At least let us be moving *somewhere*. The longer we are in this city, the greater our chances of being . . . collected . . . by the mental hospital. Surely we can find pay phones along the way. We will have other chances to contact our friends."

Rogue stopped walking and turned around to look at them. "You haven't told us what you found at the doctor's house."

"Someone who is seriously lonely," Logan said. He reached into the shopping bag and pulled out the teddy bear. Scott tried not to show his surprise. "This and a photo were the only personal items we found in his house."

"As well as a plane receipt for a flight to New York," Scott added. "He left last night."

Rogue nodded, her mouth settling into a hard white line. She looked especially dangerous in her new body, which Scott found curious. Despite the impression she usually gave—which was that of a soft-spoken Southern beauty—Rogue was one of the most formidable mutants in the world, and Scott had always judged her as such *because* of her powers. As a normal human, though, he was beginning to realize that she was just as intimidating.

That was good. He hoped all of them proved to be so strong. Because if they had to confront themselves—their bodies, their powers—and it came down to a fight, they were going to need every ounce of hard resolve to simply stay alive.

And even that would require a miracle or two.

10

ORORO MONROE, THOUGH SHE MIGHT NEVER ADMIT it, was a suspicious woman, and so when she entered the Worm Way nursery on Fifth and Tucker, and discovered that her special order of rare Gemini roses had mysteriously died during transit from South Carolina, she took it as a very bad sign. Roses never simply died. They had to be killed off. And in this case, she thought the murderer might just be Fate.

The reason was simple enough. As of this morning, every single rose in her carefully tended garden was dead or dying. Which, probably, had less to do with Fate than some irresponsible teenager who was going to end up paying for the death of her garden with some comparable sacrifice—like some hard unprotected labor on a bed of thorns.

Still, it stretched even her belief that someone she knew would go so far as to kill off a *shipment* of roses—because really, when people disliked her they went for the larger gestures, like kidnapping, torture, fights to the death.

And that brought her back, again, to signs and portents. Some mysterious message that could not be good.

As a result, she was extra careful driving home, rolling

like a woman three times her age, hunched over the wheel, watching the road for the unexpected—and getting honked at and passed for all her trouble. She felt quite foolish by the time she pulled up the long drive to the Mansion—and accordingly, summoned up her dignity so that when she stepped from the car she was once again all Goddess, confident and shining and bright with power. She tried to ignore the brittle roses by the front door.

The Mansion smelled good; someone had been baking that morning, muffins or cookies, and the sweet scent curled around her, accompanied by the loud noise of a television, laughter, the poofs and puffs of some mutant power being engaged. She saw the tip of a tail disappear around the corner at the end of the hall, and knew there were others close by, no doubt hiding from her.

"Children!" she called out, clapping her hands. "There are groceries in the car and I need help carrying them in."

It took several more announcements like that one—including a brief foray into the recreation room—before she received an appropriate response, but she soon had a nice little army of young people at her disposal, carrying bags from her car into the kitchen and unloading their contents into the correct locations.

Ororo was in the middle of supervising the placement—and protection—of the ice cream when Annie Potensky entered the kitchen. Fifteen and gawky, she was one of Ororo's best students, and a fine little telekinetic.

"Someone called while you were gone," she said,

breathless. "A woman named Mindy. She said she was a friend of Mr. and Mrs. Summers, and that they were in trouble."

Everyone in the kitchen stopped. Ororo said, "Keep working," and then to Annie, "Follow me."

When they were out of the kitchen and carefully ensconced in one of the private study rooms, Ororo made Annie tell her everything, which wasn't much.

"I spoke with Scott last night," Ororo said, recalling their brief and somewhat stilted conversation. "He did not mention any trouble."

On the contrary: Scott reported that the mutant issue in Seattle had been blown completely out of proportion, and that their trip was a total waste of time. The team was due to return later that afternoon and Ororo was glad of it. Gambit was around, but he was worse than the children. It was difficult being the sole responsible adult in the Mansion—even if it was summer and the students had the next two weeks off to relax.

"She called this morning, Ms. Monroe. I tracked the number and it was from a Seattle residence."

"Was there a name attached to that home?"

"Maguire," Annie said. "Jonas Maguire."

Ororo frowned. "That is not familiar to me, but thank you, Annie. You did a very good job."

Annie's shy smile gave way to worry. "Do you think they're all right, Ms. Monroe? Mr. and Mrs. Summers, I mean. I didn't . . . I didn't know they called last night."

Ororo tried not to show her amusement at the girl's concern. Jean and Scott were favorites among the students, who looked upon them with varying degrees of affection. Surrogate parents, teachers, and—occasionally—objects of teen lust, the married couple was the anchor of the school in ways that not even Xavier could compete with. Age probably had something to do with it. Ororo knew quite well that the students thought Charles was older than dirt.

"Everything is fine, Annie," Ororo reassured her. "Go and enjoy yourself."

Go and relax, go and think about better things than your teachers being in trouble. Leave that to me.

Not that Ororo thought Scott and his team needed help, but she still had roses on her mind, and doubt was a prickly thing. She left the study after Annie, but veered left to the secure elevators, where it was only a quick descent to the basement and the automated security center. High-tech monitors lined the wall, revealing snapshots of all the public areas in the school.

She putched a call to the Black-bird. Jean answered. Her voice sounded a little lower than usual, much like she had a cold.

"Hello there," Ororo said. "Is everyone all right?"

"Of course," Jean said. "And you?"

"Fine," she said. "I was just wondering what time you will return today."

"By lunch," Jean said, and then went silent. Ororo frowned. Jean was usually more talkative than this. Or at least, more engaged. Her words sounded a little too careful, rather clipped and shuttered.

"Well," Ororo said, trying to sound more cheerful than

she felt. "I know all the students will be happy to see you and the others."

"That's good," Jean said.

"Yes," she said, and then after a moment's hesitation, "Someone called this morning. About you and Scott. Her name was Mindy, and she said she was a friend."

Jean did not respond. Ororo said, "Hello?"

This time it was Scott who answered. "She's no friend of ours. Mindy is one of the patients at the mental hospital we visited. She . . . latched on to us."

"She must have latched on quite tightly to have uncovered our phone number," Ororo said.

"She's a telepath," Scott said. "She must have picked the number out of our heads."

Which did not make sense to Ororo, considering that both Jean and Charles had spent a long time helping each and every one of the X-Men develop their personal mental shields.

"If this Mindy truly plucked something as specific as a phone number from your heads, then she is quite powerful indeed. Are you certain she was not unfairly hospitalized? Perhaps there is something we could do for her."

"I really don't think so," Scott said. "She's beyond help."

"She must be, for you to give up so easily." Ororo's voice had more bite than she intended; her cheeks warmed. She wondered what was wrong with her, that she should be so judgmental.

"You weren't there," Scott said.

"Of course," Ororo said, though her temper still felt sour. She thought of her roses and took a deep breath.

You are a suspicious foolish woman. Do not take your insignificant troubles out on your friends.

"Were there any other mutants at the hospital?" she asked, and then, when he remained silent: "Scott?"

"No," he said, and his voice seemed deeper, not like the man she knew at all. "But we have to go now, Ororo."

The comm link clicked off. Ororo sat back, stunned. Scott had just hung up on her. Scott, who was one of the most compulsively polite men she knew. The man was too anal for anything less. She remembered something else then. According to Annie, Mindy had called the mansion from a residence, not a hospital.

Which meant that someone was lying to her. She did not, however, want to make any accusations before looking her friends in the eyes to see for herself if there was anything to be truly concerned over. She *would* get her answers, though. The truth was not something she played games with.

Ororo sat in her chair, staring at the monitors, one in particular: a shot of the garden and the withered blooms, looking as if a blight had come upon them in the night and sucked everything from them but the thorns.

Bad signs, she thought. *Or maybe something bad is already here.*

On any normal day, with any normal driver, the trip from New York City to Salem Center should have taken at least an hour. For Remy LeBeau, it took only thirty minutes—and that was because he was being careful. He had a passenger.

"You're driving too slow," Jubilee said, peering at him over the lenses of her sunglasses. Her leather jacket was a shocking shade of yellow, but at least she had developed enough fashion sense to coordinate her favorite color with hues other than hot pink and stonewashed blue. She had, instead, moved on to red and black, which Remy found almost as hideous, but which Jubilee felt was more "mature."

"*Petite*, I'm goin' more than ninety miles an hour, an' this is a country road."

"Whatever. I've seen old ladies drive faster."

"Mebbe if they were running from you," Remy muttered.

"Oh, the pain," Jubilee said, placing a hand over her heart. "You have struck a blow to my heart that will never heal."

"Good," he said. "It's what I owe you for last night."

"Puh-leese." Jubilee smirked, settling back in the Porsche's leather seat. "I saved your ass."

"You saved nuthin'. I knew exactly what I was doing."

"Dude, that chick had her hand so far up your thigh—"

"Don't finish that," Remy said. "The way you talk already gives me nightmares."

"Where do you think I learned all this?"

Logan. The X-Men. Oh, they were horrible role models. Either that, or Jubilee was just really good at talking her way into places where a fifteen year old had no right to be.

Like last night, helping him on a stake out. Real simple, too. Just a favor for an old friend who thought his girlfriend was cheating on him. Take a few pictures, jot down some addresses, and voilà! He hadn't even planned on taking anyone with him, but Jubilee seemed to have a nose for the good stuff and she wanted out of the Mansion *bad*. Without Logan to entertain her—and *mon dieu*, that man deserved a medal for patience—Jubilee was going stir-crazy and bringing everyone along with her. Very funny to watch, right up until the moment she zeroed in on you.

Which she had done, and under which he had caved like some goosey thin-skinned swamp rat fresh from the Bayou.

But the stakeout, supposed to be so easy, had gone horribly wrong. After being followed around half the night by the two intrepid spies, the girlfriend had come home at three in the morning *alone* (which was good, although maddening because it meant Remy had wasted an entire evening), only to be jumped by a group of men who had more on their minds than a simple conversation.

Remy did not like rapists. Neither did Jubilee. They made a good team.

And the girlfriend, after they took her to the hospital and waited as she filed a report with the police, was *very* grateful. Not that Remy was the kind who complained about the gratitude of beautiful women, but first, she was already taken, and second, he had a witness. A poor combination.

"Let's not talk about this anymore," he said to Jubilee. "It was a long night, an' I'm tired."

"I bet," she said, running fingers through her short

black hair. "It's hard fighting off all those beautiful chicks who throw themselves at you."

"It's a gift, *ma petite*."

"Right. Did you know there's a betting pool going on amongst the students, with the odds totally in favor of your mutant power being irresistible to women?"

Remy choked on his own spit. Jubilee laughed and turned on the radio. The Foo Fighters slammed the air and kept on playing loud and hard until they arrived home and Remy turned off the engine. The silence was broken only by the occasional tick of his cooling Porsche. Neither of them moved.

"What are you going to say when they ask?" Remy was rather worried. He had, after all, kept Jubilee out all night, and someone was bound to be displeased about that.

Jubilee grinned and Remy shook his head. He was, to use the colloquial, totally screwed.

His luck did not improve when they entered the Mansion. Ororo stood in the hall, arms folded over her chest. She looked displeased.

"Um," he said, forgetting how to be suave. He stifled the urge to throw Jubilee in front of him, and place the blame he was about to receive solely on her narrow shoulders.

"I have been trying to reach you for the last hour," Ororo said.

"My phone never rang." He reached inside his trench coat.

"Here." Jubilee pulled his cell out of her jacket. She

tossed it to him. "I pinched it off you last night when we were at the hospital. No cell phones allowed, remember?"

Ororo's frown deepened. Remy said, "It's not what you think. No one was hurt."

"At least not us," Jubilee added. "And the other guys will be fine in a month or so. No comas this time."

Remy gave her a dirty look. She pretended not to notice.

Ororo covered her eyes. Her white hair was mussed, her flowing silk wraps slightly askew. Remy thought it odd; even when upset, she was usually impeccable in her appearance.

" 'Ro," he said.

"Scott and the others will be returning soon," she said, which produced a squeal from Jubilee. Ororo did not appear as pleased. She looked Remy straight in the eyes and he saw, as he sometimes did, the memory of how he had first known her: a little stubborn girl with white hair and a face older than her years; a far-seeing gaze that was always calm, always strong. Ororo was one of the reasons he had stayed with the X-Men, and they had been friends for a very long time. He knew her moods. He knew when there was trouble in her heart.

"What's wrong?" he asked, and Jubilee's smile faded.

"Nothing," Ororo said, but her voice was distant, thoughtful. "Just little things, adding up all wrong."

"Little things that have to do with Scott and that mission to Seattle?"

"Is Wolvie okay?" Jubilee asked.

"Yes, of course." Ororo reached out and smoothed

back Jubilee's hair. "I am sorry for upsetting you. It is nothing, really. I have simply had an . . . odd day."

Remy did not particularly like the sound of that. Ororo never had "odd" days. A faint rumble passed over the Mansion.

"They're back," she said, gazing up at the ceiling, and then, softer, "This will be interesting."

Jubilee gave her a hard look. "You can stop with the riddles now."

"Yes, I can," she said. "Come, let us go and greet our friends."

Remy glanced at Jubilee and found her looking back at him in confusion. He sympathized completely. Something had happened while they were gone, and for some reason Ororo was reluctant to talk about it.

He hoped Rogue was all right. Their relationship continued to confuse him, but what he did know—the only thing he could be certain of—was that she was a friend. Quite possibly more than a friend, and if anything happened to her it would make a hole in his heart that he was not certain would ever fill up.

Better to keep her safe. Remy did not care for heartbreak.

He followed Ororo to the hangar, Jubilee close at his side. He did not bother telling her to go away, that this—whatever it was that had Ororo concerned—was for adults only. Jubilee was fifteen going on thirty, and Remy knew of few adults who had seen or done as much as she had in her short life. Besides, he knew quite well she would rather cough up her right lung than miss greeting Wolverine.

He was already off the jet when they arrived at the hangar. Jubilee raced across the concrete floor and flung herself in his arms for a giant hug.

"Hey!" she said, shameless. "You kick some butt?"

"Sure," Logan said, smiling. Remy was not entirely certain he liked that smile. It seemed . . . different, somehow. Brittle. Jubilee did not appear to notice.

Scott and Jean walked off the jet together, as did Kurt and Rogue. Remy called out a greeting to her, but she did not respond. At least, not in the way she usually did. She met his gaze only briefly, and then ducked her head with a shy smile and stared at the ground. Kurt nudged her—once, twice—until she lifted her chin. It looked like a struggle, though, as if all Rogue's great confidence had been stolen from her heart.

"Ma chérie," he said, drawing near. "What happened?"

Rogue swallowed hard. Kurt said, "She touched someone at the mental hospital. It . . . affected her. She's been like this ever since."

"You should have called," Remy told him. "What were you thinking?"

"She's not hurt," Kurt said. "She'll come out of it."

Remy did not like his tone. It was far too flippant, given the seriousness of the situation. Rogue had come in contact with the worst that humanity had to offer. If some patient in a mental hospital could hurt her this badly—make her retreat from the world inside her mind—he did not want to imagine how she had suffered in that initial touch of skin to skin.

"Why?" he asked Kurt. "Why was she touching anyone?"

"I don't know," Kurt said. "We split up."

It was a lie. Remy could taste the untruth; see it in the unsteady flicker of Kurt's golden gaze. He reached for Rogue's gloved hand and she did not pull away as was her habit. She let him tug her close. She stood very stiff in his arms, but he expected nothing less and rubbed her back. Rogue's auburn hair gleamed under the hangar floodlights, the white streak especially bright.

"Shhh, now," he whispered. "It will be all right, *chère*. We'll get you feeling better in no time."

Get her feeling better—and in the process find out just what the hell had happened in Seattle. He felt sick, thinking about it. Anything that would turn Kurt into a liar—

Remy found him staring. "What is it?"

Kurt blinked, breaking eye contact. His blue tail curled tight around his leg. "Nothing," he said, and Remy realized for the first time that his accent seemed less pronounced.

Movement caught his eye; Scott shaking his head. Jean stood beside him. She looked different, somehow. Harder. The Jean he knew, the one who baked cookies on Saturday nights or warmed milk for the students, was not the same woman he saw now. This Jean, with her mouth set in a flat line and her eyes narrow and dull, did not look as though she would care for children at all.

"Please, Scott?" Ororo asked.

"No," Remy heard Scott say. "Jean and I would like to rest awhile before we give you our report."

Ororo did not look pleased. "I have some concerns,"

she said, but Jean had already begun walking to the door, and Scott followed close behind.

"Later," he said. "I promise."

"No," Remy called out. "What happened to Rogue? Who did she touch to make her this way?"

No one answered him. Rogue pulled away from his embrace. Giving him a shy smile, she left him standing by the jet. He did not chase her, but instead watched as she and Kurt—tail uncurling long enough to lash the air—followed Scott and Jean from the hangar. Wolverine, after patting Jubilee on the head, followed them with an odd slow swagger in his hips. It seemed to him that Wolverine—though always taciturn—was especially silent.

"Did Wolvie just . . . pet me like a dog?" Jubilee asked, when the five X-Men were gone and the door had shut behind them.

"Something's wrong," Remy said, unable to shake the feel of Rogue in his arms, that look on her face: so shy, so fragile, not the woman he knew at all. Kurt, too, with his shifting eyes.

Ororo said nothing. She stared at the door, mouth pressed into a hard line. Remy felt the gentle brush of some impossible breeze, scented rain within the confines of concrete and steel. Jubilee shivered, and stepped closer to him.

"Do not worry," Ororo said quietly. "We will have the truth. One way, or another."

11

THEY TOOK ONE OF THE FREE DOWNTOWN BUSES TO Elliot Bay, north past the Spaghetti Factory, fast-food joints, and gas stations. Rogue watched the city pass, paying closer attention to the world than she ever had before. People, especially. People, on their way to jobs, out shopping, running for a bite to eat. She wondered if any of them were mutants, and for the first time in her life, could not remember why it would matter if they were. She was human now, through and through; powerless, perhaps, but not weak. She knew that about herself now. Being divorced of her physical identity for just one night had given her a clearer sense of who she was, the crutches she leaned upon in her life.

Kurt sat beside her on the bus. Their hands brushed, and she forced herself not to pull away.

"You are improving," he said, looking down at their flesh: dark and light, smooth and rough.

"Comfort is a state of mind," Rogue said. "I think I'm finally getting that."

"Don't get too comfortable, darlin'." Logan leaned over the back of their seat. "We still got problems."

"Money," she said.

Kurt smiled. "In the circus we had a saying: The lack of one penny can destroy the mightiest man. A stern reminder of what we were working for, *other* than our love of the big top."

Rogue frowned, staring at her hands. "I'm sorry, but I won't beg. I lived dirt poor for years, and never had any need to ask strangers for money. I'm not going to start now."

"No one said anything 'bout begging," Logan replied. "There are some homeless shelters around the area we're headed to. Might be able to scrounge up some things we'll need from those places."

"Just as long as we don't stay there long," Scott said. "We got lucky this morning—in more ways than one. I don't want to press it."

At Pier 90 they got off the bus and walked left across the wide tracks, which led directly to the southern entrance of Seattle's Balmer Yard. The trains were lined up like giant playing blocks, rust red or dirty blue, logos covering the ridged sides: PACIFIC RAIL, CARGO EXPRESS, EVERGREEN STEEL. The air smelled like exhaust, ocean salt; she felt a rumble in her chest and heard the high squeal of monstrous brakes. She felt very small.

"The key is to find the right car," Logan said. His fine blond hair wisped across his face and he shoved it away, scowling. "We're lucky it's summer. We shouldn't freeze to death."

"Great," Rogue said, and then pointed farther down the rail. "I see an Amtrak sign."

"Too crowded, too controlled. Security would find out

fast we don't have tickets. We need something big and empty, the kind used for cargo."

A train lumbered by; the sound of the engine forming a steel-on-steel symphony of groans and squeals and dull trembling thunder.

Logan, in the interests of subtlety, led them down a bike path that continued north alongside Balmer Yard. Through the chain-link fence they spied on the trains.

"Time for some fieldwork," Logan said. "Rogue, you're with me."

"I thought I wasn't innocent enough, sugah."

"This is the train yard. Tough and dangerous is more sexy than cute and girly."

Jean smiled. "Sorry to break it to you, Logan, but I don't care what body you wear. You might be cute, but you're never going to be girly."

"Don't kill a man's dreams, Jeannie."

An older woman sitting on a nearby bench turned around to look at them. Logan smiled and she shook her head in disgust.

"No accounting for taste," Jean murmured, which was enough to make Rogue laugh.

She and Logan left the team, following the bike path until they reached a public-access road. From there they walked past the locomotive-servicing facility to the Balmer Yard office building.

"Trying to hitch a ride in broad daylight is going to be difficult," he said, as they approached the front door.

"Do we have a choice?"

"I'd say to hitchhike, but we got too many people."

"What a mess," Rogue whispered, finally confronting the enormity of crossing the country on nothing but the kindness of strangers. It made her afraid.

Logan surprised her by draping his arm around her shoulders and planting a hard quick kiss on her temple. She flinched and he let her go, though she continued to feel the weight of his arm, his lips.

"It'll be okay, darlin'. We've handled worse."

"This time feels different."

"It *should*. You're not in your own skin."

"What do you think our bodies are doing right now?"

Logan's jaw tightened. Rogue let it go. It was a bad question; the possibilities made her feel sick.

They entered the office building; warm air washed over her face, along with the heavy smell of oil and steel. Dark boot tracks covered the lobby floor and the walls were cracked and yellow with old paint. Logan led her into the first office off the lobby. At the counter stood a tall woman with sharp cheekbones and an unhappy mouth.

But Logan, despite his new face and figure, was still a rough charmer. It was not sexual at all; simply, a charisma that had the woman in front of them smiling after mere moments in his presence. The secretary's reaction surprised Rogue; she knew that women found Logan attractive, but she had always thought that the source of his allure lay in his undeniable masculinity. After all, even though she knew quite well he was capable of turning on his charm, he was not, by habit, the most refined of men.

"We're from the university," he told her, and Rogue listened, stunned, as the hint of a valley girl entered his voice. "We're researching the rail system and how it affects economic growth in the Northwest. It's a killer course."

"But fascinating, I'm sure," said the woman. Her desk plate named her SHELLY.

"Totally," said Logan, and within minutes he had a printout of the schedules and destinations of every train in Balmer Yard. Rogue felt like getting down and bowing; it was an Oscar-worthy performance.

Just as they were leaving the office, he stopped and said, "By the way, we brought some food to keep us going today. You mind if we store some of it in your office lounge or use your microwave? Do you guys even have a space like that?" He rattled the plastic bag he still carried.

"We just got one," said Shelly, and hesitated. "Well, I don't see why you couldn't, but don't touch those other meals, right? People get territorial."

"Of course," Rogue reassured her, wondering what Logan was up to.

She found out when they actually reached the lounge—a little alcove crammed tight with a minirefrigerator, microwave, and a shelf lined with personal belongings. The other side of the space was a closet, filled with hanging coats, scarves, and umbrellas. The employee cubicles were in a completely different part of the office, out of sight of the alcove.

No one was around when they entered. Logan did not hesitate. He opened the refrigerator and threw all its contents into his plastic bag. Rogue watched the hall, sparing a glance for him as he went next to the coats, checking pockets. He found two wallets and stole cash from both.

"Logan," she hissed.

"I'm not taking it all," he said.

Maybe not, but it still made her sick—sick because she wanted that money, knew they all needed that money, but to be so desperate as to fall into thievery—

"This isn't better than begging," she said.

"And didn't I say you wouldn't have to do that?"

"What about the homeless shelter?"

"You don't pass up opportunities," he replied. The coats were too big to stick unnoticed in his bulging bag, or else Rogue thought he would have snatched those, too.

"Don't look at me like that," he said, and pulled her from the tiny lounge. Rogue kept her body between Logan and Shelly as they left; the secretary waved good-bye, never paying attention to the bag clutched tight against Logan's side.

They quickly left the office building, and only when they were clear of the doors and back into the cool fresh air, did Rogue say, "That was wrong."

"Think I don't know that, darlin'?" Logan gave her a hard look. His cheeks were flushed. "You think it's *not* going to take things like that for us to get home? What matters more to you, Rogue? Morality or survival?"

"It would be nice if we didn't have to sacrifice either one."

"Right," he said. "I think you're smarter than that."

She bit her tongue. He was right, of course, but it rankled her to no end that she could not think of an alternative. Get a job? Sure, if they had time, if the urgent press of some unknown danger wasn't bearing down on their shoulders. Strangers had their bodies, and even now at this moment, some man or woman inside her physical self might be using her powers to hurt others. She could not bear the thought of that.

And besides, you trust Logan. You know he would have taken the high road first if he could have.

Because Logan was an honorable man. A very dangerous, oftentimes unpredictable man, but decent all the same. If he thought the situation warranted sacrificing some of his hard-fought pride in order to do right by her and the others, she could not fault him.

Logan pored over the schedules as they walked back to the bike path. Rogue carried the plastic bag for him. She peered inside and saw sandwiches, soda; her stomach growled loud enough to drown out a passing train.

"Didn't need mutant powers to hear that one," Logan murmured, still reading the paperwork.

"Shut up," she muttered, embarrassed. The corner of his mouth twitched.

A white truck, spitting gravel alongside the rails, pulled up beside them. Its window was rolled down; a young man peered out. Rogue did not miss the way he checked out Logan. He barely spared a glance for her, and she wanted to laugh. Tough and dangerous was sexy, huh? Maybe in Logan's book, but not for this kid.

"You ladies lost?" he asked. She saw a security patch on his shoulder.

"We're doing research," Rogue said, "for school. The University of Washington."

He gave her a look that said quite clearly he thought she was far too ancient to be in school, and said, "You a professor?"

Logan made a small movement with his hand and Rogue—utterly bewildered that the young man could mistake her for someone of learning—said, "Yes."

"Huh." He looked at Logan again and smiled. Logan smiled back, but she knew her friend well enough to notice the hard line of his gaze, the "I just might beat the crap out of you" tilt of his head. "You need any help?"

"You know the best castbound trains for hitching rides on?" Logan asked. The kid laughed, clearly taking the question as a joke.

"I catch a lot of the old hobos on the Cascade ride. That one goes straight through the mountains and stops in Spokane. Bastards think its fun or something. I tell you, I'm just waiting for one of those idiots to fall on the tracks underneath a train. It would serve 'em right."

"I sense a lot of love there," Rogue said.

"Yeah, I'm really feeling the love when I look into a cargo box and the holds have to be hosed down because someone decided to take a dump in the corner. Guess who has to do the clean up? Me."

"Tough life," Logan said, with only moderate sympathy. "We should be going now. Thanks."

"Sure thing," he said, his gaze drifting down Logan's body. "I know we just met, but do you ever—"

"No," Logan said. "Really."

"Ooookay," said the kid, and without another word, pulled away.

"That has to be the worst security guard ever," Rogue said, watching him drive out of sight around a parked train.

"Nope," Logan said. "But he's close."

They found the bike path, but Scott, Jean, and Kurt were nowhere to be seen. A thread of worry needled Rogue's gut, growing worse as they walked, but then she heard her name called and Kurt appeared from behind a clump of bushes.

"We found a shady spot and decided to rest." He led them off the sidewalk to a small patch of ground beneath some trees. The grass was yellow, littered with bits of trash, but Rogue found that once she stepped into that soft dry spot, the rest of the world seemed to fall away.

Scott and Jean sat cross-legged on the ground. Rogue joined them, dropping the sack of food. She saw the tip of a sandwich, the plastic rim of an applesauce container. Her stomach felt like it was going to crawl right out of her throat.

"You think we can eat this now?" she asked the others.

"Knock yourselves out," Logan said, still looking at the train schedules. "Just be sure to save some of it for later."

Scott sorted through the bag, pulling out chips, soda, cookies—that lonely sandwich and applesauce—and several objects wrapped in aluminum foil, which turned out to be cold pizza.

"Lordy," Rogue said. "Nothing ever looked so good."

They had nothing to cut the pizza with, and resorted to passing each slice around so that every person could take several bites. It was, in retrospect, a gross way of divvying up the food, but they were all too hungry to care. It was the best pizza Rogue ever had.

They washed the pizza down with a shared can of Coke, and by the time Rogue took her last swallow of sugary carbonated perfection, she felt ready to run a mile. Her gut still felt hollow, but that little bit of food was going to her head like a drug.

"That pizza was still cold," Scott said to Logan. He stood up, brushing off his pants. "You didn't get it from Maguire's home."

"That's right." Logan pulled the stolen money from his pocket and handed it to him. Scott gave Logan a careful look and counted out the cash. Forty dollars. Rogue thought that might be all they had to get themselves home.

"You stole this," he said.

"I sure as hell didn't borrow it."

Scott's mouth hardened into a white line. The expression was so familiar, so . . . Scott . . . that Rogue forgot, for a moment, that he was a woman. Jean stood up.

"Don't," she said. "We need that money."

"Jean," he began, but she shook her head.

"You're a good man, Scott Summers, but now is not the time for a morality play. We need to get home."

Scott stared at her. "Morality play?"

She smiled. "Doesn't mean I don't love you."

They left the shelter of the bushes and made their way down to the heart of Balmer Yard. Logan led them on a circuitous path around the trains, keeping close to the tracks so they could duck beneath the locomotives if any security vehicles came too near. Considering what Rogue had seen of the security in this place, she did not think it would be difficult to avoid them.

"There are almost a dozen trains scheduled to leave at noon," Logan said, pausing in front of an open boxcar and pointing down the line at the nearby rear device, "but only two are heading east across the Cascades. This is one of 'em."

"Should we jump in?" Kurt peered inside the open door. "It looks clean enough."

"What are the risks?" Scott asked. "Are these cars routinely checked before leaving?"

"It's a gamble," Logan admitted, giving Kurt a boost up into the boxcar. He gestured for Rogue to follow him and she did, grabbing Kurt's hand and clambering onto the hard dusty surface. She stood in the door, blinking under the bright sun as she gazed out at the train yard, searching for anyone who might be watching. In the distance, at the edge of Balmer Yard, she saw a police cruiser parked beside a white truck. She was not entirely certain, but the security guard leaning out his window and talking to the cop looked rather familiar.

"Um," she said. "We might have a problem."

"How big a problem?" Scott asked, as Jean shoved him up into the boxcar.

"The kind that has handcuffs and that would be highly motivated to arrest us."

"Great," Logan muttered. Jean bent over to give him a leg up. He stared at her.

She smiled. "Go on now, pretty lady."

His scowl deepened. Ignoring her help, he attempted to clamber up into the boxcar by himself. It was awkward—embarrassingly so. Patty was not an athletic woman, and Logan—God bless him—had a mind that was far more willing than the body. Jean kept staring at his backside, and Rogue knew she was thinking about giving him one good push.

"I think you met your match," Scott commented, as he finally wriggled those precious last inches onto the platform. "Beaten by your own body."

Logan, feet still dangling out the door, scowled.

"The police car is moving," Rogue announced, as the cruiser pulled away from the white security truck and entered the main train yard. "He's not coming in this direction, but he's definitely looking for someone."

Scott pulled Jean into the boxcar. "Everyone get to the back. Logan, you said this thing leaves at noon?"

"It wasn't even ten when we got to that office. We've still got some time yet. You need me to play decoy?"

Scott shook his head. "I won't risk you getting caught."

"One is better than all. You can spring me when you get back home."

"When did you become an optimist?" Jean asked. "You're assuming a lot."

"I'm assuming that we might need a Plan B to get out of here, and if it means that not all of us make the trip, I'm volunteering to stay behind and get the cops off your trail. I've handled worse."

"We're sticking together," Scott said, more firmly this time. Rogue briefly wondered if Mindy had ever looked so resolved—so hard—or if the inner person really did mold the outer. Mindy's face was almost beginning to resemble the real Scott.

For the next two hours they sat at the back of the boxcar. They did not speak, but peered through slits in the wall planking, keeping watch for any movement outside the train. Twice, they heard voices—engineers, employees—but those men and women did not linger. Rogue was just beginning to think they were safe when she heard the loud crunch of gravel, the growl of a car engine. She peered through a narrow opening in the wall and saw a white truck. A car door slammed.

Logan moved. Scott made a grab for his arm but he was too slow. Rogue, after a moment's hesitation, followed him.

They made it to the entrance of the boxcar at the same time as the security guard. It was the same young man.

"Whoa," he said, startled. "What are you two doing up there?"

"Research," Logan said. "We wanted to see what the inside of one of these things looks like."

Rogue edged closer to the edge of the platform, blocking the young man's view of the shadowed interior. He glanced up at her for only an instant before focusing on Logan.

"It's a good thing I stopped here," he said. "This train is due to leave in just a couple minutes. You could've gotten stuck up there."

"Nah," Logan said. "We were just leaving anyhow."

"Cool." He reached his hand out to Logan, who stared at it, unblinking.

"Um," said the kid, blushing. "You need help down?"

Logan opened his mouth. Rogue cut him off with a quick "Yes." She ignored the dirty look he gave her. After a moment, Logan grimaced and took the young man's hand.

Rogue jumped down on her own. The security guard still held Logan's hand and was trying to lead him back to his truck. "Come on," he said. "I'll drop you guys off at the front gate."

"That's all right," Rogue said. "We can walk."

"It's a long walk," he said, "and this time of day there are a lot of trains moving out. It's not that safe, especially for you guys. You don't know all the rules."

"We know enough to stay out of the way of a moving train," Logan said, prying his hand loose. She half-expected him to wipe it on his jeans, and sure enough, he did not disappoint. She almost felt sorry for the young man, who watched Logan's apparent disgust with flushed embarrassment. He glanced at Rogue and she gave him a small smile.

"Yeah," he said softly. He began walking toward Rogue, and she stepped backward, startled.

"What are you doing?" she asked.

He gave her a strange look. "I need to check the inside of that boxcar."

"We were just in there," Rogue said. "It's very . . . clean."

"That's good. I still need to check, though. It's part of my job."

So much for being a lousy security guard. Rogue blocked his path.

"Before you climb up in there, do you think you could answer some questions? We're in a bit of a hurry."

"So am I," he said, in a sharper tone. Rogue thought he was just beginning to process the sting of Logan's rejection. "This train is going to leave any minute."

Rogue heard a loud metallic groan from down the line, a hiss and loud clack, like the tumbling of a giant lock. The young man swore, pushing past her. "That's just great. Now I've got, like, five seconds to check this thing out—"

Rogue could not stop him in time. He hoisted himself onto the edge of the boxcar and peered inside. Swore loudly.

"Hey!" he shouted. He looked over his shoulder at Rogue and Logan. "What the hell kind of game are you playing? There are people in there! Why didn't you tell me?"

The train moved, a sharp rocking jolt, and the young man jumped off the platform. "I gotta report this," he said, reaching for the walkie-talkie belted to his hip. "God, I hate this job. And you two, don't move. I can't believe you did this to me."

"It was easy," Logan said, and slammed his fist into the young man's face. The young man's breath escaped in a rush and he hit the ground hard. He did not move. Rogue, watching him, felt her stomach twist painfully in her gut. She remembered her hands around a man's head, pounding his skull into the floor with all her strength because she was human—and human was not strong enough to kill—

She ran to the young man and fell to her knees on the hard gravel. She checked his pulse. It still beat, slow and steady. She remembered how to breathe again.

"Come on," Logan muttered. "Help me get him in his truck."

"We don't have time for cleanup." Rogue looked at the train, the boxcar inching ever farther away. Scott, Jean, and Kurt leaned out the door.

"Make the time." Logan lifted the upper half of the young man's body and with Rogue's help carried him to the truck and shoved him inside, very much out of sight unless one stood right beside the truck. Logan slammed shut the door—

— and then they ran.

The train had picked up speed. The gravel was difficult to run on. Rogue pushed hard, reaching back to grab Logan's arm and haul him with her. He was having even more trouble than her, and that was unacceptable, impossible, because if Rogue got on that boxcar Logan was going with her, or else she would just stop running now. She refused to leave him.

They reached the boxcar door; Jean, kneeling, stretched out her arm. Rogue grabbed Logan and shoved him in front of her. He protested, but Jean grabbed the back of his shirt and threw herself backward, hauling him off the ground. His kicking foot clipped Rogue in the shoulder and she stumbled to one knee. Pain shot up her leg into her hip; gravel cut her palm.

Someone shouted her name. She forced herself up. The boxcar had moved impossibly far, but she started running anyway—fast, fast, she had forgotten what it was to be human and slow, and what she wouldn't give to fly again—

Somehow, miraculously, she ate up the distance between herself and her friends. She did not feel her knee anymore; the pain in her hand was distant, faint like the sounds of those voices calling her onward, drowned out by the rumble of the moving train, those tracks, and then Rogue was close enough to reach out an arm and brush Jean's fingers, and Jean shouted "Closer! Just a little closer!" and Rogue threw herself forward, gasping, and Jean's hand closed around her own and pulled, pulled so hard she flew off her feet and slammed into the edge of the platform, her legs dangling close to the moving wheels, the grind of steel on steel, and then someone else grabbed the back of her pants and she was flying again—flying and landing hard on a vibrating floor that swayed and swayed with the rocking of the rail. She lay there, clutching at that floor, gasping for breath. Parts of her body felt burned from the inside out.

Rogue heard low muttering by her ear. She flopped onto her back and looked up into Kurt's concerned face. He crossed himself and said "Amen."

"Yeah," she breathed, closing her eyes. "I'm with you on that one, sugah."

12

THE TRAIN MOVED THROUGH THE CITY LIKE A SLOW-rolling caterpillar, following street bridges, crawling toward the Lake Washington Ship Canal, where Kurt got a nice view of the water and the boats. Later, passing through a pleasant neighborhood of small well-kept homes, he watched a green park shimmer on the edge of Puget Sound, and smiled as kites fluttered high in the blue sky, children screaming and laughing below them.

Kurt thought it might be nice to go to a park such as that one, looking as he now did, and just . . . be. Be a man, be anonymous, be something other than a mutant. Not that he minded what he was. Everything was part of God's great plan, including him, and to regret his circumstances, to wish himself different, would be to go against that which God had meant for him, and him alone. Every living person was blessed with individuality. Kurt was simply more individual than others.

And yet, still, that wistful wonder. He could not help himself, even if it was something he did not indulge for long.

The train increased its speed. Kurt stopped watching the view—Puget Sound and clay bluffs, great blue herons perched on rocks—and focused instead on Rogue, sleeping nearby. He tried not to imagine what would have befallen her if she had not made it on the train. He thought he might have jumped off to be with her. His sister.

It was not something they ever really discussed, though the knowledge was there—had been for years, ever since discovering that Mystique had mothered them both. Sometimes he wished they could talk about it, but his few attempts had accomplished nothing. Rogue was not ready to speak of their mother. He did not take it personally. Only, it was times like this that he wondered if she thought of him in the same way, as blood.

Jean sat down beside him. Long dreadlocks hung past her broad shoulders; her skin looked very dry and her lips were rough. Her eyes, though, were light with intelligence, and he could not help but smile when he looked into her borrowed face.

"That's one of the things I like about you," Jean said. "I can always count on you seeing the sunny side of any situation. I can always find a smile."

Kurt shrugged, studying his dark human hands. "I grew up in the circus, Jean. You learn how to smile through anything. You learn how to smile and mean it."

"I didn't take you for a cynic."

"A cynic is one who believes the worst of people. I believe the best. Only, we are not always faced with the best."

"Like now?"

"Oh," he said, and felt another smile creep close. "This situation is not entirely bad."

Jean studied his face. After a moment she said, "I can tell you believe that."

There was a peculiar tone to her voice, as though the importance of that statement depended more on her own ability to read his face, than on his sincerity. He understood, and was not hurt. Jean had lost her telepathy; he could not imagine the difficulties she faced adjusting to this new—and no doubt, isolated—life.

Rogue stirred, mumbling in her sleep. Kurt said, "I am the same man you have always known, Jean. Haven't I always believed what I say?"

She flushed. "I didn't mean it that way, Kurt. I just . . ."

He touched her hand, and for the first time in his life—because he did not count his mother—his skin looked the same as the person sitting beside him. It did not matter to him, but he noted it because it was new and different, something to remember.

"It is all right," he said softly. "I simply want you to remember that even if you cannot hear us," and he tapped his forehead, "you are not alone. Nor have we changed. Be confident in that, Jean. Besides, it is not as if you went around reading our thoughts before you lost powers."

"Of course not," she said. "But I *could* feel something, whether or not I wanted to. Energy, maybe. I suppose . . . I suppose that even though I never acted on it, just knowing I could was reassuring."

"Because it meant that no one could hide from you." Kurt smiled. "It will be all right, Jean. Look upon this time as a lesson."

"In humility?" She gave him a wry smile.

"I was thinking in terms of learning new skills, but I suppose yours is the more profound thought."

She shook her head. "My powers didn't emerge until puberty. Up until that point, I was just like everyone else, and when I first went to Xavier's I told myself that would never change. That I would never forget what it was like to be . . . normal. But . . . this . . . all of us . . ." She looked down at herself, touching her flat chest. "I forgot, Kurt. I got so wrapped up in being 'other' that I forgot what it was like to be just . . . regular."

Kurt was far too polite to belittle her feelings, but he said, "I suppose that depends on your definitions of normal and regular. I, in my original state, do not look normal or regular, but I feel like I am those things."

"So what you're saying is that I need to change my point of view."

Kurt heard a sound on his left. Logan, rolling over. His eyes were open and he stared at Jean.

"No, darlin'. What he's trying to say is that you're full of it."

"Hey," Scott said, from his place in the corner.

"It's true," Logan said, "and Jeannie knows it. Being a mutant may have given her different life experiences, but she's the same damn person she always was, with or without them. She's got a better heart than ninety-nine percent of the world around her, and that kind of thing doesn't depend on mind-reading or lifting objects or shooting cosmic flames up someone's rear end. Don't you feel sorry for yourself, Jeannie. Your powers don't make or break you. Right, Kurt?"

"I suppose," he said, though he would have chosen different wording. Logan's approach, however, was more effective, and it was something Jean needed to hear. Having a strong sense of identity—knowing the heart of one's self apart from gifts and powers—was essential to staying sane during such hard times. Better than moping, at any rate.

Then again, perhaps he was asking too much. Kurt had been born different—had grown up different—but the circus had raised him as an equal, a valued friend and son, and had never treated him as anything else, despite his appearance and powers. Jean, on the other hand—like most mutants—had lived her life a certain way, and then overnight been forced to change. No smooth transition, no lifetime spent learning how to be comfortable in one's skin, *apart* from one's skin—simply, a transition that seemed more like a violent rite of passage into adulthood than like the blessing of some extraordinary new ability.

Under those circumstances, Kurt was not surprised she was having trouble adjusting. She had been conditioned to live one way, and now that conditioning was being shattered and she had nothing to fall back on but ideas and memories and notions of what was normal and human.

None of that mattered. At least, not to him.

"Logan." Scott stood up.

"It's all right," Jean said. "He has a point."

Rogue cracked open one eye. "Are we fighting?"

"Just a little," Kurt said, patting her shoulder. "Go back to sleep."

"Actually, don't." Scott crouched beside them. "We need to plan."

"Plan what? How long we're going to ride this train? What we're going to do for food or money? How we're going to contact the Mansion again? Don't know if that requires a plan so much as finding opportunities and acting on them." Logan leaned on his elbow. His shirt rode up his ribs, revealing a great deal of skin and the hint of a breast. Kurt did not think he noticed or cared. Still thinking like a man. Which . . . was probably a good thing.

Jean tugged his shirt down. He gave her a questioning look and she said, "It's nothing."

Kurt participated in the planning discussion, but not for long. He had little to contribute, and like Logan, believed that events would play out as they must, and that the road home would be won by taking opportunities, by living bold.

So he sat and watched the train roll through the limits of a gray city that smelled like chemicals, pulp and paper manufacturing, past that into green trees, the Snohomish River valley. Farther, through the Cascade Tunnel under Stevens Pass, where the agricultural valley shone bright under the sun, lovely and peaceful. Kurt felt as though he was dreaming with his eyes open, such was the beauty.

Then he closed his eyes and dreamed for real, and when he awakened he saw mountains capped in snow, rivers rolling past small hamlets lost in evergreen forests, and then he closed his eyes again, lulled by the rocking of the train, and when he opened his eyes once more, some time had passed because the mountains were gone, far behind them, and the train was arriving at its destination.

"We're in Wenobee," Logan said. "Right on the edge of the Columbia River."

In the distance, Kurt saw a large arching bridge crossing the wide blue river to connect one cityscape to another; monotone suburbs surrounded by parks, and deeper, toward the city heart, brick and steel and glass. The train moved quite slowly.

"Now what?" he asked, to no one in particular.

"You shouldn't have fallen asleep," Logan said, crouching beside him. "Then you'd know."

Kurt smiled. "Then let me make some assumptions. First, we will disembark from this train, and then second, we will look for another that is headed farther east, and board it."

"You're missing the part where we all get some grub and try to make some phone calls."

"Is there anyone you can contact who would help us?"

Logan shook his head. "I would try SHIELD, except their access number is secured by voice recognition. They've even got random automated questions so no one can pretape anything. If someone calls who isn't recognized, they're patched through to an answering service."

"That is better than nothing."

"Maybe, but SHIELD has got so much red tape and so many cranks who hack their number off the internet, I doubt they'll pay much mind to a woman who says she's Wolverine—or who tries to make any claims of knowing him."

Just then Kurt spotted other trains, parked in the distance like large rusting bricks. He watched as their train slowed to a crawl and curved around the gravel lot. He glimpsed vehicles in the distance. White trucks. A lot of them.

"We should get off this train," he said, uneasy. "Now, in fact."

Logan peered over his shoulder. "Crap. They must have found that kid I clobbered."

"We knew they would. He probably informed the authorities that we were on this train."

"Crap," he said again, and looked back at the others. "We have to jump."

"The train is moving," Rogue pointed out.

"Yeah, and if we wait until it stops, that'll be too late. We've got maybe one minute tops before we round this bend, and after that, all those security guards are going to see us jump. It has to be now."

Logan grabbed Kurt and pulled him to the edge of the platform. The slow-moving ground made him slightly dizzy; the gravel looked sharp. Rogue limped up close behind him. His own knee felt better, but he was not sure what such an impact would do to it.

"Come on," Logan said, pushing on his shoulders. "Sit down on the edge and then push yourself out. We've done this before. I shouldn't have to explain the mechanics."

"The last time was with aliens from outer space," Kurt said, declining to add that he usually teleported his way out of situations like this. He sat down and swung his legs out over the moving ground, took a deep breath, and jumped.

He hit the ground hard—his knee protesting—and then Rogue was there beside him, staggering, her face pale with pain. Kurt watched as Scott and Jean jumped, followed closely by Logan, who held the plastic bag to his chest. All of them hit the ground wrong, their legs and bodies forming awkward angles, and it was clear that knowing the correct way to jump from a moving object mattered only half as much as having a body that was fit enough to do it.

They picked themselves off the ground and hobbled between trains—narrowly avoiding security and other yard employees—until they reached the last of the railcars and gazed upon the edge of a business district that was pleasantly decorated with trees and painted murals.

"Maybe we're overreacting," Jean said.

"Maybe not," Scott said, looking around. Kurt glimpsed the wheels of a truck speeding quickly down the gravel pathway on the other side of the nearest train. "Come on, let's get out of here. It's not safe for us right now."

"When is it ever," Logan muttered, but they jogged—as best they could, given their aches and pains—across the street. They hit the sidewalk, took a quick left, and disappeared down a wide clean alley that was breezy and lined with the colorful back doors of shops and restaurants. Tables had been set out; well-dressed men and women smiled and laughed over their drinks and food. Kurt's stomach rumbled. He forced himself not to look. He thought, from the corner of his eye, that people watched them. Subtle, yes; no one stared outright, but he felt the quiet scrutiny nonetheless, the dip in conversation as they passed.

He could not imagine it was their clothes that drew attention; they still looked relatively clean, though Kurt knew that would not last. He wondered, too, if their faces had been on the news. That would be enough to cause anyone to look twice.

Or maybe it was nothing at all. Kurt, however, felt as though he had blue skin again. As a mutant, it was rare that people stared outright. Those around him always ogled without looking, consciously making the effort to look past him—as though studied indifference did not count the same as rudeness.

"Logan," he said quietly, "are people watching us?"

"Yeah," he said. "We look poor. Our skin isn't the right color, either. Must be a bad combination in this part of town."

"You cannot be serious."

"You mean, how people can still be that way? Why do you think mutants have a problem?"

"But we look human."

"Human ain't got nothing to do with it. We look different, Kurt. I'm not saying they're holding that against us, but difference always attracts the eye. In some parts of the country we'd be the most 'different' thing for miles."

"I suppose I am naive," Kurt said, staring at his hands, those dark human hands. "I thought such things were past. When I think of what is said and done to mutants, anything else feels . . . archaic."

Logan clapped him on the shoulder. "Don't let it get

you down, Elf. If it wasn't race, it would be mutants, if it wasn't mutants, it would be religion, if it wasn't religion, it would be something else. Just the way it is. And who was it giving Jean a lecture this morning about feeling good about herself?"

Kurt said nothing. He could understand fear and ignorance of mutations because the physical distance was, on occasion, quite wide. It took time for people to become accustomed to the radical. But to be human and *still* be looked at strangely . . .

Well, that was just wrong.

They walked for a long time, without much purpose other than to keep moving. Kurt's knee hurt; he did not think Rogue felt well, either. All of them were tired and hungry.

Scott stopped at the first pay phone he found and dialed the Mansion. Waited. And then his face—that stranger's face, which was becoming not so strange—paled.

"Hello," he said, and though his voice did not waver, his expression was so troubled that Jean reached out to touch him. "I'm a friend of Ororo. Is she around? No? Are you sure?" He paused, and then quickly hung up. He stared at the phone.

Jean said, "Scott," and he looked at her, at all of them, and Kurt knew what he was going say, felt sick in his stomach with fear, dismay.

"That was me," Scott said. "That was me who answered the phone."

"Jesus," Logan said. "And he wouldn't let you talk to 'Ro?"

"He recognized my voice. His voice. Whoever. He knew who I was. He said my name. Mindy's name, anyway." He closed his eyes. "They must be censoring the calls that come in."

"What do they want?" Rogue asked.

"They want to ruin us," Jean said. "Or even if they don't, that will be what happens. Can you imagine? The government and public already distrust us. If someone goes out, using our bodies with an agenda—"

"We might as well shoot ourselves in the head." Logan clenched his hands, digging his nails into his palm. Kurt could feel his friend's rage grow strong, tight, and he touched Logan's shoulder.

"Calm yourself," he said quietly. "You cannot afford to lose your temper." Nor did he have a healing factor to fix him if he tried to drive his fist through a wall.

"Who said anything about losing my temper?" Logan growled. "I just want to kill someone."

"Later," Scott said, and there was a hard quality to his face that was mirrored in everyone around him. Kurt wondered if he shared that intensity, that sharp resolve; all he knew for certain was he felt sick at heart, ashamed for deeds committed that were out of his control. With his face, with his body, with his power—the stain would be his to bear, as well.

"We need to steal a car," Logan said. "Something, anything to get us moving again. Fast."

"And if we get caught?"

"What do you think is more important right now?"

Getting home. Kurt could see it on Scott's face. He

did not like the idea of stealing—hated it, in fact—but he felt the same powerful urgency infesting his teammates.

"So we steal a car," Jean said, taking a deep breath. "Fine. Go at it, boys."

"You the new cheerleader for the poor and criminal?" Logan asked, walking away from the pay phone.

"God help me, but I am," she said.

They found a grocery store. Scott and Kurt went inside to buy food. They spent less than seven dollars and came out with two loaves of day-old discounted bread—as well as half-price doughnuts of the same age—peanut butter, one gallon of water, a tiny bottle of antibacterial hand gel, and a package of toilet paper.

"I hate to admit it," Scott said, "but it's been a while since I had to pinch pennies like this. I used to be good at it."

Kurt said nothing, juggling the water for a better grip. In the circus, everyone was poor, but no one minded because you always had as much as the person performing next to you. He missed that sometimes. Life had been much simpler.

Logan, Jean, and Rogue sat outside on a bench, waiting for them.

"Do we do this now?" Logan asked, and then in a lower voice, "There aren't any security cameras in the lot."

Scott looked at the sky. "It'll be dark in two or three hours. I would feel more comfortable waiting."

"There's a gas station down the road," Rogue said. "I don't know about you guys, but I could use a bathroom."

"I could use some clean underwear," Jean muttered.

"Turn it inside out," Logan suggested. "You can make it last twice as long that way."

"Gee, thanks," Jean said, giving him a dirty look.

The gas station was large and well maintained. Not much business, though. Another station, just down the road, was filled with cars.

When Kurt saw the clerk he understood why.

"Hey," said the young lady, when they entered. She leaned on the plastic counter, a magazine in her blinking hands.

"Hello," said Kurt, trying to keep track of all her eyes. Her face was covered with them, as was the rest of her body. Blue, brown, green—eyes of different colors and sizes, all of them staring in different directions.

"Can we use your bathroom?" Jean asked.

"Sure," said the girl. She glanced at Kurt and frowned. "Are you staring at me?"

"Yes," he said. "I'm sorry. You have a fascinating face."

"Hmph," she said. "Do you want to buy something?"

"I'm afraid I don't have enough money."

"Then keep talking."

Kurt rested his elbows on the counter; the girl did not move. She stared at him. Really, really stared.

He said, "It must be easy to hurt yourself. Eyes are so sensitive, after all."

She studied his face. It was difficult to read her expression, partially because eyes covered it up.

"Sometimes it's trouble," she finally said. "That's why I try to keep this place clean. You a mutant or something?"

"No," Scott answered for him. "But a lot of our friends are."

"Oh," she said. "You must not be from here, then. There aren't a lot of us in town."

"Trouble?" he asked.

"People here don't cause trouble. They ignore it, sweep it under the rug. No, there just aren't a lot of mutants. Not many born, not many who come. I guess they feel safer in the bigger cities."

"And you?"

"Lived here all my life. Married my high-school sweetheart. This is our place."

"People don't treat you differently?" Scott asked.

All her eyes narrowed. "Why would they?"

Rogue and Jean came out of the bathroom. Scott said, "All I meant—"

"I know what you meant. And no, people don't treat me differently. If they do, they're not the kind I want to know, anyway."

"Are you causing trouble?" Jean asked her husband. She looked at the clerk. "I'm sorry. Sometimes my . . . wife . . . gets a little too nosy."

"Sure, no problem." The girl looked down at her magazine. She did not talk to them again.

"Smooth," Logan said, when they left the gas station. "Your skills as an X-Man really shone through back in there."

"I didn't notice you saying anything," Scott said.

"Exactly. Why would I? Any idiot could tell that girl's doing fine."

"She's a mutant."

"Not everyone feels persecuted," Kurt murmured, but he knew that would be difficult for his friend to take as truth. Scott's experiences told him otherwise. Of course, as difficult as it was to be the persecuted, even the hunted could be guilty of the same sin, in another form.

Scott shook his head. "Fine. Let's move."

They walked to a nearby park and sat on the grass where they opened up the bread, dipping it into the peanut butter jar. They did not speak, but dozed in the waning sunlight, waiting for night. Kurt watched children play. No kites, but Frisbees and baseballs. He liked listening to their laughter, which was happy, unrestrained. They were not yet old enough to know about holding back, the disease of self-consciousness. Kurt had experienced it briefly in his teens, but the circus had no patience for shyness. At least not in public.

When it grew dark they went back to the grocery store and sat in the bushes on the edge of the parking lot, watching who went in and out. Ten minutes of doing this, and a beat up little Corolla pulled into a nearby space. The driver, a young man who looked barely out of high school, wore the store uniform. He never noticed his watchers; he had headphones on, and strutted his way into work.

"Bingo," Logan said. "That one's not going to be out for hours."

It did not take him long. The boy had forgotten to lock his door and everyone clambered into the car.

Ten minutes later, they were on the freeway headed east.

13

THE WAY LOGAN DRANK HIS BEER WAS NOT THE FIRST indication that something was wrong, but it was the most significant, and Jubilee could not help but consider it a minor sign of the apocalypse when she sat beside him and watched his little pinky lift off the can. It was very slight, barely noticeable, but it was that subtle delicacy that made her antenna go boom-boom. She watched him take a long swallow of beer with the same startled interest reserved for particularly nasty cases of foot fungus, dudes dressed as Klingons, or old white guys who thought it was okay to run around with their shirts off.

She said, "Hey, are you feeling all right?"

"Peachy," he said. "Why do you ask?"

"Nothing. You just seem a little . . . different . . . since you got back from Seattle."

"Just your imagination."

"Right." She scooted a little closer. "So, remember that talk we had before you left?"

He never looked at her, just drank his beer. The sports channel was on, but he switched it to the news.

"Wolvie?"

"I heard you. Remind me."

"Oh," she said, disappointed. "You were going to take me to Japan this year. When you visit Mariko."

Mariko, who was dead and gone. Jubilee still remembered a rainy night, years past, when Logan had huddled over her grave, sobbing his heart out like he could bring her back with tears or pain. Every year he visited her, every year on a special day. He always went alone. He always left without telling anyone. This time, Jubilee wanted to go, too. Not to intrude, but to be that friend she thought he needed.

And besides, traveling with Logan—no matter how sad the circumstances—was always an adventure. She needed one of those right now. Bad.

"Mariko," he finally said. "Sure thing, kid. It'll be nice to see her again."

Jubilee blinked. Logan picked up the remote control and changed the channel. Gunshots filled the air and he grinned.

She stood up and left the room. Logan did not say good-bye.

Jubilee found Remy in the garage, stretched out on the ground beneath his car. She grabbed his ankles and yanked hard. Something thumped, she heard him swear, and then he rolled the rest of the way out, holding his head.

"Make this good or else I'm cuttin' your new jacket."

"You're evil," she said, "but not as evil as Wolverine. Dude is *not* the same."

Remy sat up. "Tell me."

Jubilee resisted the urge to hug him. Things like this were why she liked Gambit second-best only to Wolvie. He took her seriously. He always listened. She scooted close, and in a low voice said, "First of all, he's holding his beer like a girl. Like, not a real girl, 'cause he's not all dainty and stuff, but there was some pinky action going on, like, a real honest-to-God pinky lift, and then he needed me to remind him of this conversation we had, which never happens because Wolvie always remembers everything—no exaggeration—and this was big, Remy, real big, because I asked him to take me to Japan with him this year, you know, when he visits Mariko's grave, and when I said that—when I said that, do you know what he told me? He said, 'It'll be nice to see her again.' And I was like, holy crap. *Nice to see her again?*"

Remy frowned. "Maybe he meant to say it a different way. Maybe it just came out wrong."

"It came out wrong like a fifty-pound baby, Remy. Wolvie doesn't do wrong like that. He says what he means."

"Okay, then." Remy briefly shut his eyes. "Okay. So something's different. He's not the same man. You don't mean that literally, do you, *ma petite?*"

"Don't ask me!" she said. "Jeez, who's the adult here?"

Remy gave her a dirty look. "We need to talk to 'Ro."

"No kidding. Have you noticed anything weird? Like, with Rogue?"

"I haven't seen her much," Remy confessed. "She's been staying in her room a lot."

"I find that highly suspicious."

"That's not sayin' much. Mood you're in, you'd perse-
cute a kitten."

"Right on, dude. Down with 'em all." She stood up,
gesturing for Remy to do the same. "Now move it! We're
in the middle of *Invasion of the Body Snatchers*, here. No
time to relax."

Remy grumbled something unflattering. They went to
find Ororo.

The phone rang as they entered the main hall. There
were several public phones placed through the Mansion;
easy access for anyone who needed to make a call or answer one. Jubilee was only three steps away from the receiver when Scott came bursting out of a side office. He
blocked the phone with his body and picked up the receiver.

"Hey," Jubilee said, smacking him on the shoulder.
He ignored her. She *hated* that.

She heard him say the name "Mindy" and then everything else was a garbled mess and he hung up the phone.

"Who's Mindy?"

"A wrong number," Scott said, turning around to face
them.

"We don't usually get wrong numbers," Remy said.
"You sure?"

"You think I wouldn't be?" There was a challenge in
his voice that didn't sound like him at all, and made Jubilee uneasy. She grabbed Remy's hand and tugged him
away.

"S'kay, Cyke," she said. "We believe you."

"That's better," he said, in a self-important tone that

for a moment carried the subtle hint of an odd accent. Giving them one last hard look, he returned to his office and shut the door.

"You were sayin' something about Body Snatching?" Remy said.

"Uh-huh," she said, sick.

It went unsaid between them, but as they walked through the Mansion they took care to avoid the rest of the team, those who had gone to Seattle. Jubilee was not quite sure how to hide her suspicions from a psychic like Jean—it was possible, even, that she was already aware that Jubilee was getting Freaked Out. If that was the case, then the game was up. Until she found out for certain, though, her strategy was simple: avoid, avoid, avoid.

And then, if she had to, kick some butt. Yeah, baby.

They found Ororo in Xavier's study, sitting behind his desk like she belonged there. For a moment, Jubilee felt a pang of anxiety, and then Ororo looked up from the paperwork in front of her and smiled. A real smile, genuine and utterly familiar. Jubilee sighed.

"You feel like going out for dinner?" Remy asked, closing the door behind him. "I know a great little spot in town you haven't tried yet."

"I do not think so," Ororo said, looking curiously at him. "One of us has to stay here and watch the students."

"Ah," he said, and looked at Jubilee with a smile tainted by bitterness. "You just told me all I need to know, 'Ro."

"Excuse me?"

"You don' trust them, either. Scott, and the others."

Ororo's breath caught. Jubilee said, "You didn't even think about it, did you? You completely marked them off."

"No," Ororo said, but Jubilee shook her head.

"You did. It's like us. You feel that weird vibe."

"More'n a vibe," Remy added. "Something happened on that mission to Seattle. The others came back . . . different."

"Rogue's silence can be blamed on trauma," Ororo began, but Remy raised his hand.

"It's not just Rogue. It's Kurt, too. Scott and Jean. Wolverine? They're different, 'Ro. I can't tell you how, but it's real. Haven't you noticed?"

"Maybe," Ororo conceded slowly. "I must admit, I turned on the psychic dampeners when I entered this office. I would say, in all likelihood, that this is the only safe place in the Mansion for us to talk."

Jubilee's eyes widened. "You went that far and you're still arguing with us?"

Remy frowned. "You think Jean's been compromised?"

"Compromised? I don't know if anyone has been 'compromised.' Only, you're right. Something *is* different with them. Something . . . not right."

"Duh," Jubilee said. "I think you can leave the understatements at home, Storm. Now is the time for big honkin' gestures."

"Like body snatching," Remy added.

Ororo raised her eyebrows. "I do not think so."

"I *totally* think so," Jubilee said. "Have you been paying attention to the way they're acting? Wolverine is off his rocker. In tiny ways, maybe, but off. So is Scott. I haven't seen Kurt lately, but if he's anything like the others, I'm gonna start sleeping with a knife under my pillow."

"This is ridiculous," Ororo said. "Remy?"

"I'm beginning to agree with her, 'Ro. Considering all the crazy and powerful people we've met over the years, can you really discount the possibility?"

"That five of the most powerful mutants in the world are being possessed by some unknown entity? I don't want to consider the possibility. It makes me sick to my stomach." Ororo closed her eyes, pinching the bridge of her nose. "Let's say you are right. What reason would someone do this?"

"Power, money, out to ruin us . . . does it matter? The real question is, has it been done, and if so, how do we reverse it?" Remy reached into his pocket and pulled out a deck of cards. He started shuffling, which was a pure sign of anxiety in Jubilee's book.

"How about Professor X?" Jubilee said. "He could figure this out in no time flat."

"I have been trying to call him," Ororo said. "I keep receiving a busy signal on the other end."

"You sure it's the other end?" Remy asked. "Maybe there's a reason you can't get ahold of him. A reason that starts here."

Ororo's jaw tightened. "Ever since they returned, I have been trying to convince myself that the differences I sensed were due to some trauma none of them wished to

discuss. I was going to respect that, and wait. Now . . .
now you have me scared."

"Good," Jubilee said. " 'Cause I'm ready to pee my
pants."

"Yes, well." Ororo stood, smoothing out her dress. "I
think it is time for a field trip. Every single student here at
the Mansion needs to attend, don't you think?"

"*Absolument*," Remy said. "Something overnight? Perhaps in the city?"

"I have a dear friend in New York who might be willing to help chaperone. She has a rather spacious town-
house that would accommodate all the children who are
here during break. Jubilee, I would also be counting on
you to help her."

Jubilee coughed back a laugh. "You have got to be kidding. No way, Storm. I'm staying here."

"No."

"Yes. You need all the help you can get."

"You're only fifteen."

"And who taught me everything I know? What age
was I when I first joined the X-Men? You never treated
me like a kid, then."

"I do not have time for this," Ororo said, but Remy
shook his head.

"Let her stay, 'Ro. She's right. We need help."

"You might as well have me keep all the students
here," she muttered, but then shook her head and said,
"Fine. You may stay."

"Cool." Jubilee shot Remy a grateful smile.

"I need to make some calls," she said. "Why don't you

two start investigating the logs in the jet. Find out exactly what happened in Seattle. Perhaps, even, find out where Logan's contact got his information."

"On it." Jubilee saluted her.

"Please be careful," she said to them. "If things are as bad as they seem, we cannot predict the behavior of our friends. They could be capable of almost anything."

Which was a sobering thought. Jubilee said, "If everyone really has been body-snatched, then where did they go? Is Wolvie still inside there, fighting to come out?"

"I hope so," Remy said. "I don' want to think about the alternative."

"Neither do I," Jubilee said, but she had a feeling she just wasn't that lucky.

14

THEY DROVE ALL NIGHT, TAKING TURNS AND STOPPING just once in Spokane, for gas and a change of cars. By four that morning, they were well into Montana.

"No speed limit. I love this state." Logan sat in the passenger seat as Rogue drove. He glanced over his shoulder; the others were dozing. Uncomfortable as hell, probably, but they were too tired to care where and how they got shut-eye, just as long as they did. Logan could relate. This body of his just wasn't used to long hauls.

"How are you doing?" he asked Rogue.

"You asked me that ten minutes ago, sugah. Maybe you should get some rest."

"I've been telling myself the same thing. I just can't seem to fall asleep."

"I thought you were the kind who conked out pretty fast."

"I am, but maybe that's a body-specific thing."

"Maybe. How do you like being a woman? Any deep thoughts?"

"Darlin', if you're expecting deep thoughts, you're talking to the wrong man."

Rogue laughed, but there was a tightness to her eyes

that made Logan squint against the shadows. It irritated him to no end that his eyesight was no longer good enough to see in the dark.

"What is it?" he asked softly. "What's troubling you, darlin'?"

"Nothing," she said. "What makes you ask?"

"Instinct," he said. "And I know you too well. Come on, Rogue. It's a long drive and with those sleeping beauties back there, it's just you and me. Spill."

She hesitated. He had some idea of what she would say and he was not far wrong.

"It's that man I killed," she told him. "I can't stop thinking about him."

"Yeah?" he said. "Nothing wrong with that."

"Everything is wrong," she argued. "He's dead."

"We already discussed this, darlin'. You were trying to stop him from killing someone. It was in self-defense."

"It's more than that. It was arrogance, Logan. My arrogance. I thought this body," and she stopped, gesturing at herself as though she were something distasteful, "wouldn't be strong enough to kill. I didn't hold back."

Logan sighed. Rogue was one of the finest women he knew, but she could hold on to guilt like it was a second superpower. It did not make sense to him to feel bad about things you could not change. Better to learn from mistakes and just move on. Of course, he was a different kind of animal from Rogue. She was more civilized than he.

"Let it go," he said, trying to make her understand. Her lips tightened into a thin line and he shook his head, exasperated. "Forget it, then. I give up, Rogue. I don't know how you do it. How you manage to be the oldest woman I've ever known while living in such a young body."

"You can stop now."

"Fine." He leaned away from her and stared out the window, watching shadows pass along the freeway. A moment later he felt a warm hand touch him, fingers curling around his fingers.

"Thank you," she said softly. "I do appreciate it."

Logan squeezed her hand. "Anytime, darlin'. Anytime you need to talk. I'll always be there for you."

Rogue pulled over at the next rest stop and everyone clambered out to stretch their legs and use the restroom. The parking lot was full with semitrucks, red and yellow edge lights twinkling like it was Christmas. It was still early enough for the sky to be dark, though the birdsong had changed.

The building itself was almost empty. Logan thought he glimpsed some tall figure in an alcove looking at maps. It was almost four in the morning; most everyone, especially the truckers, were tucked snug in their cabs and cars, fast asleep. Logan began to follow Kurt into the men's bathroom and was saved by a loose arm draped over his shoulders. Rogue, steering him into the woman's bathroom. Personally, he did not see how it really mattered where he went.

"Remember your place," she whispered, her breath tickling his ear. She glanced at Scott, who was just now emerging from the bathroom. He had been the first to jump out of the car, charging into the rest stop like there was some Sentinel inside needing its tin metal butt kicked. Scott said nothing, but Logan thought he looked infinitely more comfortable.

The bathroom smelled and the toilets had seen better days—better ends of a bleach bottle, too. He *really* missed standing up.

"You okay over there?" Rogue called over the stall, her voice monstrously loud. "I'm not hearing any tinkle-tinkle."

"Ain't none of your business what I'm doing in here," he said, still standing up. He had already done this multiple times, but it never got easier. It felt so wrong.

"Sure thing," Rogue said, clearly proud of her own wondrous ability to relieve herself. Her toilet flushed and then she was out, washing her hands. He heard her slap water on her face.

"You going to be okay if I head back to the car? Logan?"

"Sure," he said, gritting his teeth as he finally went through the motions. "Just get away from me. I'm concentrating."

She chuckled, and he heard the door swing open. Less than a minute later someone else entered. He wondered if it was Rogue, but kept his mouth shut. The last thing he wanted to do was talk to some stranger.

He finished, flushed, and left the stall. Stopped.

A man stood in front of him. Tall, with a narrow face and hollow cheeks. He wore a tight T-shirt and jeans. Logan thought he looked familiar, and placed him as the map-reader.

"You're not supposed to be in here," Logan said, already planning his moves, the classics: throat, nose, groin. He shifted to the balls of his feet, hands loose and ready at his sides. Great. Didn't seem to matter what he looked like; he always attracted the weirdos.

The man smiled. His teeth were very sharp. Too sharp.

Logan thought, *Oh, crap*, and then he had to dart sideways because the mutant attacked. Logan slammed his fist into the soft part of his throat, following up with another blow to the nose. The combined impact did not slow his assailant in the slightest. His fingers lengthened, scraping Logan's shoulders, searching for a hold. Logan batted away those hands. He got in another punch and then one more, and he watched the man smile, so wicked, confident and smug, and he realized those blows meant nothing to him, weren't even tickling his skin. Jerk was a mutant and he needed a mutant to fight him. That, or Logan was going to require something stronger than two small fists of fury.

He was not fast enough, not in this body. Impossibly long fingers wrapped around his ankles and he hit the ground hard, slamming the back of his head into the tile. Stunned, dazed, he still tried to kick, to scoot backward. The man fell on top of him, fingers uncurling from ankles and snaking upward to wrap tight like rope around Logan's soft arms. Logan snarled, trying to buck him off. Nothing worked. Enhanced mutant strength. For one moment, Logan understood why humans hated his kind.

"Get off me," Logan growled. The door to the bathroom rattled. Logan head Rogue's voice, asking if he was all right. He shouted out to her and got head-butted for his trouble.

"Shhh," hissed the man, speaking for the first time. "Be still."

"You idiot," Logan said, struggling. "You must be the worst rapist ever."

The man smiled. His mouth was close and hot and wet. Soft, he whispered, "Who said anything about rape?"

Logan watched those lips peel back, those teeth glint white and sharp. He thought he saw meaty bits plugging the gaps between them.

The door rattled again. Logan shouted as that scraping mouth touched his cheek.

And then a boom rattled the air, a concussive blast that knocked something out of the door, and Jean and Scott burst into the bathroom. Jean held a gun—that gun she had taken off the pimp—and she aimed it at the mutant holding down Logan and said, "Get off him right now or I will shoot you in the face."

He hesitated. Jean said, "Now."

And then behind them another figure entered, a man—

—a gun went off. The mutant's head exploded and Logan got a mouthful of blood that had him spitting. He heard Scott say, "No," and Jean added, "I didn't do it."

Logan was blind with blood in his eyes and could not move his arms to wipe it away. His ears were fine, though, and he heard a low voice, the voice of a stranger, and the man said, "Hope you don't mind, sir, but I always wanted to kill me a mutant."

And Logan was fine with that. Really.

His name was Duke, or at least, that was what he called himself. Logan did not imagine his mother had given him that name. Duke drove a semi for a furniture company. He always carried a gun, and he did not like most mutants. Some were okay, but the rest could just go hang themselves because they were too dangerous to live, and if he couldn't even trust his sheriff not to be corrupt, or his wife to be faithful, or the local politicians to keep things on the up and up, well, he didn't put much stock in the ability of mutants with superpowers to keep from abusing the little guys. It was just a fact of life, according to Duke. Power made people corrupt. Why, look at that Magneto fellow, or the Brotherhood of Whatsit. Even those X-Men probably had some fishy deal up their sleeves.

"Probably," Logan said, shaking his hand. "Thanks, Duke. You sure you'll be okay?"

"Yeah," he said. "Like I told you, the sheriff around these parts doesn't like mutants too much, and I got a dozen witnesses here says you were being attacked. Or at least, he was on top of you when I shot him. I'll just say you got scared and ran away. Nothing's going to happen to me, sweetheart. Won't even make the papers."

Which was disturbing, and under any other circumstances, worthy of an in-depth investigation. Except, Duke and the men backing him up—all of them truckers who had heard the ruckus and come running—were trying to be good people. Had been, too. They just had a different perspective on things, and Logan really couldn't blame them. Hell, psycho cannibal mutants like that corpse in the women's bathroom did not do much for making a good impression.

Scott, thankfully, kept his mouth shut. Logan could tell he was itching to say something, to speak up for the goodness of all mutant kind, but this was not the time or the place.

Duke said, "You take care, Patty. I hope you and your friends make it home safe, without the law on your tails."

Because none of the X-Men wanted to risk encounters with the police, and Duke seemed like the kind of man who understood why it wasn't always good for some people to have face time with the cops.

They got into the car and drove away, fast. Scott was at the wheel, Jean in the front seat beside him. Crammed in the back with the others, Logan felt like a little kid about to get a lecture from his mommy and daddy.

"What happened back there?" Scott asked, the moment they were back on the freeway and gunning it at ninety.

"Someone took a look at me, thought victim—or maybe just Happy Meal—and decided to go for it. Might have taken a chunk or two if Rogue hadn't come back to see how I was doing."

"I didn't think anyone, even you, couldn't possibly take that long," she said, squeezed up tight against him. Logan felt grateful for her good Southern common sense. He glanced at Jean, noting the lines of her pensive face.

The gun was in the glove compartment. Logan wondered if she really would have shot that mutant, and decided yes, if push came to shove.

"He didn't even get a chance, though," Scott said. "That man, Duke, didn't ask any questions. He just shot that mutant, and was happy for it."

Logan stared at the back of his head. "Did you miss the part where I was going to be eaten alive?"

"All right, so the situation merited some defensive measures. My point"—here Logan could barely hear him over the low shocked laughter from the rest of the car—"is that it could have been something completely different. That mutant—and yes, I know this wasn't the case, but let's be hypothetical—could just have been trying to help you. Maybe the situation merely looked bad. You can't justify a 'shoot first, ask questions later' policy, just because it involves mutants. And then the way they were going to sweep it under the rug—"

The soapbox was coming, and Logan did not feel in the mood to hear Scott rant about injustice.

"Scott," he interrupted. "If it makes you feel better, I would have killed him myself if I'd had the chance. In cold blood. You don't let psychos like that run loose. All they do is cause pain."

"Is that your professional opinion?" Scott asked, his voice cold. "You think the same hasn't been said about you?"

Kurt made a soft sound of protest. Logan said, "I know it has. Doesn't bother me, because they're partly right. I am a dangerous man. And one day, if someone puts me down for being dangerous, I'll know they probably had a good reason. Thing is, Cyke, there are the kind who are dangerous just because, and the kind who are dangerous because they get off on it. Those are the ones you should be worried about. Those are the ones you shouldn't feel sorry for. That was the kind of man who had me pinned down on the floor of that bathroom, and who was going to take a bite out of my face. You can bet I'm not the only one he's cleaned his teeth on. So don't you dare ask me to sympathize, and don't you make me apologize for being alive."

"We're not vigilantes," Scott said. "We can't take justice in our own hands. No one should be able to do that."

Logan said nothing. He and Scott had never seen eye-to-eye on certain issues, this being one of them. Logan was the kind of man who did what had to be done, no questions asked. Scott was the same, except he asked the questions. Which, when he thought about it, was probably the reason why he was team leader, and why Logan respected him for it. Scott could be a pain, but he usually knew what he was talking about.

Except for now.

"You're thinking too much in black-and-white," Logan said. "Those guys back there are good people."

"If you're not a mutant."

"Maybe so, but imagine the kinds of experiences they've had with mutants. Tonight might be the closest any of them has come to one, and what do they see? A murderer, a cannibal. What do you expect them to do, hold hands and sing the praises of forgiveness? I don't think so, bub."

"So it's okay? They've got carte blanche to discriminate and kill anyone who they think *might* be a threat?"

"Don't you twist my words, Cyke. You know that's not what I'm saying."

Scott remained silent, stewing. He was good at that. Logan wondered if he ever tried to pull that shit with Jean and decided he wouldn't dare. At the moment, she watched him sternly, and if Logan had not been certain she was no longer telepathic, he could almost swear she was giving him some kind of mental lecture.

She probably is. He just ain't hearing it.

"So," Rogue said, breaking into the silence with a wry smile for Logan. "How long until we get there?"

"You're only allowed to ask that question once a day," Logan said. "We're about twenty-four hundred miles from home. That's, what, almost thirty-five hours of road time. If we don't stop much, we'll be home the day after tomorrow."

"We'll probably run out of money before then," Scott said. He seemed calmer, more in control. Logan gave all the credit to Jean's nontelepathic vibrations.

"Too bad we can't sell this car," Rogue muttered.

"And then steal another?" Logan gave her an amused look. "Have I created a monster?"

"The monster was always there," Rogue said, and there was a slight edge beneath the humor, enough to give him pause. He did not push her for more, though. Logan was not a big fan of dredging up issues. If people wanted to talk, they did. Simple as that.

The sun came up, illuminating rock and tree, mountains bright. Logan rolled down his window, inhaling the scent. Homesickness swelled inside his heart—not for New York, but for this, this precious solitude—and if the situation had not been so dire, if he had been whole and healthy inside his body, he would have forced Scott to stop the car and let him out. Let him go, deep into the wild to disappear for a day or a year.

They pulled over at a truck stop in a little town outside Bozeman. It was midmorning and the tank was banging on empty. They had only ten dollars left and all of that went to the gas.

"What's our food look like?" Scott asked, leaning on the car. His black hair looked a little on the greasy side, but his skin was clear and his dark almond eyes had that glint in them that was pure Fearless Leader.

Kurt peered into the plastic bag. "We still have some bread and peanut butter left, but the doughnuts are gone and we're almost out of water."

"We could always fill up inside a bathroom faucet," Logan said. "Food is another matter. We might just have to go hungry until we get home."

Jean pulled her dreadlocks back, twisting and knotting them into a bun. "There are some pay phones over there. I'm going to call the Mansion."

"Okay, but if one of us answers, hang up. The less we talk to them, the better. No need to give our counterparts an excuse to start looking for us, or tracking our location."

"I'm going to the bar," Logan said. Everyone stared at him.

"Bar?" Rogue asked. "There's a bar?"

"Sure," Logan said, amazed they hadn't noticed it. "Look over there by the gas station."

Rogue squinted. "That's a shack, sugah. I've seen tool sheds in better condition."

"Yes, but this one has beer. They've got it advertised with a nice little neon sign."

"It's ten in the morning."

"And there are cars parked outside."

"You're broke."

"Who says I'm going to buy?" Logan hefted the water bottle. "I'll be back."

Scott frowned. "I better go with you."

"Oh, Lord." Rogue looked at the sky, while Kurt crossed himself. "Save us now."

"Laugh it up," Logan said, and marched off toward the little bar which did resemble some rough toolshed, but no doubt carried the scents of cigarettes, liquor, and cheap women: *parfum d'Logan.*

It was all of those things when he went in, minus the cheap women. Just a bunch of men sitting at a tiny counter that barely had room for a bottle of vodka, let alone glasses and elbows. The rest of the bar's floor space was taken up by an emerald holy grail, illuminated by perfectly placed track lighting that seemed to light that gleaming surface from within.

"That's some pool table," Scott said, peering over Logan's shoulder.

"Sure is," he said. Men stood around, holding their cues like spears, weapons of war. They looked at Logan and Scott, looked with the eyes of men unaccustomed to having their inner sanctum invaded by outsiders, and Logan suddenly had a brilliant idea. He glanced at Scott, and smiled.

"Oh, no," he said. "Logan—"

"Hello boys," Logan said. "Nice sticks you've got there."

They had to leave the bar for several minutes in order to tell the others where to park. Logan also used it as an opportunity to give Scott some instructions.

"Unbutton your shirt," he said.

"Excuse me?"

"You don't have much cleavage, but if you unbutton your shirt a little more that won't matter. See? Look at me."

"I cannot believe I'm doing this."

"Think of yourself as breadwinner. Like some boxer from the thirties, throwing himself into the ring to bring money home for the wife and hungry kids."

"It's a little different," Scott said. "You want me to sell my body."

"I don't want you to sell your body. I want you to sell an image. When they buy that image, then kick their butts."

"What are you doing to my husband?" Jean asked, meeting them as they walked to the car.

"He's trying to make me sexy," Scott said. "Is it working?"

Jean closed her eyes. "I don't want to know. Really, I don't."

"Did you get through to the Mansion?" Logan asked.

"Busy signal. I must have called twenty times, using different room extensions, and it was always busy. I think they've cut off the school."

"Makes sense, if they were worried one of us would get through. Crap. I hope the others are okay."

"Who's there right now? Ororo?"

"Gambit," Jean said. "Jubilee."

"Jubilee," Logan said, clenching his fists. "She's going to figure it out."

"Why would that matter?"

"Kid's going to spend one minute with my alter ego and know that something's wrong. And then she's going to start making some noise."

"If we're lucky, all of them will figure it out and start taking action."

"And the busy phone lines? That's not the kind of action I was hoping for, Cyke."

Rogue and Kurt waited for them outside the car. Logan looked for cops. He didn't see any, but it made him nervous, the car sitting out in the open for any length of time. Driving felt different, but this was like being a sitting duck.

"We're paid and ready to go," Rogue said, and then, "Scott, honey, your shirt is undone."

"Yes," he said. "You need to park the car over by the bar. Logan and I have . . . business in there. It may take a while."

"Business," Jean said, raising an eyebrow.

"Oh, no." Rogue covered her mouth. "We're not *that* desperate."

Scott shook his head. "Just . . . move the car."

"I want to know what this is about," Jean said.

"Earning some easy cash," Logan said. "They got a pool table."

"Oh," she said, and then, "*Oh.*"

"Exactly."

Jean looked at her husband and mussed his hair a little more. She tweaked his shirt, pulling the tail from his jeans and tying it in a knot around his thin waist.

"Go get 'em," Jean told her husband with a crooked smile.

The men in the bar certainly appreciated the new look. Whistles accompanied Scott and Logan's entrance. Jean waited outside with Kurt and Rogue. Having male friends join them at the pool table would ruin the illusion of sweet innocents just wanting to pass the time, to try their hand. They had no money to add to the betting pool, but that did not matter. No one expected them to win, anyway. Taking their money in a bet would have been . . . ungentlemanly.

But that did not mean Scott and Logan couldn't collect.

Logan played only two games, losing both. Scott went up next, and Logan let the bartender buy him a beer as he sat back and watched the show.

One of the lesser-known facts about Scott Summers was that the man played pool like a god. Even Logan knew better than to compete with him. It had something to do with his powers, his ability to know exactly how objects would move, rebound, deflect. A side effect, perhaps; Logan had seen him hit mission targets that were out of sight, simply by calculating the best angle at which to release his energy beams. Bing, bang, bong.

A couple of balls and a cue were child's play.

Following Logan's example, Scott lost the first two games, fumbling miserably as his opponents smiled, enjoying the spectacle of having a beautiful girl at their table, trying so hard to be as good as them. Oh, how cute. Oh, don't worry, you'll get better. Oh, Harry, cut the girl some slack.

And then the wager hit one hundred dollars—not a lot of money, but enough to get them home—and Scott stopped losing.

He did it subtly, no grandiose gestures that screamed "hustler." Just a ball here, a ball there. In retrospect, Logan wondered if that was the key mistake, the one thing they did wrong. They did not leap about and cheer every time a ball went into the hole. They did not cry out for support. They did things quiet, because that was their nature, and neither of them, for all their big talk of looking sexy, could change that one aspect of themselves. Logan knew plenty of women who were exactly the same, but those were professionals, not young things who supposedly didn't know much of anything about playing pool. It was all about perceptions and expectations.

The game was an easy finish. Scott, doing a decent job of acting surprised, smiled tentatively at the men and reached for the money.

"I think we should play again," said his opponent,

Fred, moving just enough to block his hand, "Double or nothing."

"I would love to," Scott said, "but we need to get back on the road. Besides, this was a lucky finish. I don't think I could win a second time."

"That so?" said the other man, a local lumberman named Daniel. He stroked his pool cue, thoughtful. "I'm not sure I believe in luck."

"Now, now," said the bartender, as Logan got off his stool. "There's no need to be sore losers."

"What, exactly, is the problem here?" Logan asked.

"The problem is that I think you cheated."

"Cheated?" Logan gazed around the room. "You telling me there's a way to cheat at pool?"

"There is if you've played before and now you're lying about it."

"And what makes you think we're lying?"

The bar's door opened; light flooded in from the outside, blinding them all. Logan blinked, recognizing the outline of a body that stood in the doorway, the silhouette of dreadlocks reminding him of old Greek tales about Medusa.

Scott, again, reached for the money. Fred tried to grab it first, but Scott was faster. He snatched the cash and then he and Logan started moving to the door, ignoring the protests that erupted behind them. Logan had anticipated this part, though usually it didn't happen unless the wins were bigger. One of the men he had been sitting beside at the bar stood up and tried to block the door. Logan said, "You better move," and when the man just smiled and reached out his hands, Logan did not mess around, but slammed his fist into that jaw, rocking the drinker back on his heels so that he stumbled and hit the wall.

His hand hurt but he didn't dare rub it. He turned in a slow circle, meeting hard gazes that flickered and then broke away. It was like playing a game of chicken with his fists. After pulling that first bluff, no one wanted to play for keeps, especially if it required hitting a woman. Fine by him.

Outside, Scott said, "You always make things sound so easy. And then people start hitting us."

"You should be used to that by now." Logan turned to Jean. "You could have helped. They accused us of cheating."

"Big surprise. Now come on. I was coming to get you. We have to get out of here."

"Police?"

"Worse," she said. "Cerebro."

15

THE HARDEST PART OF DEALING WITH BODY SNATCHERS
was that you had to pretend they were your friends at din-
nertime. Which meant that Jubilee stopped going to dinner. Frankly, she did not think anyone was keeping
regular meal hours; since their return from Seattle, she
had run into Scott only once in the kitchen. Jubilee had
stayed long enough to grab a box of Twinkies and then
made a run for it back to her room, looking over her
shoulder the entire time to see if Scott followed her. He
did not, but she still felt wary. There was no telling what
they wanted.

She even, for a time, stayed away from Wolverine.
That did not last long, but when she did go to him she remained on the periphery, occasionally talking, but most
often just observing. Wolverine—or whoever he was—
did not seem to mind. The more she was around him,
the more it seemed that he treated her like a pet, some
lonely little puppy that was cute to have around, but only
as long as it didn't become annoying. Even with the possibility that her Wolvie was a completely different man,
Jubilee did not question her ability to handle him. Nah.
Wolvie was easy.

The real problem was Jean. Jubilee had already taken certain precautions—the kind that involved a wrench and a screwdriver, and the unhealthy application of such tools to certain highly revered pieces of technology—but that was not going to help anyone living in the Mansion.

"Dude," Jubilee said to Remy, less than a day after their first meeting with Ororo. "She's going to read our minds and find out we don't trust her. We might as well give up now."

"Mebbe," he said, with a curious lack of expression. Could be exhaustion; he'd been up half the night helping Storm drive the kids into the city for their "field trip."

"Mebbe?" she mimicked. "What aren't you telling me?"

Remy brought Jubilee to his room. It was certainly not the first time she had gone into the teachers' wing, but she had never been to Remy's room before. She expected luxury, designer furnishings, New Orleans flair.

The reality was quite different.

"Wow," Jubilee said, when Remy opened his door and turned on the light. "I feel cheated."

" 'Cuse me?"

"Nothing," she said, closely examining the fine clean lines of the polished wood floors, the simple curve of two black leather armchairs. The bed was plain, the sheets cotton and white. It was all very austere. Not what she had envisioned at all.

Remy shut the door and walked across his room to the

closet. Jubilee got a glimpse of dress shirts and jeans, several long coats, and a set of body armor, and then he pulled down a box from the top shelf and kicked the closet shut. He sat down on the floor and Jubilee joined him. She studied the box in his hands.

"I've been saving these for something important," Remy said, and opened the lid. Jubilee peered inside and saw three small black discs the size of her thumbnail cushioned in gray foam pads.

"What are they?" she asked, stroking one with her finger. Remy pried the disc from the foam and placed it in her palm.

"Psychic dampeners," he said. "I acquired them just last month."

"Cool," Jubilee said. "If I wear this, not even Professor X can read my thoughts?"

"That's what they promised me." There was an odd note in his voice that caught her attention. Jubilee tore her gaze from the disc and looked into his eyes.

"Why do you have these?" she asked, not sure she wanted to hear the answer.

"Really, you want to know?" His smile looked faintly bitter. "Because, *ma petite*, best friends make the worst kind of enemy."

Jubilee sat back, staring. "You've thought about this happening. You anticipated it. You thought they—the psychics in this place—could go bad."

"Everyone can go bad. The pace is slower for some, that's all."

Jubilee sucked in her breath. She did not know what

to think about this new revelation, how to respond to the idea that Remy might not trust even her, but she swallowed down the hurt and stuck out her hand with the disc glinting dull and black beneath the light. "Can you help me turn this thing on?"

He did, working silently as he placed the disc behind her ear. Jubilee felt it vibrate once and then go still.

"Is it is working?" she whispered.

"*Oui.*" He picked up a second disc and placed it behind his own ear.

"Storm," she said.

"Of course," he said, and they went looking for her all over again.

Remy did not like exposing his secrets; that Jubilee now knew he had made contingency plans in case his friends ever turned on him was a deeply personal fact that had hurt to share. Part of the revelation had resulted from Jubilee's own perceptiveness, but the other was entirely his own fault. He had said more than he should. Oddly, he felt no desire to take it back.

He and Jubilee did not linger in Ororo's office after giving her the dampener. Remy did not want to allow his friend an opportunity to comment on his paranoia, his morality. It was enough that her thoughts would be safe when she left Xavier's office.

"So now what?" Jubilee asked.

"The Blackbird," he said. "I want to check to the logs."

The lights were off inside the hangar; they left them

that way as they walked to the jet, listening for anyone else who might be in there. Jubilee, after a moment, whistled the theme to *The Twilight Zone*.

"You can stop that," Remy said. "Really."

"Sure," she said, and he realized that she was trying to cover for her own uneasiness. When the Mansion was full, there were usually any number of people down in the hangar—either learning something new about the machines, doing maintenance, or taking flying lessons via the simulator in the corner. This new silence felt unnatural. He did not trust it.

The interior of the Blackbird was as he remembered. Nothing looked out of place; he saw no signs of a struggle. Quick, uneasy about lingering long, he made a search of the logs and found several recordings Scott had made upon arrival in Seattle. He played them.

"Boring," Jubilee said, lounging in the pilot's seat. She looked over the controls and blinked hard.

"Hey," she said. "Remy, you need to look at this."

He bent over her shoulder, staring where she pointed. It was the fuel gauge, and the arrow tilted at empty. No one had refueled the jet.

"Oh, yeah," Jubilee murmured. "Someone is going to get it."

Remy shook his head. "Refueling the jet as soon as you return is a fundamental safety procedure. Even *you* know that."

Because too many emergencies arose that required the X-Men to depart the Mansion at great haste. Running out of fuel in midair on the way to saving lives was not a good situation to find oneself in. Right now, there was barely enough fuel to fly into the city.

Jubilee tapped her jaw. "So finally there are people on this team even more irresponsible than me. I'd be happy about that, except it's another sign of the end times."

"End times?" said a new voice. "That's a little melodramatic, don't you think?"

Remy whirled, stepping in front of Jubilee. Scott stood at the back of the jet, his body cast in shadow. There was a slight tilt to his mouth, an almost-smile that was cold and hard. For just an instant, Remy did not recognize him; the person inside was so different that the physical resemblance had become meaningless.

"What are the two of you doing here?"

"Maintenance check," Remy lied easily. "It's my turn."

Scott made a humming noise. "Do you do all your maintenance checks in the company of teenage girls?"

"Hey." Jubilee narrowed her eyes. "I don't like the sound of that."

Neither did Remy. "She's my student, Scott."

"So was little Lolita, once upon a time."

Jubilee raised her hands; Remy glimpsed light in her palms and he grabbed her wrists.

"*Non*," he murmured. "Not now."

Scott moved closer; his smile changed into something sly. "So. Have you found anything that needs maintenance?" He looked at Jubilee. "Or did I get here too soon?"

"Remy," Jubilee said. His hand tightened on her wrist.

"Get out of here, Scott," Remy said. "You need to leave, right now."

"And miss out on the fun?" His mouth widened, white and cruel. "Where should we start?"

Remy let go of Jubilee and punched Scott in the face. It was a blow Scott should have been able to block— Remy was too angry, his swing wild—but he slammed Scott's face before the team leader had a chance to raise his hands, and the man went down hard on the floor. Remy stood over his body. His heart thundered and he held cards between his hot fingers.

"Don' you *ever* talk like that to Jubilee or me," he said in his softest voice. "Don' even think it."

"Or what?" Scott asked, touching his bloody mouth. "You'll kill me?"

Remy felt his heart sink into a dark place. This man in front of him was not Scott Summers, but the body was his, and he could not be certain that the man himself did not still reside there, lost beneath the cruel light in the eyes of the person looking up at him from the floor.

But there were some things Remy would not tolerate, no matter what, and he said, "Yes, I will kill you, Scott."

Scott scooted backward until he could stand with some distance between himself and Remy. Remy watched him carefully, waiting for him to retaliate. Scott never did.

"Later," he said, backing away slowly. "Later, you and I will do this again."

Remy said nothing. He watched Scott leave the jet and did not relax until the X-Man left the hangar. Remy slapped the ramp panel and raised the door. When the airlock sealed, when they were protected by steel, Remy leaned against the wall and felt a long shaky breath escape his throat. He heard footsteps. His gaze slid sideways to Jubilee. Her eyes were huge.

He reached out and drew Jubilee against him.

"It's okay," he whispered.

"No," she said, her voice muffled against his chest. "It's not."

16

EVEN THOUGH JEAN NO LONGER HAD HER POWERS, SHE remembered what it was like to have her mind probed. The sensation always changed, depending on the telepath; Emma Frost, for example, felt like a blood-starved limb, all prickly with pain, while Charles's psychic touch produced incalculable warmth, a baby blanket for the mind. Jean, up until this point, had no idea what her touch might feel like to others, only that it would leave a mark.

And so it had, one that she was astute enough to catch.

"I think my counterpart—or whoever has my body—is looking for us," Jean said. "I felt her tickle my brain."

"How do you know it is you?" Kurt asked. "There could be another telepath in this area. Perhaps the two are confused?"

"No, it's me. I can't explain it. It's like . . . a familiar scent or hearing the voice of someone you thought you'd forgotten. It feels like home."

"I think I'm jealous," Rogue said.

"She must be using Cerebro to expand her range." Jean twisted in her seat so she could look at the others. All of them were pale, tired, with dark circles under their eyes and a hollow quality to their cheeks that was probably part of the same hunger than gnawed her own belly. "I think she's doing it badly, though. Of course, it's hard to tell, but it felt like she was on me for only a moment or two."

"But that could be enough, right? If she knows what she's looking for." Scott's knuckles were white on the steering wheel.

"But why would she? If my counterpart had no supermental abilities before the transfer, then how would she possibly know what my mind feels like?"

"And if it's Jonas Maguire using her? He certainly knows your mind."

"If he was the one who transferred it."

"Let's just say he did until we can prove otherwise," Logan replied. "So the other Jean is using Cerebro and she touched your mind. I don't think we should rule out an accident, or that she had some purpose for using Cerebro *other* than finding us. Think about the power she's got. She could go after anyone with that thing. Maybe she's just training herself to use it."

The car sped up. Jean looked out the window and saw golden grassland bathed in sunlight, rolling hills that hid mysteries, always just on the other side. There could be a hundred people only yards away from the road, and no one would ever know. Good ambush country. Not that she thought anything like that would happen to them. At least not here, and not with people springing out from behind hills or trees. A police roadblock, a gun in her face? Maybe her own powers used against her? Yes, all of that was a distinct possibility.

"There's no way to protect ourselves from Cerebro, is there?" Rogue sat between Kurt and Logan. She looked uncomfortable. Jean could only imagine what it was like, suddenly able to touch and then to have it forced upon her in the form of continuous close contact. Jean still had trouble coping with her mind blindness. Sleeping was horrible, because with her eyes closed the world truly fell away, and she was reminded of those first moments in the mental hospital when the world had felt so cold and empty.

Stop it. Stop feeling sorry for yourself. The others were right. So your abilities are gone. You were relying on them too much if this is the kind of reaction you're having. Take this time as a lesson to toughen up.

"No," Jean said to Rogue. "There's no way to hide, not unless we have some natural shielding. Kurt, when he teleports, is always hard to find. Gambit, too. His brain . . . scrambles things. I doubt we're that lucky."

"So if the police do not stop us, then we risk having our minds destroyed." Kurt sighed. "Lovely."

"We don't have any options," Scott said. "We have to go home."

And what a shame it had to be under such terrifying circumstances. Jean knew the exact process of destroying an individual's mind. It was something she had contemplated quite often—not because she wished to harm anyone, but because she wished to know exactly what to do in order to avoid some accidental, and quite devastating, use of her telepathy.

To destroy a mind, to rip from it the essence of personhood, was the ultimate in tortures—and crimes. Jean did not want to consider it as the possible end for herself or her friends. She would rather face death than that, which was no better than being a zombie; a body, a shell, with nothing inside but the most rudimentary instincts.

Late that afternoon they passed into North Dakota, and it was there, caught within a parted sea of hot golden grasses, at least thirty miles from the nearest town, that their little car blew out its tire. The trunk did not have a spare.

"Pack it up," Scott said. "We're walking."

"We better find a way of getting off the road before some cop checks out this car. Minute they run anything on the plates, they're going to figure something's fishy. And if we're the only ones on the road . . ." Logan's voice trailed away.

It was simply one more blow against them. Jean thought she should probably count her blessings that they had made it this far, but it was difficult to think about the positive when the sun began to set and the few cars on the road sped by with drivers and passengers who looked at them as though they were bogeymen, or the prime suspects of some horrible highway ax murder. Jean wanted to yell "Boo!" every time she saw their expressions.

"You can't really blame people," Rogue said, wiping sweat from her face. "I mean, there are a lot of crazies out in the world."

"Fear should not hinder compassion," Kurt said.

"That's easy enough for us to say," Logan countered.

"We're trained professionals. We fight space aliens with our bare hands, for Christ's sake."

"Does compassion mean less when you're a superhero, then?" Kurt wondered out loud. "Without that inherent risk, that choice of possible harm, does a kind act from one of us count as much as the kindness of a normal human being?"

"Kurt," Scott said. "Does it matter?"

"*Ja.*" Kurt turned around, walking backward so he could look at them. "We are powerful people. Or at least, we were. But how often do we use that power to help those without? Our focus is always on mutants, and that is right and good, because there are also mutants who have nothing. But what else? What else have we done?"

"Saved the world," Logan said.

"Several worlds, actually," Scott added. "Maybe the universe?"

"Now you're exaggerating."

Kurt threw up his hands. "You see? We have saved the world, but did we actually do anything to make it a better place? We shelter mutants at the school, but do we teach them how to interact with humans? Do we encourage them to make friends with different kinds of children? If we isolate them, do we teach compassion or superiority?"

"Kurt," Rogue protested. "We're trying to create a world where mutants and humans can live together."

"Perhaps, but I am no longer convinced we are going about it in the right way."

Logan grunted. "We do what we can, Kurt. We do the best that we can, with what we've got."

Kurt began to respond, but instead narrowed his eyes, staring up the road. "I believe there is a car coming." There was no excitement in his voice. Just a dull announcement of yet another vehicle that would speed past and leave them to the mercies of the oncoming night. Jean wondered how cold it got out here.

Much to their surprise, though, the approaching truck stopped in the middle of the road. A man looked out at them. He had gray hair, blue eyes, and a nice mouth. A dog sat in the passenger seat. It had the same coloring.

"Was that your car that I saw broken down back there?"

"Yes," Scott said. "I don't suppose you could give us a lift into town?"

The man hesitated, studying them.

"I could," he said slowly. "What kind of people are you?"

"Excuse me?" Scott said. "I don't understand."

"Are you good people?"

It was a surreal question. Not many people ever asked Jean if she was "good," though she found it rather refreshing that the old man expected a straight answer.

"Usually," Logan said, looking him in the eye. "Depends how good the other side is."

"Fair enough," said the man, seemingly satisfied at the answer—or the reaction to it. "You can sit in the back of the truck."

"Thank you," Jean said. "Thank you very much."

The man shrugged. The dog watched them, careful.

"You see?" Kurt said, when they were moving and the

wind blew long and hard against their bodies. "Compassion. One normal man, helping five strangers on an empty freeway."

"Let's not start this again," Logan said. "If it makes you happy, we'll send him a medal when we get home."

"I would prefer instead that we emulate his kindness."

"I thought you said that wouldn't mean as much because we're mutants," Rogue pointed out.

"It still means something," Kurt said. Jean felt sorry for him, but remained silent. Philosophical differences were always impossible to argue, and at the moment, she was content with merely watching the world go by, savoring the warmth of her husband, soft and small at her side.

And then, unexpectedly, she felt a strange tickling sensation in her brain. Like fingers, scraping the surface of her mind, looking for openings. Startling, to say the least. The prelude to an invasion, maybe. For some reason, she did not feel afraid.

"We've got company again," she said, and tapped her forehead. The tickling stopped. Everyone, even Logan, looked at her in concern.

"Are we being tracked?" Scott asked.

"I wish I knew. It's impossible to tell. All it felt like was someone brushing past my brain. I don't think anything more was done."

"I hope not," Scott said. "We're dealing with a lot of unknowns here, not the least of which is whether we'll be able to make it home."

"We're moving in the right direction, aren't we?"

Logan said. "What more do you want? Just give it one step at a time."

One step. Easy enough. Jean knew how to be stubborn. It seemed to be a mutant power all its own, one shared by all the X-Men. It was a wonder Charles ever got them listening to anything at all, and probably explained the occasional soap opera atmosphere of the Mansion.

They drove in silence until they reached town. Or rather, the one lone gas station perched on the edge of the freeway. Sunset had come and gone, but the darkening sky, pricked with the first stars of evening, still bled prairie purple with a blush of gold.

Their driver pulled off the freeway and turned into the gas station. He parked beside one of the pumps and got out. So did they.

"Not much around here," said the man, unscrewing the gas cap.

"We'll make do," Scott said. "Thank you for taking us this far. We can help pay for the gas."

"Nah," he said, quiet. "Wasn't out of my way." He paused for a moment, and then added, "You all looking for work?"

The question surprised Jean. She did not know how to answer, and for a moment, the rest of the X-Men shared her confusion. They looked at each other.

"It's not a hard question," said the man. "And you certainly don't have to say yes."

"We're trying to get home," Scott said. "Back to New York. It's an emergency."

"You all have the same emergency?"

"We're family," Jean said, irritated by his subtle skepticism.

"Fair enough." He started pumping gas. "Even if you don't want work, you're all welcome to stay at my place tonight. Just me and the dog."

Scott said, "I think we might intrude."

"And I think you'll be spending a cold night on the prairie if you don't take me up. That's your choice, though. You might get a ride, but I doubt it."

"Is there a reason you're so keen on having us at your home?" Logan asked.

"Every man has a reason for the things he does," he said.

Scott looked at them, and Jean saw her own feelings mirrored on his face. Yes, they needed a place to stay— even better, a way to keep moving—but this was just . . . odd. Even Kurt, for all his talk about compassion, seemed reserved.

You're jaded. Maybe, but for a good reason.

"Thank you for your offer," Scott said. "Really. What we need, though, is transportation."

The pump clicked. The man removed it and screwed the cap back on. His movements were careful, deliberate.

"I might be able to help you with that, too. That is, if you'll help me with something. Shouldn't take long. Just a couple of hours."

"It's not illegal, is it?" Rogue asked.

He smiled. "No. Just a little something that needs more hands than I got."

"That why you pulled over?" Logan asked.

"Maybe. What do you say?"

Scott hesitated, and then, slow, stuck out his hand. The man looked at it for a moment, smiled again, and shook.

"Okay," he said. "Let's go home."

He said his name was James and that his dog was called Dog, and that they had been alone for a week. The wife was dead, gone from a heart attack because there was no hospital close enough to help. In this part of the country, he said, you lived on your own and you died on your own, and that was the way of it, the price for solitude and minding your own business.

His house was very small and old and white, with real wood siding that had seen better days and some pots filled with red geraniums that desperately needed water. The house and the nearby barn were the only structures for miles, and so they had some warning, even in the waning light.

The yard was dusty. Jean sneezed twice and wiped her eyes. Her body ached as she uncurled from the hard seat of the truck cab.

"Come on in," said James. He walked right into the unlocked house, and Jean was the first to follow him. The interior was dark, but pleasantly decorated with an elegant spare hand that believed in the quality of old hardwood, white walls, and the occasional splash of color. Jean thought there might only be four rooms: the kitchen, the living room, a closed door that was probably a bedroom, and beyond that another closed door. A bathroom, maybe. She hoped it was a bathroom. She needed one.

"Are you hungry?" James asked. "There's not much here, but you're welcome to it."

"That's all right," Scott said. "Perhaps you'd like to tell us about the work you need done?"

James nodded. "I suppose now is good. I've been . . . putting it off. From doing it myself, you see. Too difficult, even though it shouldn't be. You're all young, though. Younger than me. I appreciate this."

He walked to the first door on Jean's left and opened it. Inside, on the bed, she saw a body. Jean did not know what shocked her more: that the body was dead, a corpse, or that it was not quite human.

"Whoa," Logan breathed.

James entered and sat on the edge of the bed. He touched a wrinkled limb, one of many, folded like thick ribbons on the still narrow chest.

"This is Milly," he said into the breathless quiet. "My wife."

Jean walked to the end of the bed, and felt her friends follow. Except for Logan's outburst, they all remained quiet, respectful of the reverence in the old man's face.

"Wasn't she beautiful?" he asked, and laid his hand on Dog, who nudged close between his legs.

Milly did have a lovely face; Jean thought she must have been a true beauty in her youth. The rest of her body, though, was nothing more than a series of tentacles attached to a slender torso that had no discernible arms or legs.

"She must have been resourceful," Jean said, gentle,

unsure exactly what to say, what was appropriate under such unusual circumstances.

"Oh, yes. She had to be." James smiled. "We were together almost forty years. Sweet baby."

He finally looked at them and his eyes were bright and wet. "I don't want Milly at the local cemetery. They never understood her, anyway. She was just a sideshow. So I want her here, where she was happy. Where we can be together. That's the job I have for you. I need help digging the grave."

"Of course," Jean said, gazing down upon that still face, the deformed body. "Anything."

"I got some shovels in the barn. I'll show you the place. The ground is real hard, which is part of the reason I kept waiting."

He took them to the barn. Outside was dark and cool, the sky heavy with stars. There were no floodlights, nothing to see by, but James led them with an unerring sense of direction and the barn, thankfully, did have a light. It was clear that livestock had been kept there in the past, but now the floor and stalls were clean and dry, and held only the faintest scent of animal.

The shovels were by the door. Three of them, plus two pickaxes.

"The perfect number of people," James said. "I got lucky."

"There wasn't anyone you could ask for help?" Logan shouldered a pickax.

"None I wanted to ask," James said. "Milly and I were pretty much alone out here. She had no family, and mine gave me up when I married her. We never had children. Milly just wasn't built that way. It would have been nice, though."

He led them to a small tree that grew behind the house. Jean could barely see it in the darkness. She touched the leaves and found them smooth and cool.

"Lilac," James said. "Her favorite scent. She waited all year for this thing to bloom."

And then he pointed at the ground and they began to dig.

He was right: the ground was hard. They rotated jobs; Jean and Kurt worked with the pickaxes first, breaking up the ground, and then the others went in with the shovels, hacking and scooping, steel ringing as it occasionally hit rock. James sat on the side and watched. Every now and then he left to bring water, and when one of them had to rest he took up the slack and worked until the weary could start again.

"What did you all do before you found the road?" James asked.

Scott stopped chipping at the earth. "I suppose you could say we were in the profession of helping people."

"Or not," Logan added, with a smile. "Some people need to be helped in . . . different ways."

James smiled. "Milly and I knew people like that, but they left us alone after a while. Got tired of it, I guess. Or maybe they grew up."

"Some never do," Jean said.

"I suppose. There were others, like her, who also treated us impolite. I took her to the city, to places where they had all kinds. I thought it would be better for us there. Less lonely for her, anyway. But Milly was too unique, even for them. I think that hurt her more than just about anything, so we came back here and never left."

"That's not right," Rogue said.

"That's the way it is. Those other kind, like Milly, they look different and they got different skills, but they're human where it counts. They're human in all the ways that make us mean and hard, loving and kind. Why else do you think this world has so much conflict? It's because when we look at people like Milly, or heck, all those hero folks on TV, we know we're looking at ourselves, and we know all the dirty things we'd do if we had that kind of power. Now Milly, she just looked different. She could also do miracles with sweet potatoes, but I think that was another gift entirely on its own."

Jean laughed, and James said, "Good. I'm glad someone can smile when I talk about her. She was a sweet woman. She deserves smiles."

It took them until midnight to dig the grave. James went into the house and spent a long time there. Jean and the others lay in the grass, stargazing while they waited for him.

After a time, they heard a whistle. James stood at the back door. He had a suit on, and a nice hat.

"She's ready," he said. "Maybe you could help me carry her."

James had wrapped Milly in a white sheet. She looked smaller, bundled tight, and Jean picked her up before anyone could offer help. Milly was heavier than she looked, but Jean bit back any complaints and carried her from the house to the grave. There, it took some effort to lower her into the ground. Everyone got on their stomachs and grabbed a sheet corner. Careful, slow, they let her down, deep into the earth.

And then they stood, and listened to James say his last words to his beloved wife.

They did not discuss the promised transportation. It seemed inappropriate. James told them to go into the house and get something to eat, to clean up if they wanted because there were plenty of clean towels and a lot of soap. James did not go back in with them. He sat on the ground at the foot of Milly's grave, staring at the fresh-turned pile of dirt. Dog stayed with him.

"That poor man," Rogue said, slumped at the kitchen table. A wet towel lay over her shoulders. She sipped coffee.

Jean sat beside her, also drinking coffee. She had taken her shower first, and it was good to be clean—though rather startling to see herself naked. Logan, the last of them to bathe, was still in the bathroom.

Jean thought of James, sitting alone in the dark at the grave of his wife. She thought of him and Milly, living their lives in isolation because the only place they could find true acceptance was here, with each other. Perhaps that was enough for them. James, certainly, did not seem to have many regrets. Jean, on the other hand, tried to imagine herself in their shoes and could not. People consumed her life and that was fine, because despite her gift, she did not like to be alone.

"I'm going to go check on James," she said. "Maybe he'll want something to eat."

The night air felt colder than she remembered, though digging deep holes in the hard earth tended to distort one's perception of temperature. She stumbled along in the dark, and knew she was getting close when she heart Dog whine.

She tripped, and even as she fell to the ground she recalled the sensation of her foot catching something soft, and no, that could not be true, she hit the ground hard and did not stop moving, just rolled and got to her hands and knees, crawling to the soft lump she had missed seeing in the darkness, and she called his name but he was quiet, and she felt his neck and for a moment there was nothing, but then she moved her fingers and felt a pulse, sweet, and she called his name again and James finally stirred, whispering, "I was trying to die. Now is a good time when I have someone to bury me right."

Jean lay on her stomach, breathless. "Do you want to die?"

"No," he said. "I feel like I should, I loved her so. But I don't want to die."

"Then don't try," Jean said, and watched him hold something up in his hands. "It's too dark, James. What is that?"

He gave it to her. It was a syringe. "An air bubble kills you quick. Goes right to your heart."

"Death is a bad way to fix something that's broken," Jean said, her own heart pounding.

"I know." He took a deep breath, still staring at the stars. "I've seen the way you look at that girl. Mindy is her name? You love her?"

"We're married," Jean said. "We . . . grew up together."

James smiled, slow and bitter. "Milly and I were the same. She never did look quite like the others, but it wasn't until her teens that she made the full change. It was real hard on her. Hard on me, too, I guess."

"But you made it," Jean whispered.

"Sure did. She wouldn't want this. Me, thinking about dying. I can't help it, though. I'm alone out here, and those people in town . . . even if one of them did find me, they wouldn't bury me here at her side. They would take me away to the cemetery. Heck, I don't even know what to do about Dog." He looked at Jean so very solemn she wanted to cry. "Be careful, son, when you get older. Take care of the people you love. Find some good friends. The kind who will watch over you after you've gone. You don't want to end up like me."

"Was it such a bad life?" she whispered, trying to imagine James and Milly, both alive and full of love in that little four-room house.

"No," he breathed. "I wouldn't trade it for anything."

17

EARLY THE NEXT MORNING, JAMES DROVE THEM TO Bismarck, a fairly sizable town in the middle of North Dakota. He bought them breakfast at a truck stop. He tried to pay them money for their night's work, but Scott refused. It did not seem right to take anything for burying a man's wife.

"I was going to give you my car," James said. "I didn't think I would have much need for it after you took care of my Milly."

Because I was going to have you bury me, too.

James did not have to say it. They all knew the truth; James had given Jean permission to tell them.

Scott borrowed some paper and a pen from the waitress. "Here's our address in New York, and this is the phone number we can be reached at. It's, uh, not working right now, but it should be up and running in a couple of weeks. If you ever need anything—*anything*—contact us and we'll be there for you. You can even come live with us if you want. You might like it."

James examined the address, reading off the list of names that were not the ones Scott and the X-Men had given him, and then he said, "Xavier's School for Gifted

Youngsters? That sounds familiar to me, for some reason."

"It's a good school," Jean said. "We teach there."

James studied them. "I thought you were homeless."

"It's complicated," Scott said. He thought James would press him for more, but after a moment's quiet contemplation, he smiled.

"Fair enough," he said, and asked for the check.

They walked him back to his truck. Dog poked his head out the passenger window and Scott scratched his neck.

"I'm sorry I can't do more for you folks," James said. "Especially after all you did for me. I just . . . I just can't stay away from Milly for that long. Long enough to drive you home, anyway."

"We understand," Jean said. "You take care."

James climbed into the truck. He looked tired. Dog leaned up against him.

"Sure is going to be strange," he said softly, and Scott could only imagine he meant home, that empty little house that still bore his wife's touch. James started the engine, put the car in gear, and waved good-bye as he drove away. Scott watched him go, and could not muster a shadow of disappointment or frustration that another stone had been thrown in their path.

"So now what?" Logan asked. "Walk?"

"Let's look around," Scott said. "Maybe someone will give us a ride."

"I see a bar across the street."

"No."

Logan grinned. "No gambling, I promise. It's the best

place to scope a ride, though. Give me a little money, sit tight, and I'll see what I can dig up."

"It won't be much, looking the way you do," Rogue said.

"Why don't you come with me, sweetheart. You can charm the men with your aging assets."

"Sweet talker."

But she did go with him, and while Scott used a pay phone to call the Mansion, Jean and Kurt sat on a bench outside the truck-stop restaurant to watch for opportunity in whatever form it might take. Scott was not very optimistic.

He was even less so when all he got was a busy signal.

He scowled and slammed the receiver back into its cradle. It terrified him, the idea that five X-Men were being impersonated. Walking and talking, using their bodies, their powers. He was scared to check the news, but he bought a newspaper and brought it back to the bench.

Much to his surprise, there was barely a mention of any mutant-related criminal activity or catastrophes. Just a side note about the conference in Geneva, as well as a small mention about the mutant-rights march planned for the day after in New York City. Scott knew all about it. The X-Men were scheduled to attend—not as participants, but as security.

"What is it?" Jean asked.

"What's what?" he replied absently.

"You look like you just had a bad thought." She reached and touched his forehead. "You're all wrinkled."

He caught her hand and kissed her fingers. "That mutant-rights march is mentioned in here. Remember?"

"How could I forget? The children are dying to attend."

"We're supposed to be there," Scott said, looking at her and Kurt. "What if we are?"

"Why is it, *mein freund*, that I do not think you are referring to present company?"

"Because I'm not." Scott shook his had. "I don't know why I'm even thinking about it. Because really, it wouldn't make sense. Why would someone steal our bodies just for that event?"

"You're right," Jean said. "It doesn't make sense. Maybe our counterparts aren't even planning to go."

"Then what are they doing?" Kurt leaned forward, clasping his hands. "I have prayed a great deal about this, but so far, God has not yet provided me with any insight."

Jean pointed. "They're coming back."

Not just coming, but running. Rogue's expression, a combination of red-faced embarrassment and anger, alarmed him.

"What happened?" Scott asked.

"No time," Logan said. "There's a guy who's leaving in two minutes. He works for a manufactured-home company and he's transporting part of a house to Minneapolis."

"An actual house?" Kurt asked. "That sounds much better than stealing a car."

"Yeah, I think this one classifies as breaking and entering. You guys ready to go?"

They followed Logan out into the vast parking lot, which seemed more like a way station for an army of semis. Toward the center, surrounded on both sides by two trucks bearing the sign OVERSIZED, they found one half of the manufactured home. The other side of it squatted several wide spaces to the left.

"Does it really matter which one we take?" Scott asked.

"Guess not." Logan pulled a pocketknife from his jeans—a gift from James, who had also given them clean clothes, some food to carry, and a backpack for their few belongings. Scott could not take money, but those other things seemed less . . . offensive than cold hard cash.

You're too technical—and you're a hypocrite.

Very true. He was also an anal-retentive control freak, but not everyone could be perfect.

Plastic sheeting covered the inner half of the home; Logan cut a small slit into the farthest edge, a space just large enough for them to fit through, and held it open as they squeezed into the house. It was not that easy. The actual floor was at least three feet off the ground, requiring a bit of maneuvering that was difficult with hard plastic shoved tight against his back. Scott missed being tall.

Despite some difficulties, less than a minute later they all sat in a back bedroom, the farthest spot away from the white plastic barrier separating them from the road. Logan occasionally peered out the windows.

"I thought that guy was leaving soon," Rogue muttered,

when after several minutes the truck still had not moved.

"What happened in there?" Scott asked, peering into her red face.

"Nothing," she said. He looked at Logan, who shrugged and scratched his head.

"Some, uh, derogatory language was used by our ticket out of here. He saw you three sitting on that bench and thought it was funny."

Rogue sucked in a deep breath. "He made me so mad I wanted to hit him."

"Nearly did, too. That's part of the reason we ran out of there so fast."

Somewhere distant they heard voices; a car door slammed and then an engine roared to life. The house vibrated.

"Perfect," Logan said. "This is slow, but we'll get to Minneapolis by tonight."

"You're right, that is slow." Scott tapped the newspaper against his thigh. "I feel as though we've got a deadline. Thing is, I don't known when it is."

"And if we're too late?" Logan asked.

Scott felt everyone stare at him, but he did not say a word. He felt just as lost as they did.

Rolling down the freeway in a manufactured home was not, Scott decided, such a bad way to travel. Except for the fact that it was agonizingly slow. So slow, he wanted to pull his hair out—a feat he could actually accomplish for the first time in his life, given that his hair was now a length suitable for gripping.

"I can't stand this," he said to Jean. "Not knowing what is going on at home is driving me crazy."

"Me too," she said, stretched out on her stomach. The carpet had plastic over it, which crinkled every time they moved. "There's not much we can do about it, though."

So for the rest of the day he tried to rest, to strategize a response for an imaginary series of events that would likely never take place, but if it did, was currently out of his control. Such as assassination attempts on the President of the United States, or some other world leader; declarations of aggression against all humans; joining the Brotherhood of Mutants, which, now that he thought about it, might very well have orchestrated this little body crisscross. The only problem with that was the Brotherhood were usually much flashier—and they liked to brag a whole lot more. Scott could not imagine one of them pulling this off without coming to the mental hospital to rub it in their faces.

And if it was the Brotherhood, the X-Men would probably already be in the newspapers by now.

Unless it was something else they were after. Technology, maybe. Secret files that Scott and Jean would most certainly have access to. The possibilities were endlessly troubling. He needed aspirin.

He took a nap and dreamed about James resting inside a grave full of writhing tentacles, smiling and crying, with Dog perched on the edge, howling at the moon. He woke up, gasping, and felt Jean do the same. She held her head.

"What is it?" he asked, reaching for her. It was getting

easier to look into her stranger's face and feel desire. It also helped that they were alone; the others had retreated into the living room for a game of cards, another of James's gifts. The bedroom was all theirs.

"That sensation in my head. It was stronger this time. There was a definite focus."

"Do you think she—whoever—got anything from you?"

"I don't think so, but it has me worried. At first I could tell myself it was an accident, but now it's looking deliberate." She hesitated, looking at her hands. "I suppose it could be something else."

"What?"

"Well, it occurred to me that if our counterparts inherited our physical abilities, like my telepathy, for example, then we should also have inherited some of theirs. As in, their mental illnesses. Patty, for example, is supposed to be a paranoid schizophrenic, while you apparently suffer from some debilitating social disorder, which is vague enough to be completely unhelpful. Rogue's chart, according to Kurt, has her diagnosed as suffering from an acute bipolar disorder. And I'm just mean and delusional."

Scott waited for more. Jean sighed. "My point is that even if our consciousnesses have been transferred, we should still be suffering from the same physical abnormalities as the people we are occupying. Just because the thinking minds are different, does not mean the brains are."

"So you're saying we should be crazy."

"Yes. At the very least, displaying *some* symptoms of mental illness."

"And if some of us have always been a little crazy?"

"Logan doesn't count, Scott." Jean tried not to smile. He nudged her with his elbow, forcing her to make room against her much larger side. It was odd being the smaller person in their relationship. He was getting used to it, though he liked it better the other way around.

"So," he whispered, angling his mouth close to her ear—*his ear, a man's ear*—and shutting his eyes, "I understand what you're saying, but unless we start frothing at the mouths and speaking in tongues, I don't see how it matters. Science isn't going to get us home. The man who did this, on the other hand . . ."

"We'll figure it out," Jean whispered. "Now rest a little, Scott. Go to sleep."

Lulled by her voice, her touch, he did.

18

FOR SEVERAL DAYS, STORM SPENT MOST OF HER TIME in Professor Xavier's office. The psychic dampeners gave her a sense of security she could not find elsewhere in the Mansion, and while Remy's portable dampeners were another comfort, the large airy room continued to be the only place she felt safe. She blamed it on the lingering presence of the professor, that sense she always had around him that everything would be fine, that the answer to all life's difficulties was always close, part of every person.

She told herself those same things whenever Scott and Jean or the other three X-Men came to see her and inquired about certain things going on the school. Like why hadn't Storm cleared the field trip before allowing the children to run willy-nilly through the city, and why was she in this room all the time—it must be stifling, come out, come out, and play.

Ororo did not feel like playing, and there was something in the way Jean looked when she asked the question that gave her the unsettling sensation that she meant another kind of play entirely. One that would be inappropriate and utterly unappreciated by her husband.

And her roses continued to die.

Of course, it also occurred to her that she was completely overexaggerating and that all these differences she sensed—subtle, inexplicable—were simply figments of her imagination. Figments, too, of Gambit and Jubilee's minds. After all, the three of them did have similar backgrounds, having grown up on the streets, victim to the various humiliations and desperations associated with such hard living. Maybe they suffered from a shared psychosis, some paranoid delusion as a result of that experience.

Or maybe their friends really weren't the same people.

"They're not the same people," Jubilee said, during one of their brief meetings inside Xavier's office. The girl was painting her nails and popping gum, although there was a darkness in her eyes that bothered Ororo— a heaviness of spirit that she had never thought to see in Jubilee.

"You still think they have been . . . body-snatched?"

Jubilee looked up from her nails. Her eyes were hard. "Yes, Ororo. I do." And then she relaxed, the darkness melted away, and Ororo no longer knew if it was a mask or the real girl when she said, "Dude. I know you're still on that trauma kick, but have you even asked Jean or Kurt if anything bad happened?"

"Yes. They . . . didn't give me any details."

"Then there wasn't any trauma. Those two can't keep their mouths shut around you. It's like, you show up and they start going a mile a minute. Blah, blah, blah."

Ororo narrowed her eyes. "Must I remind you, Jubilee, that you are speaking to an elder? You should be a little more polite."

Again, Jubilee stopped painting her nails and gave her a look that was far too old. Remy said, "If anyone acts traumatized, it's Rogue. She hasn't talked once since her return."

"Body-snatched," Jubilee said. "She has a nefarious purpose."

"I think she is genuine. The others?" He waved his hand. "*Je ne sais pas.*"

"Could they be shape-shifters, then?" Ororo wondered out loud. "Are our friends being held captive somewhere else?"

"If they are shape-shifters, they're really bad at the whole impersonation thing," Jubilee said. "Do you know what I saw this morning? Wolvie in the gym, standing in front of the mirror, ogling his body. Do you have any idea how disturbing that was?"

"*Non,*" Remy said, dry. "What don' you tell us, *ma petite.*"

"But before you do," Ororo said, cutting her off, "I want to know if you two have learned anything about Seattle."

"Nada. Scott—" Jubilee stopped, swallowing hard. "Scott made some dinky little voice records a day or two before coming back. Something about how they still hadn't found what they were looking for, but they were going to the hospital that night to look around."

"Which hospital?"

"Belmont, Belvue—"

"Belldonne," Remy said. "We called. They said no one fittin' their descriptions had stopped to ask questions, or been seen. They weren't really talkative, though. Seems they lost some of their patients recently. Police are out lookin' for them."

"No relation to our people?"

"Don' see how."

"Unless Wolvie and the others were transferred into their bodies and they've made their break."

Ororo looked at her. "Do Scott and the others act mentally unwell?"

Jubilee shared a quick glance with Remy.

"Mentally unwell?" she said. "How about Scott accusing Remy of having sex with me just because he saw us together?"

"Talking," Remy clarified. "Together talking. And he didn't exactly accuse us of sex."

Jubilee gave him a look. "He was a total pervert, Remy."

Ororo covered her mouth. "How could he? Scott knows better."

"Exactly," Jubilee said.

Ororo sat back, stunned. Remy said, "You should know, 'Ro. None of those who came back refueled the jet."

"What?"

"Don' worry," he said. "I did it. But I did check the levels and matched them to those lil' numbers Scott likes to keep about how much fuel we burn, dependin' on the distance. There wasn't enough gas in that tank, *chérie*. Not by a long shot."

"What are you trying to say, Remy? They went somewhere else first?"

He shrugged. "Seems that way to me. Unless someone on that plane dumped some fuel or started getting a taste for it in their drinks."

"What kind of diversion from the flight schedule are we discussing?"

"At least a hundred miles. Not far in the Blackbird, but it burns the gas all the same."

Ororo slumped back in her chair. This was looking quite bad.

"Yo," Jubilee said. "We still have another problem. Bobby and the others aren't answering their cell phones. I've been trying to reach them and all I get is a busy signal. Now, Bobby is a big talker, but still. You were having the same issue with the Professor, right?"

"I have been in the control room, but I can find nothing wrong."

"I also looked for the problem," Remy said. "Dug deep, too. There's nothing wrong wit' the system, which means it's an outside source causin' the problem. I think they're using one of our scramblers."

"Scramblers" were a useful tool that Hank McCoy had invented for those missions when the team wanted to be sure that no one could call out from a particular location. It supposedly scrambled all communication devices, though Ororo had never actually seen it used.

"I checked the lab," Remy said. "I don't know exactly how many Hank kept around, but there's an empty spot on the shelf. Worse yet, they must have found a way to patch into our private cell-phone network, because I tried makin' calls from town, at a pay phone, and still got nothin' but busy."

Troublesome, because all the scattered X-Men still on active duty relied totally on those cell phones to keep in touch with the school. Not that anyone would be making the effort, or even notice that something was wrong. A little busy signal, if you yourself were not having an emergency, was just an annoyance.

"Dude," Jubilee murmured, for the first time looking afraid. "They must think we're totally stupid not to notice something's going on. That, or they think they can take us."

"I do not know," Ororo said, deeply disturbed. "They have been keeping their own distance from us, except on those rare occasions when Scott thinks I have done something out of the ordinary and comes to check on me."

"I think Scott did that with me and Remy," Jubilee said.

Ororo stood and began pacing. To sit any longer felt claustrophobic, as though the desk in front of her already pinned her legs and the walls, those walls of her life, were settling down upon her shoulders, suffocating her.

"All right," she said. "So something is wrong with our teammates. They might, or might not, have been . . . taken over. Whoever this entity is, has done a good enough job insuring that they know enough to pass, at least superficially."

"Mebbe they know more than that," Remy said, solemn. "If they could fly the Blackbird *and* find—and rig—one of Hank's scramblers, then we got security issues. Files, contacts. . . . Cerebro."

"Cerebro's cool," Jubilee said, screwing the cap back on her polish. Both adults stared at her, waiting. She blew on her nails.

Remy coughed. *"Ma petite?"*

"Yeah? Oh, I mean, I took care of it. First thing. 'Cause, you know, body snatchers and long-range psychic enhancers aren't a good combination."

Ororo had trouble speaking. "You . . . took care of it?"

"Yes. You guys think I never learned anything when I was hanging out with Hank? Last time he tuned up Cerebro, he blabbed for like an *hour* on all the different weak spots in the wiring and casing and how it was going to take him at least a month to fix them." She grinned. "Heh. It's gonna take him longer now."

Remy planted a hard kiss on top of Jubilee's head. She batted him away. Ororo covered her mouth.

"Very good," she said. "Though I sincerely hope we are able to salvage whatever wreckage you left behind."

"Looks the same on the outside, and the inside is just missing some guts. If these jokers don't know enough to imitate Wolvie to the letter, they're not going to be able to fix Cerebro."

"If they wished to use it. Their purpose may be quite different."

"Sure, whatever. I just want to get the real deals back."

"Maybe they are already there, and simply cannot act. They can listen, but nothing more. Utterly suppressed."

Which was the preferred possibility, because anything

else meant that their friends might be lost forever. Minds, after all, could not stay adrift in the wind and remain whole. At least, she did not think so. The X-Men, on occasion, defied logic in their ability to survive extraordinary circumstances.

"So, what? We try to break through to them?"

"*Non*," Remy said firmly. "*Petite*, I want you to stay away from Wolverine for a while. At least until we figure this out."

"Remy—"

"I'm serious." He glanced at Ororo. "Isn't there some event we're supposed to attend tomorrow?"

"A mutant-rights march in New York. I do not think we will be going."

"And Scott and the others?"

"I cannot say for certain, but they haven't left the Mansion since they returned. I would assume they will not leave tomorrow."

"Which means that what they want is here."

"So are we going to take them out?" Jubilee asked.

Ororo hesitated. "I would like to know more before we make any efforts to control them. It is possible there is no need for violence, that this is something that can be resolved through negotiation. Whatever 'this' is. I still feel quite confused by the situation."

"There's not much to be confused with," Remy said. "We have a problem. Mebbe we can't define the problem, but it's there, an' it looks exactly like five of the most powerful mutants on this planet."

"You think we're next?" Jubilee asked. "I mean, not

that they'd go after me, 'cause I'm just a kid or whatever. But . . . I don't want to lose myself."

Ororo could not answer that. Remy, very gently, said, "I think they would've done that by now if they could, *ma petite*. An' I know I'm still me. Got every confidence in both of you, too."

For now, Ororo thought.

There was nothing more to discuss. Remy and Jubilee left the office, presumably to continue investigating on the sly. She was sorry to see them go; she worried for their safety. Hers, too. It was maddening, being unable to pinpoint anything concrete, a specific action that she could see with her own eyes that was wrong. Yes, the Blackbird had not been refueled, yes, the phones were down—*all* their phones—and yes, the behavior of their friends was . . . off. Ororo could not deceive herself. She was wearing a psychic dampener, after all, and had silently applauded Jubilee's foresight in breaking Cerebro. She avoided Scott and the others as much as they seemed to be avoiding her. All of them, dancing on eggshells, hoping the other side did not notice how much they really knew.

Which, when Ororo thought about all the wicked men and women they had dealt with in the past, did not seem very professional at all. Possession was a subtle art, but once employed, either continued to be subtle, flawless, or went to the other extreme: utterly radical behavior that screamed "wrong." None of that was present in this situation. If the X-Men had been possessed or replaced, they were dealing with an amateur, one who knew just enough to be dangerous, but not in any way perfect.

For a moment, she thought about their students, if any one of them could be abusing his or her powers. The children were safely away in New York on a field trip to end all field trips, but they had still been present when the five team members left for Seattle—the assumption being that whatever had transpired to alter them had taken place during that trip.

Ororo squeezed shut her eyes. Her head ached. Air—fresh air—that was what she needed. Perhaps a walk would make her feel better, clear her head for inspiration.

She turned on the psychic dampener, a sticky little device that Remy had planted behind her ear. She was going to talk to him one of these days about where he found such things. The dampener—along with the rest of his toys—was far too advanced to belong to any place but the military or some highly specialized research lab . . . and no doubt actual mutants had been used to test the thing. Not that she was going to tear it off in protest.

Without the children around, the Mansion felt eerily quiet. It had been like this once before, in the years when the school had admitted only a select few, when it was less of a school than a front for clandestine activities. Sometimes Ororo missed those days, but she could not deny the joy she took in raising the next generation to be strong and educated and unafraid in the use of their abilities. Everyone had the potential for greatness. It was merely her job to make sure that the young people in her care took advantage of that, in the best ways possible.

So she walked the lonely halls, unable to shake the sensation of being watched, and left the house for bright sunshine, green grass, the buzz of bees and the thrush of hummingbirds, zipping through the garden. She passed the vegetable plots first—a school project, to teach the children the value of the food they ate. Ororo, having grown up hungry and in a country where famines were common, thought it important that no one take for granted the bounty set before them.

Of course, she herself had never been forced to grow her supper. What she needed, she stole. Which was easier and much more fun. Not very ethical, though, and she was trying to set a good example.

Past the vegetables, she entered a wild labyrinth of stone paths and overgrown flowers, bursting with fragrant blooms. Every now and then, Ororo stopped to pull moisture from the air, generating localized rain and mist to aid those plants whose leaves drooped, or curled up, brittle with thirst. She was quite intent on this—as well as the pleasure of being distracted—when she noticed movement from the corner of her eye.

Red hair shining in the sunlight. Ororo waved her hand and the rain cloud hanging above the petunias disappeared. She followed Jean.

She did not have to go far. She stopped on the edge of the garden and watched as Jean sat on a stone bench. Ororo's roses grew nearby; her Geminis and Red Rubies, the Blue Teas, Moonlight Maidens, the Bonny Bonnets and Isle Stars; formerly lovely and now drooping, petals shucking into the grass, stems flaccid like string.

Suspicious, suspicious—all her trouble had begun with the roses. Ororo was half convinced that if they had not begun dying, none of this, her problems with the other members of the team, would have taken place. The students would still be here, Jubilee would be getting into trouble of an entirely different sort, and the house would feel safe and normal.

Jean did not appear to notice Ororo's presence. She had a book in her hands, but sat too far away for a clear view of the title. She seemed, for the most part, to be enjoying the sun, the quiet solitude. Ororo wondered, once again, if she was overreacting. Surely this was not the action of someone possessed, or plotting harm?

And then, so slow she almost missed seeing it, she noticed her dying roses droop even more. All her roses, that shriveled decaying line of them, moving as one like a descending curtain, blossoms and stems sinking even lower, leaves curling up with a brittleness second only to shriveled mummy lips.

And there, in the center of that silent death, sat Jean with her book, and a very small smile on her face.

Long ago, while they were still alive, Jubilee's parents told her that every person in the world had three things they were good at. Three things all their own, however small, that no one could do better than them. Jubilee's mother, for example, could cook dumplings like no other, play mah-jongg like a gambling queen, and chew out her father like nobody's business. Jubilee missed her mom.

Jubilee, on the other hand, had a rotating list of her

best three things—rotating because, heck, she was only fifteen and learning new stuff everyday. And besides, three was such a limiting number.

At the moment, number one was stealth. She could do stealth like the Invisible Woman—all whoa, that chick is gone. Number two on her list was sheer crazy stubbornness. When she wanted something, there wasn't a force on earth that could change her mind—except maybe Wolvie—which brought her to number three: She was the only person in the world who could reach that man when he went all "Grrr" and acted like an animal. Berserker rage? Not a problem. Fourth Horseman of the Apocalypse? Easy.

Which meant that Remy, as much as she liked him, did not know anything about her and Wolverine, and there was no way, nohow, she was going to stay away from him if there was any possibility he was still in there, fighting for a way out.

She could do it. She could reach him. She tried not to think about Scott. Her powers of conviction, however strong and unearthly, were limited only to Wolvie, and until she got him back, she could not risk his impersonator—or controller—knowing that she was on to him. All she could do was be present, a focal point, and let her friend do the rest.

As long as he was in there, of course. Jubilee preferred the idea that he was. She did not want to think about the alternative. The alternative . . . hurt too much.

She found him in the gym, which seemed to be his new hangout of choice.

"Hey," Jubilee said, watching him watch himself as he did a set of biceps curls in front of the mirror.

"Hey," he said, not even sparing her a glance. She wandered over to the weight rack and picked out a twenty-pound barbell. Sat down beside Wolvie and began curling. She got tired after the first three, and had to lift the weight with both hands. That got his attention.

"You're puny," he said, and his voice seemed lighter than usual. No gruff growls, no deep-throated rumbles.

And he was calling her puny? Her?

Body-snatched, she reminded herself, taking a deep breath.

She smiled and said, "I guess I need to work out more. I'm more of a gymnast, anyway."

He looked her over. "Yeah, I can see that. You're skinny enough for it, I guess. Thought those kinds of girls were tough as steel, though. Twenty pounds shouldn't be any problem."

"We use a different kind of strength," she said, unlocking her jaw so she didn't grind her teeth right out of her gums.

"Whatever," he said. "You want to show me some moves?"

Anything to keep him interested. She took off her jacket and moved to the wide mat. Took a deep breath and then executed a series of jumps and somersaults that had the world spinning, her body feeling like it could fly.

"Interesting," he said, wandering over. "You look fast."

This entire conversation was wrong. If Jubilee had not been convinced before that something was off with

Logan, then the last few minutes had finally cemented it in her head. Even during those first days of their acquaintance, hiding out from the Reavers at that base in the Australian outback, he had never patronized her. Not like this.

For one brief moment she felt afraid, but she pushed it away, unwilling to let herself entertain the possibility that even the body of this man could be used to hurt her. If Wolvie—her Wolvie—was really in there, he would stop it. He would stop his possessor, his impersonator, from hurting her. Because that was the kind of man he was. Logan moved heaven and earth to help his friends when they needed him.

And maybe, just maybe, that was what he needed. Some motivation.

"I'm really fast," Jubilee said. "Faster than you."

"Really." Logan smirked. "I doubt that."

"Yeah?" Jubilee bounced on her toes. "You wanna bet? I say, if we spar right now, I'll kick your butt. Big time."

The smirk faded. "I don't think so, kid."

"Chicken? Afraid you'll lose to someone so . . . puny?"

His expression changed, and suddenly, Jubilee was quite certain this was a bad idea. As in, the I'm-gonna-die kind of bad. She wasn't going to back down, though. Not when Wolvie needed her.

And if he's not in there?

That was just a chance she would have to take. If the situation was reversed, she knew he would do the same for her.

There was no warning except that look in Logan's

eyes, and it was good she paid attention because when he leapt at her, his claws out, it took every bit of speed and agility in her body to keep from getting stabbed. Shocking, that killing stroke. A part of her never expected it.

Jubilee blasted him in the face with a series of plasma bursts, but he shrugged off the fireworks and kept coming. There was nothing coordinated about his movements—Logan, when they sparred, was all about playing dirty to teach her the best defenses—but this, this was worse because it was driven solely by some crazy rage and she could not predict his movements. Even when Logan went berserk, there was always a pattern to the way he fought, some indefinable brutal grace. Not now. Now he was a rabid caveman, with swords sticking out of his knuckles.

"Wolvie!" she cried out, ducking under his wildly swinging arm. She threw fireworks in his face, plasma blasts that ignited and burned his skin, but it was nothing, nothing at all, and he screamed at her and the voice was different, higher, the accent like a woman—which was wrong, really wrong—and he came at her again fast and she stumbled, distracted, because she was still thinking about that voice and he scratched her with his claws, cutting right through her shirt so that she felt blood well past the pain and then he was on her again and she rolled but he caught her, flipped her up, and straddled her stomach.

She blasted him in the face but not with everything she had, because this was still Wolvie and even though she was categorically terrified, she could not bring herself to burn his face off no matter how much he currently deserved it. He shrugged off her blast, parts of him leaking blood and other fluids, and sheathed his claws to catch her wrists. He pinned her down on the ground.

"There are some things I've been wanting to try with this body," he whispered, flecking her face with his spit. "Maybe I'll start with you."

"Wolvie?" she whispered, staring into those hateful eyes, seeking some sign of the man who was like a father to her, the one person in the world she trusted with her life. She looked and looked, and for the first time, allowed herself to believe that he might not be there.

His fist slammed down into her face.

19

ROGUE, OF COURSE, WAS IN HER ROOM. REMY WAS NOT quite sure why he continued to seek her out—probably, he thought, for the same reason Jubilee remained fixated on Logan and his sacrilegious pinky. He knew Rogue, he cared about her, and this behavior—no matter if it was trauma or the personality of another—bothered him because it was wrong. It was wrong in such a fundamental fashion that it hurt him to think of it, of his Rogue, his friend, his lady, gone or buried. And yes, for all his talk of body snatching, of invasion and replacements and danger, a part of him wanted to believe that the woman who opened her door to him was the same woman, and that it was only the others who needed to be feared and that a kind word, some time spent together, would be all it took to bring her back to him. He could not help himself. He was a romantic, that way.

He stood on the threshold, gazing upon the crown of her head, and reached out to touch her hair. She stirred, but did not look at him.

"How you doin' today, *chère?* You want to take a walk with me? Sky is a beautiful blue, and more pretty when it's hanging over you. Windows don' do the world justice."

She just stood there staring at her feet. Or his. It was hard to tell. He glanced down at his boots and they were dirty, scuffed with age and mud.

He sensed movement at the end of the hall. Kurt, stopping to lean against the wall. His arms were folded over his chest. Something about his posture wasn't quite right, but that was the new normal. Nothing at all had been right since Seattle.

"You can't seem to stay away," Kurt said.

"When did a man have to stay away from the woman he loves?"

Words to win a woman by. Rogue finally looked at him—momentary, lovely—and deep warmth spread through Remy's heart, sweet as her green shy eyes.

Kurt moved closer. His yellow eyes glinted with a cold light and Remy, though he smiled, felt the dagger in his heart, his own cold readiness to fight and win should Kurt, this new stranger in a friend's body, provoke him.

But he did not. All he said was, "Rogue, do you want to go for a walk?" and Rogue hesitated. Kurt held out his hand and after a moment she took it and allowed herself to be drawn from her room past Remy into the hall. Kurt smiled, as if to say, *She listens to me, not to you, and how does that make you feel?*

Like going for a walk.

"That sounds like a lovely idea, *mon frère*." Remy gathered up Rogue's other arm and tucked it against his body. He felt her quiver, but she did not pull away. Kurt looked disappointed, and Remy wondered if someone had forgotten to inform the blue teleporter that Rogue was his sister and therefore certain behaviors toward her might very well be inappropriate.

The three of them walked down the hall in silence, descending to the stairs to the main entry hall. Remy said, "I haven't been smelling much sulphur lately. You cuttin' back?"

For a moment Kurt looked confused, and then he said, "I've just felt like using my legs more, that's all." His accent was barely discernable and his voice was rough, a noted contrast to his usual soft-spoken nature. Remy wanted to laugh. Kurt, liking to use his legs? Even when the man was not teleporting, he somersaulted through the air, traversed halls in a series of cartwheels, flew through the house like it was nothing but a circus tent and he was the main attraction. Kurt might seem unassuming, but that was more of an act than the act.

Past the lobby down another hall. Remy would have guided Rogue out into the fresh air, but it was clear that Kurt had another destination in mind, and he was content to follow and observe. Anything he learned here might be useful—and soon. He could not see the status quo continuing much longer.

As they drew near the gym a strange sensation overcame him. Premonition, maybe. He felt nauseated. Sweat prickled against his back and a cold hard band tightened around his heart.

He heard something, then. Thick, like fists on flesh.

Remy let go of Rogue's arm and ran down the hall. He reached into his pockets for cards, for his retractable staff, for all those things he fought with because that horrible feeling was strong now, high in his throat, and when he rounded that corner into the gym it was worse than he could imagine because it was something he had never thought to see, something he could not bring himself to believe.

Wolverine was beating Jubilee to death. She was trying to fight, still struggling, but his fists were strong and fast and—

Remy did not stop running. Cards cut his fingers and he fanned them bright and hot, hot and willing and furious, and as Wolverine looked up with that sick mad look in his eyes and blood flecking his chin, Remy barreled into him and shoved those cards into his mouth.

He flung himself backward, still moving, still flying, and grabbed Jubilee without a pause in step, holding her tight against his body. She breathed, "Wolvie," and then the cards went off and Remy fell to his knees as the shock wave pushed him down. He glanced over his shoulder. He could not see Wolverine's face, but his hands still moved.

So did Remy. He climbed to his feet. Kurt and Rogue blocked the gym's entrance. Rogue's expression was horrified, but he did not know if it was for Wolverine's benefit or Jubilee's. Kurt showed nothing at all.

Hoisting Jubilee higher in his arms, Remy reached into his pocket for more cards. Held them up for Kurt and Rogue to see and in his head he said, *If you try to stop me I will kill you I will blow your heads off I will set you on fire and it will feel so good,* and he felt those thoughts enter his gaze, his walk, the line of his mouth.

He thought they would let him pass, but Kurt grabbed his arm and Remy spun with cards burning between his fingers and he threw them at Kurt—through Kurt, because he teleported in a cloud of smoke—and the gym shook again with an explosion that sent Rogue huddling to the ground with her hands over her head, shaking. Remy ran into the hall, cradling Jubilee tight against him. He heard air pop, felt a rush of something cool against his neck, and he turned in time to see Kurt bounce off the wall at his head.

Remy ducked, barely avoiding a set of sharp fingernails that raked the air near his cheek. Kurt said, "Come on now and play," and the voice was different, higher, without any hint of a German accent. Jubilee stirred in Remy's arms and a moment later Kurt screamed. Remy glanced over his shoulder, still running, and saw a glittering cloud of plasma eating through Kurt's clothing, burning his skin.

Remy reached the infirmary and he slapped the intercom, yelling for Ororo to come find him in the medlab.

He lay Jubilee down on the bed and her red eyes were open, conscious, utterly horrified. Bruises marred her swollen face, while her lips looked like one large cut. He thought her nose might be broken.

"He's not there," Jubilee breathed, and the heartbreak in her eyes made him want to go back and kill the bastard for good. "Remy, he's not in there."

"*Ma petite*," he began, but she shook her head.

"No. He would have stopped himself if he had been in there. Wolvie would have stopped. He would never hurt me. *Never.*" Tears trickled from her eyes and Remy smoothed them away with a light touch.

"*Jamais,*" he soothed. "You are right. Wolverine would never hurt you, *ma petite.* Never."

"You sure about that?" said a new voice. Scott. Remy snarled, whirling on the balls of his feet, moving away from Jubilee as fast as he could because Scott had his hand on his visor and red light shot from his eyes, punching a hole through the wall where Remy had stood only seconds before.

Cards sparked hot between his fingers and he flung them hard at Scott, who dodged back into the hall while explosions rocked the walls and floor. Remy stumbled, catching himself, and then raced toward the doorway, grabbing a sheet from the end of a bed and bundling it tight against his chest, burying his hands in cotton and feeling it burn with power. He fought to hold it in, to keep the energy contained, and he tasted blood in his mouth as he bit his lip. He entered the hall and saw Scott sprawled on the ground, trying to stand. Remy smiled and ran right over Scott, draping that sheet on his body as he passed, and he knew the moment it should explode, knew it like the beating of his own heart, but when he heard the final roar, the thunder, the sound was muffled and the air did not shake. He turned and saw Jean at the end of the hall, her hands outstretched, face screwed up in concentration. Scott was still in one piece—unconscious, maybe—but charred bits of ash, the remains of the sheet, fluttered on top of him like dark snow.

"*Merde,*" Remy said, and Jean's face relaxed into a

smile. He felt himself picked up by a hand—her hand, flexing—and he hit the wall hard. Slammed again and again, and he heard Jubilee's faint voice call his name. Jean laughed and he looked at her through the haze of pain, looked and saw her hair begin to rise. Remy felt electricity gather in the air.

Thank you, he thought, just as a bolt of lightning seared the ground near Jean's feet. Remy dropped to the ground. So did Jean, staggering to her knees. He saw Ororo appear from behind her. She held a piece of the torn-up floor, and she brought it down hard over Jean's head.

"Perfect timing," Remy said to her, stepping over Scott's still body.

"I thought so," she said, and ran into the infirmary.

Everywhere Ororo saw a war zone, but nothing was worse than the first moment she saw Jubilee.

"Goddess," she murmured, looking at the girl's ruined face. "Remy, who did this?"

"Wolverine," he said, grim.

"No," Jubilee whispered.

"His impostor," Remy corrected himself. "The impostor did this."

"I'll be fine," Jubilee said weakly. "Really. This just . . . looks bad." She hesitated. "Does it look bad?"

"Badges of war," Remy said gently.

"Oh," she breathed. "That bad."

"I am surprised you are still conscious," Ororo said, fighting for control. Thunder shook the room, accompanied by a cold wind that made her shiver in anticipation. The power tickled her skin; she knew what her eyes would look like if she had a mirror. She was ready—more than ready—and she wanted a fight. One look in Gambit's eyes told her that he felt the same.

First, though, she had to remember Jubilee. She had to focus on what was most important. Everything else was merely icing on the cake. Ororo hurried to the counter where Hank kept his most advanced medical devices, some of which had been borrowed from the Shi'ar. Alien technology could not be beaten in terms of efficiency.

"I'm still conscious because I'm tough," Jubilee said, though Ororo noticed a slight slurring to her words. She thought Jubilee might have a concussion.

"Yes, you are quite tough," Ororo said, in a voice more gentle than she felt. "It is one of your many remarkable talents." Ororo gave her several shots of medicine that Hank always used for those X-Men who had had bad run-ins with tougher and larger adversaries than themselves. She touched Jubilee's hand and said, "Rest. By tomorrow you will feel much better."

"What about the others?" she asked. "What about *him*?"

She could not say his name. Remy swallowed hard. Ororo said, "They are done here, Jubilee. They are done and gone, as of now. I promise you. I will not let this stand, no matter whose bodies they wear."

"Rough," said a familiar voice. Ororo and Remy turned. Scott leaned against the doorway. Remy held up an array of cards.

"Don' move," he said. "Game's over, Scott. Or whoever you are."

"You don't know who I am? I thought the face made it obvious." Scott smiled, cold. He glanced down at Jubilee. "How bad is it?"

"Go to hell," Jubilee said, before either one of them could answer. Her jaw was stiffening up; in another ten minutes she would not be able to talk at all.

"What she said," Remy added.

Scott continued to smile and it was eerie how his expression did not change. Unnatural, as though it had been pasted on his face for him and he could not move his mouth until given permission. His eyes certainly did not reflect that tight smile. His eyes were dark with fury, with rage, and Ororo realized that the hard edge of anger was something she had seen for quite some time now, in all their faces. Subtle, though. Reined in.

She heard movement in the hall behind Scott, and Jean appeared: cold, face sharp. Blood trickled down the side of her temple. Ororo's hair stirred and she knew it was not her own power, but Jean, teasing her, playing without humor. Kurt arrived, followed by Rogue, and finally, as she knew would happen and dreaded, Logan entered the infirmary. Most of his face was missing, but the parts that remained were knitting together before her eyes. His skull glimmered beneath a light sheen of blood.

He did not look at Jubilee, which Ororo found odd. She could not take that as a sign of guilty feelings; rather, almost, as punishment.

Jubilee tried to sit up straight when Logan entered the

room, but Remy put a hand on her shoulder, squeezing gently. She did not relax. Her eyes, what little Ororo could see of them in her swelling face, were haunted.

"What is this?" Ororo asked, preparing herself for battle. She stood straight, tall, summoning the Goddess within her as shield and weapon. She gazed into the faces of those who should have been her friends and said, "Why have you become strangers? Why enemies? Who are you?"

"I don't understand those questions," Scott said. "Why are you asking us these things?"

"Because you are not who you say you are," she whispered, and the quiet in her voice was merely the lull, the prelude to something bigger, devastating. Remy knew her well; he inched closer to Jubilee.

"Maybe *we* don't know who we are," Jean said. "Maybe we're just as confused."

"And maybe I am also tired of games," Ororo said, and let go of her control, tearing down those hard-fought walls she kept around her emotions, those deadly emotions that were the wellspring of her gift, that gave it power. To feel too much was a killing thing—like now, like her rage—and there was no buildup, no slow kiss of wind, but a hurricane ram that knocked the men and women in front of her off their feet, slamming them hard against the wall. Hail cut their faces deep, drawing blood.

She expected them to fight back, looked forward to it with visceral desire, but they did nothing. They lay against the wall like dolls and allowed Ororo to punish them. It made no sense.

" 'Ro," Remy said. "Ease up. Somethin's not right here."

She did not want to ease up. "They should be punished, Remy. For Jubilee, if nothing else."

"Storm," said the girl, but she was cut off by a new voice, a deep voice, one that rang clear as a bell even over the howling of her winds.

"Yes," said that voice. "Yes, that was my thought, as well, given their lackluster performance."

Storm cut the winds. The impostors slumped to the ground as though their wires had been cut. Between them, stepping over them, a man entered through the open doorway. He was tall and elegant, with sharp brown eyes and strong hands. He might have been handsome had it not been for the sickly cast of his skin, the gauntness of his cheeks. He looked tired, but beyond that, deeper, she saw iron resolve.

"Who are you?" Ororo demanded. "How did you enter this school without the alarms going off?"

He smiled. "My name, Ms. Monroe, is Jonas Maguire. I was able to enter this place because I was invited."

"By them," Remy said, gesturing at the group still resting limp on the floor.

"Yes," he said. "I suppose you mind that a great deal."

"*Oui*," Remy snapped.

"And if I told you I was a mutant? Would that make a difference?"

"Not particularly," Ororo said. "What have you done with our friends? Our real friends?"

"They're still alive, though no doubt uncomfortable if

they haven't managed to escape the place I put them. Another special school for gifted youngsters." He smiled. "I was a teacher there myself, though that was not my job description. After observing what you people do here, part of me hopes your friends do escape. I think it would be nice for those five to come back and see the home they can never be a part of again."

"So they're alive," she breathed. "You stole them from their bodies, didn't you? Why? What is the point of such deception, especially one so poorly done?" She wanted to attack him, to slam lightning in his eyes, but she suddenly could not move and her powers refused to respond. So much for the psychic dampener.

"Poorly done?" He looked amused. "And I tried so hard. Oh, well. I won't care much about the execution, as long as I get the job done. And I think I will. I actually think I will be able to do this thing." He held up the newspaper and Ororo saw the front page's news, a discussion of the mutant-rights march. "I had hoped the X-Men would be attending this. It wouldn't have mattered, either way, but this is official. This means the press and the public will be playing close attention to all of you."

Jonas smiled. "Maybe I shouldn't have revealed myself like this. I thought I could wait. I had been waiting for so long already. I did think, however, that the charade would last a little longer. I thought that, despite your suspicions, you would play dumb to see what could be wrong with your teammates, your *friends*. I thought I could do all these things, to learn more about you, but I did not anticipate *my* Wolverine's reaction to the girl.

"If it comforts you," he said to Jubilee, "I did my best to rein her in, but she was too far gone. Her temper is quite fierce. I apologize for that."

"Wha?" Jubilee asked, frowning.

"I need to go," he said. "I'm going to make you all sleep now. I would do more—there are some lovely people the three of you would be perfect in, but my resources are limited. This is the finest balancing act I have ever committed myself to, a great feat of puppetry."

Lassitude swept over Ororo's mind, her body, and she struggled to move anything, including her mind, those heavy thoughts. Those psychic dampeners were worth nothing at all. Jubilee already looked unconscious, while Remy had fallen to one knee. His eyes were half-lidded and Ororo found that she, too, could not keep her eyes open. She saw enough, though. She saw the five fallen X-Men finally stir, rising to their feet and rubbing their heads and eyes as though they had been in a deep sleep. Jonas did not look at them. He stared only at Ororo, and his gaze was wild and dark.

"I am sorry about your roses," he said, "but my boy, your Jean, had to practice certain skills."

"What do you want from us?" Ororo asked, her words slurred.

She heard him say "Nothing. I want nothing from you at all," and then he patted her cheek and told her to sleep. Her eyes drifted shut.

They arrived home after a night of near relentless driving, cramped in a car they stole in Minneapolis, which was a junker on the outside, but had a beauty of an engine that made Logan consider keeping the old sweet Bess when they got back to the Mansion. Not right, of course, but life threw him so many curveballs he thought his karma must really suck. Might as well tack another onto the chopping block of his life.

The closer they got to New York State, the quieter they became. Nerves, fear of the unknown, a lack of certainty about their reception. Hell, they might not be able to get through the front gate and wasn't that going to suck. If that happened, Logan planned on chaining himself to the bars and waiting for the Professor to come home, or for someone to call another telepath. One good mental sweep should do the trick. Wasn't like anyone could mistake his mind for someone else's.

That was the positive side of his thoughts, the ones that led to the good outcome. The other side, the darker side, worried that the Mansion as they knew it would be gone, that all their friends would be hurt or dead, and that the X-Men as a team, a symbol, would never live again. All that work, all those dreams, flushed down the toilet for a reason none of them could yet suss out.

Again, he thought about having to spend the rest of his life as a woman. The prospect still did not appeal. Walking in other people's shoes was an overrated exercise, especially if the only purpose was to build a well-rounded character. He had plenty of character, thank you very much. He did not need any more.

And then, on the fifth morning of their pseudo-captivity, Scott drove up to the gate of their home. It was open, which was slightly unusual, but they pulled in and followed the winding driveway to the house. Everything was very quiet.

"Where are the children?" Jean asked, and they all had the same terrible thought, that one of them, all of them, perhaps, with their bodies, had wreaked some terrible harm upon the young people.

The school still stood, though, and Logan did not see any discernable signs of a firefight. Except for the dead roses—which, if he remembered correctly, had all been very much alive on the day of his departure—nothing seemed out of ordinary. The front door, however, was unlocked.

"I am worried," Kurt said.

"Yes," Scott said, and they entered the house. The security system was off and Scott punched in the code, reinstating the alarms. A warning, if nothing else, to give them time to prepare. Although, in Logan's professional opinion, if they were forced to go up against themselves—which seemed likely, at some point—preparation would not help them in the slightest. Only luck, only resolve. Those were the kinds of things that kept a man living through hard times, and even though they were home, Logan did not think their lives were about to become any easier.

Indeed, the more he walked through the Mansion, soaking in the unrelenting quiet, the unending lack of "presence," familiar or otherwise, the more he prepared himself for something truly horrible, the kind of thing that would create another anniversary, the sort that requires flowers on a grave to mark the passing of another year gone without a dear friend or lover. Logan was far too good about those anniversaries. He never forgot.

"It's like everyone picked up and left," Rogue said.

"I hope they just left," Logan muttered, and ignored the dirty looks his friends gave him.

The first place they found that indicated some kind of trouble was the gym, and there were two clues that made Logan's mouth go dry and his bowels loosen: a yellow leather jacket, and a spot some distance away that was covered in blood and bits of flesh.

He did not wait for the others. Holding the jacket tight against his chest, he raced down the hall toward the infirmary, and when he entered and saw who lay on the bed looking like death warmed over, who lay on the floor on either side looking not much better, a loud shout escaped his throat.

A thin layer of water covered the infirmary's entire floor. He slipped on his way in, falling hard, but crawled the last bit of distance. A quick glance showed him that Ororo and Remy still breathed, though the expressions on their faces looked like trouble had come knocking. He tried shaking them, but they did not respond. Their sleep was unnaturally deep.

Logan stepped over their bodies and sat gingerly on the edge of Jubilee's bed. It was difficult for him to peer into her swollen, beaten face, and he imagined what each blow must have looked like to make those marks. The attacker had been violent, brutal, and unrelenting. The attacker was also someone Jubilee knew, because the kid was too good to be taken down by anyone less than a friend, someone she would be reluctant to hurt too badly.

Logan looked at his hands, soft and round and female. He had a bad feeling about the person who had hurt Jubilee. Very bad.

"What happened here?" Jean asked, leaning over his shoulder to get a better look at Jubilee. "My God. Did one of us do that to her?"

Logan said nothing and Jean gave him a sharp look. "Logan?"

He shook his head, still unable to give voice to his fear, his certainty. He might be wrong, but he doubted it. Things like this he had instincts for. He knew what the work of his hands looked like. Jean squeezed his shoulder.

Scott and Kurt crouched over Ororo. Kurt held a small cup of water.

"I do not know about this," he said.

"Unless you want to start getting physical, use the water."

He did. Ororo stirred. Kurt placed her head in his lap and gently smoothed back her hair, whispering nonsense in German. Slowly, Ororo opened her eyes—

—and froze.

"Who are you?" she said. Her voice sounded hoarse, misused.

Kurt smiled, ever so gently. "I have been away too long, Storm. Maybe I am not blue, maybe I am no longer handsome, but how could you fail to recognize the twinkling light of my eyes? The eyes do not change, *meine schoöne Frau.*"

Ororo blinked. "Kurt?"

"The one and only."

She reached up with a careful hand and touched his face. Tore her gaze from him to stare at the others. She took a deep shuddering breath.

"These last days have been difficult without the five of you," she whispered.

"Have our bodies been here? Where are the children?"

"The children are fine, everyone except for . . . for Jubilee. And yes, your impostors have been here. You need to go after them. I do not know how long I have been unconscious, but the man controlling your counterparts mentioned the mutant-rights march. He is going there. I think he plans on having his impersonators do something that will damage us all." She tried to sit up and Kurt settled her against his chest. "He is a telepath. His name is—"

"—Jonas Maguire," Scott said. "Yes, we know."

"I have something of his," Logan growled. "Maybe a couple somethings."

"Logan?" she said, startled. "Is that you?"

"What? You can see the resemblance?"

She narrowed her eyes and Logan gave her a brief smile before turning his attention back on Jubilee. He felt her watch him and he knew she wanted to say something. He did not ask. He did not let her.

Rogue said, "Remy won't wake up."

"We don't have time to wait on him," Ororo said. "We must go into the city and stop Maguire."

Scott checked the clock. "It's after ten thirty. Isn't the march supposed to start at eleven?"

"Yes, I—" She stopped talking. "I can't move."

"Your spine—" Kurt began, but Ororo shook her head.

"No, he did something to me. My body won't listen." Tears leaked from her eyes. "You need help."

Kurt shook his head. He gave her a quick hug. "As you said, we have no time. We will be fine."

Logan agreed. They were going to be fine because they were too pissed off for anything less. Maguire was going to get stuck on a stick, and roasted like a marshmallow.

Plus, it would be one more for the road. The five of them, finishing what they had started.

Logan did not think that was such a bad way to die.

20

IT WAS GOOD BEING IN A PIECE OF TECHNOLOGY NOT acquired by anything other than cold hard cash. Jean, while she might miss the train ride, did not think she would ever recall those moments of vehicular theft with the kind of fondness that would make her go back for a repeat performance. She also much preferred flying to driving.

"You're thinking dramatic, aren't you?" Scott said to her, when she took her seat beside him at the controls of the mini-jet.

"I'm thinking big," she said. "Epic."

"That's good," he said. "We're going to need something epic in order to get out of this whole and intact."

"Pessi—" She stopped, sensing those fingers in her brain, light and full of fire. So familiar, so—

Jean shut her eyes. Scott said her name, again and again, and she lost the connection in the sound of his voice. The fingers disappeared. So close . . . she had been so close to figuring out what was in her head.

"What is it?" he asked, and he looked so concerned she could not bring herself to be mad at him for interrupting her concentration. They could not read each other's minds anymore, which was a loss that Jean thought they had overcome during the journey. For most of her life she had relied too much on her mind and not on words, not paying attention to the subtleties of an expression or the clear quality of a gaze. Not anymore. Even if she somehow managed to regain her body, she was not going to let herself forget.

They entered the city and Scott put the mini-jet in stealth mode. They found the mutant-rights march without much difficulty. It had been in the works for almost a year, planned for by a coalition of people whose one common bond was that they believed mutants and humans could coexist in respect and peace, each side helping the other in mutually beneficial ways. It was a goal that Charles Xavier supported wholeheartedly, and the X-Men had agreed to be present at the event, both as security and as role models.

"Is this what our body-snatching has been all about?" Rogue wondered out loud. "Just as a means of destroying our reputation?"

"It won't just be our reputation. If the X-Men are seen going wild, it will reflect badly on all mutants, including Maguire." Scott frowned. "Somehow, I don't think he cares."

"We must have burned that guy something good," Logan said quietly. He had the teddy bear in his lap and was staring at it with the same intensity he usually reserved for really good beer, the Super Bowl, or a beautiful woman. Jean smiled. She had seen the teddy bear several times on their trip; Logan occasionally removed it from the sack to stare and prod. Jean thought he and the bear had developed a special language; it told him things about Maguire that it told no one else.

The sun disappeared behind the clouds and the air coming in from the vents smelled sharp, like rain. Jean closed her eyes, drawing in that scent. She summoned up all the strength left to her, everything she would need to fight, and she imagined sharing that strength with her friends. The odds were against them. Only human now, out of shape and exhausted—while their real bodies, those they had been born with, were both gifted and at the top of their form. Jean knew why Ororo was concerned for them, but she also knew that this was their job, to do or die.

We are *going to die*, she thought, but for some reason, the idea did not frighten her. The past few days had soothed her soul in ways she could not yet describe—only, she knew now what she was made of, and though her hardships had not been as great as she thought they would be, it was not strife or fighting that made her feel so polished on the inside. It was living human, being with her friends and seeing how far they could go on so little, and realizing that in her life, they and her husband were all she needed.

And even if she did not have others, she had herself. Herself, stripped down to nothing, no distraction of power, until she could see her spirit clearly. It was a good feeling, that self-knowledge. It made her feel strong.

The heart of downtown came into sight and Scott flew the mini-jet like a sport's car, bending around buildings at breakneck speeds that would have made her sick had she not been concentrating so fiercely on finding their counterparts.

"There," Logan said. "Down below on that rooftop."

Jean looked, and sure enough saw six figures standing on the rooftop edge of an office building, gazing down upon the main core of the parade. She did not know why they were there, rather than on ground level with the other participants, but it made their lives easier. Jean preferred to fight out of the public eye. Too many people could get hurt that way.

Logan said, "Come on, Cyke. What are you waiting for?"

"Nothing," he said, and flashed Jean a quick grin that still managed to warm her toes. "We're going in. Everyone, hang on tight."

She appreciated the warning. A moment later the mini-jet dived toward the earth, streaking past the noses of the impostor X-Men and their handler, winging them in the face with their tail wind. Kurt grinned.

"I am going to enjoy this," he said, "even if it is the last thing I do."

"Might be," Logan said, but he was smiling, too, and Jean knew that his agenda involved a mighty punishment upon himself—or rather, his impostor. Jean did not know how to resolve the paradox of hurting their own bodies as punishment for crimes others committed while using them. It was like hurting themselves—literally—and if they ever were transferred back into their own selves—

That doesn't matter now. The only thing that matters is

keeping these people from hurting innocents, keeping them from ruining the X-Men with their actions. There is more at stake than your lives. You have to do what must be done and don't look back.

The mini-jet rattled, swinging wildly. Scott muttered, "That's it. Chase us, you arrogant little jerks. Come on."

Again, that wild rattle, turbulence so severe Jean thought the jet might come apart. It was her, she realized. Herself, Jean Grey, using telekinesis to rip them apart. Her method was clumsy, though; Jean sensed a lack of any true focus. Only a generalized intent that reminded her of when she had first started using her powers for real and found her mind a clumsy and unwieldy tool.

"They don't know how to use our powers," she said in wonderment, as Scott struggled to find a place on the roof to land. "They have some superficial knowledge, but they're learning about themselves as they go along."

"You sure about that?" Scott asked.

"Yes," Jean said. "Otherwise, I would have disintegrated this jet by now."

"I'm sold," Logan said. "Land this thing, Cyke. Let's end this."

Scott landed on the rooftop, less than a hundred yards from where their counterparts stood, their attention temporarily off the parade. It was a bad area to fight in, but Scott had not wanted to take the risk of trying to lure them away, only to have the impostors stay behind to continue with their plan of discrediting the real team.

Of course, if these men and women were as unskilled

as Jean thought they were, the small fighting space would work to their advantage. The real X-Men were a team of friends and family, and they worked like one. Maguire might have spent the past year prepping his patients to make them more malleable for time in their bodies, but Scott doubted he had taught them other skills. He doubted he had taught them trust.

Trust, which could only be learned through hard experience and shared suffering and joy—things that served to strengthen the bond between his teammates, to turn them into something more than their parts.

Logan was out first, teddy bear in one hand. Rogue followed close at his side, with Kurt beside her. Jean went next, but Scott caught her hand before she left the jet and drew her close for a long hard kiss.

"We'll do that again when this is over," he said.

Jean smiled, caressing his throat. "We'll do more than that," she promised.

The air smelled cold and wet; strong winds whipped their bodies, gusts that threatened to spin Scott's small body end over end. He eyed the competition. Funny, he had fought all these people more than once in Danger Room simulations—and in the flesh—and though he believed he knew their every weakness and how to exploit them, he felt as though all those exercises had to be thrown out because the minds inside the bodies were different, and the psychology of these men and women was even more different than the normal.

Ororo had called Maguire a telepath. A telepath of remarkable strength, if he was able to transfer minds or souls into different bodies willy-nilly. Was he also strong enough to force a mentally disturbed individual into a kind of healing? Temporary or fixed, that was the only way Scott could explain how five individuals with such difficult consistent problems, could stand before him looking competent, ready to fight, like soldiers.

Scott looked at Maguire, but found that the man was focused entirely on the teddy bear in Logan's hand. A look of such haunted despair passed over his face that, for a moment, Scott forgot why they were there. The expression disturbed him; it felt like a reminder of all those times he thought he had lost Jean, and had suffered through the gamut of unbearable pain, mourning the loss of the only woman he had ever loved.

Of course, Jean always managed to come back from the dead. It was a gift of fate that had served her well over the years.

"Where did you get that?" Maguire said to Logan. His voice was low, cultured. "You've been in my home?"

"Yeah," Logan said, hugging that bear to his chest. "Funny, your home. The only two things in it that seem to mean something to you are this bear and the photograph on your desk."

"Give me the bear," he said quietly.

"This bear and I have gotten to be real good friends," Logan said, ignoring Maguire's request. "Real good. Looks to me like it used to be someone else's real good friend. I'd say that someone was a sight smaller than me, though. I'd also guess that the woman in that picture was your wife. And I think I might also guess that something very bad happened to those two people, something that involves us, that created a connection you just couldn't get out of your hair. You couldn't let go. Am I getting close, Jonas? Does any of this ring a bell?"

Scott stared at Logan. Everyone stared, including Maguire. He wore the face of a broken man, but even as his throat worked, his fists clenching tight against his thighs, Scott saw his face go as hard as he had ever seen a man look, and Maguire said, "That would be accurate. You . . . you and your team had a fight with some . . . some renegade mutant. Some *idiot*. My wife and child got in the way. Innocent bystanders. I couldn't save them. I tried. I tried so hard to find bodies to place them in because that's what I do. Just like wrapping a gift, wrapping up my wife, all of her, everything, her soul— and then doing the same to my baby, holding them all inside me, stored so carefully, until I could find them a place to live." He shook his head. "They were too close to death when I got to them. I put them inside me but there was not enough time and they . . . trickled away. I could feel them inside my head, just like sand, and I couldn't save them."

"So you go after us?" Scott said. "You ruin our lives?"

"My wife would still be here if it hadn't been for you and your methods. Every time you fight with someone, an innocent gets hurt. Your powers are simply too great, and the destruction you cause—" He stopped, still looking at the teddy bear. "No, I won't discuss this. You are criminals. If nothing else, you are guilty of manslaughter. Every time a bystander dies when you fight another mutant, you are guilty of such a crime. I want you punished. I want people to see you, always, for what you are."

"All you will do is create more difficulties between mutants and humans," Kurt said. "Surely that is not worth this. Surely your wife would not—"

"You did not know my wife," he said in a deathly quiet voice. "Don't you dare say another word about her."

Scott studied their bodies, the impostors. Not one of them had moved since the beginning of the conversation with Maguire. They stood like statues, without expression.

"You're doing it to them, aren't you?" he said to Maguire. He pointed at them. "You've got all five of their minds inside you right now. That's the only reason they're acting even a little sane. You're controlling how much goes into the body. You're letting in only the good parts, the healthy bits."

Maguire's breath caught. " A good analysis. Yes. Yes, that is what I'm doing."

Jean shook her head. "You'll kill yourself doing that, or go crazy. I don't care how talented or strong you are, one person cannot cope with maintaining five distinct individuals inside their head."

"I don't have to do it much longer. After today, I'll let their minds go. If you want, even, I'll put you back where you belong. Or not."

Jean frowned, looking at her counterpart. She touched her head. "You may not have much of a choice," she said, and Scott gave her a curious look. There was something in her eyes that felt like a promise. Maguire did not notice. He looked at Logan again and held out his hand.

"Make me," Logan said, and reached behind to tuck the bear between his belt and lower back.

Maguire narrowed his eyes.

"Enough," Scott said. "You can't fight all of us, Maguire. Your head is too full."

"That's all right," he said. "This has gone on long enough."

He snapped his fingers. Their counterparts jolted into wakefulness, like watching windup dolls.

"Well," said the impostor Cyclops, sneering. He gazed at Jean. "Isn't this surreal. I never knew what I looked like in real life, outside a mirror."

This was getting too complicated. Scott had assumed that the transfer was a simple crossover, that the woman he now inhabited would inhabit him, and that Cyclops would be quiet, so quiet.

But that would never be believable. That would never work.

Scott gazed at their counterparts and noticed one of them staring at her feet. Rogue. There was no mistaking that quiet avoidance, the shy phobia. An interesting choice. Very calculated. Rogue's power did not require any action on her part to work. All someone around her had to do was drag a person over to be touched.

Wolverine had his claws out, sharpening them on each other like steak knives. He looked at Rogue, their Crazy Jane, and winked. "My body treating you well, *darlin'*?"

Rogue cracked her knuckles. Logan said, "You better

put that focus on me, bub. I'm the one you need to worry about."

"Really. Is this body yours?" Wolverine smiled. "I like it. I like what it can do to people."

Scott watched terrible rage pass through Logan's face, and he thought of Jubilee on that infirmary bed. Oh, yes. Someone was going to pay for that. Dearly, and on many different levels.

Cyclops touched his visor and let off a blast at Scott's head. Scott had never thought anyone could be a bad shot when all you had to do was look at your target, but Jean was right. His aim went wide.

"When I get you?" Cyclops said. "You're dead."

"Maybe," Scott said. "Or maybe you'll be surprised."

The thing about fighting crazy people, Logan thought, was that they behaved in crazy ways. Crazy, unpredictable ways that nonetheless could be counted on for certain constants: Crazy people fight crazy, fighting crazy means fighting the unpredictable, and if you can't predict your opponent, you better stay the hell away because he will take your sorry butt.

Unless, of course, you were just as crazy as he was.

Being all kinds of crazy, Logan was fairly certain he qualified, which meant that he had every confidence the fight would turn in his favor. It had to. There was no way he would let this scumbag keep walking after beating the crap out of a friend.

Wolverine flashed his claws, striking a pose like some wannabe martial arts fanatic: arms over his head; one leg in the air, poised to kick. The Crane, maybe. Logan thought he looked like a fool.

Wolverine sneered. "You scared to come at me?"

"Sure," Logan said. "I'm real terrified."

"Good," he said, too crazy to understand sarcasm. "I'm gonna gut you like a pig."

"Come on, then," Logan said, and kissed the air between them.

Wolverine snarled and lunged. The first time Logan moved fast enough.

The second time, he did not.

Rogue saw the impostor's claws come slashing down against Logan's side; she forget her own obligations, her priority to take care of herself, and ran to him. Around her there was chaos in miniature: Scott, dodging the wild, ill-aimed strikes of his impostor, which also threatened to take out some of the team. She saw Scott get close enough to ram his shoulder into Cyclops's gut; both men tumbled to the ground, grappling with each other.

She came up fast behind Wolverine, the impostor, the real Crazy Jane, and grabbed his head and neck. She remembered the hospital when she touched his bristly hair, the sensation of killing someone by breaking open the skull. She had spent the last few days trying so hard not to remember, to bury it deep like she did most of the unwanted things in her mind, but touching Wolverine brought it back because he moved with the same crazed abandon, the same rage, and he flung her off before she could get a proper grip and take him down.

Wolverine turned on her, claws flashing. Logan rushed him from behind; his face was red and blood streamed down his ribs. For a moment he looked into Rogue's eyes and the message was clear: Get away. Right now.

So she did. Scott and Cyclops still wrestled on the ground, while Jean and her counterpart appeared locked in a staring match. Rogue did not see Maguire anywhere.

She found her impostor standing in the rooftop corner, a lonely slender figure who stared at her feet. Rogue wondered if she had ever appeared so whipped; it was not a good look on her. She stood for a moment with some distance between them, and said, "Hey."

Nothing. Rogue knew quite well what her impostor was capable of; it scared her, she scared herself, but she stepped even closer, and still there was no eye contact, no movement, not even when she nudged her with the tip of her shoe.

"Come on now," she murmured to the impostor. "Sugah, I got better things to do than this."

Still, nothing. Rogue suspected she might be able to put a gun to this woman's head and pull the trigger, all without a single reaction or attempt to escape. Shaking her head, confused, she turned her head and spied Kurt. He stood in the middle of the rooftop, watching Nightcrawler teleport.

With one last glance at her counterpart, she turned and ran to him.

"Hello," Kurt said to her. "No luck with your impersonator?"

"She won't lift a finger against me," Rogue said. "You?"

"I won't let you catch me!" cried the impostor, as he continued to bounce in and out of the sky. Rogue waved a hand in front of her face. The air smelled horrible.

"Doesn't teleporting like that make you sick?" she asked him.

"*Ja.*" Kurt smiled. "Just wait."

She did, and several teleportations later, Nightcrawler dropped out of the sky like a rock and landed between herself and Kurt. He vomited. Rogue nudged his tail with her shoe.

"I expected a little more," she said.

Jean felt as though her brain was on fire. Truly, with flames licking the inside of her skull, little fingers searching the soft tissue for a place to push down burning roots.

The woman across from her said, "I love this."

Jean said nothing at all; if she opened her mouth it would be to scream, and she refused to give her the satisfaction. The impostor was already far too satisfied with the abilities that had been given to her, and Jean knew with quiet certainty that she was being played with. There was nothing subtle about the way that woman used her telepathy. She slapped it about like a great big bat; but she was still kicking Jean's butt, so there was no way for her to feel too superior.

For a moment, though, Jean felt something cool wash through her head, a different kind of fire, and it felt familiar, like home, like all those little touches that had accompanied her on the long journey from Seattle.

And then her counterpart made a flicking motion with

her hand and threw Jean off the side of the building. Jean imagined she heard Scott cry out her name, but the wind was strong and the roar like a train, like that rolling mountain train, and she looked down and the city was rising to meet her like a city parting from the sea, and the fire was gone from her head but she felt those light fingers again and then something deeper, something that made the force of her heart swell and then draw away, sucked outward until a new fire kissed her face, old as the universe and catching her arms like wings, and she cried out—

—and then she was on the roof again and her body was engulfed in fire and her mind felt the touch of the universe singing down into the root of her soul, that old soul, those voices—six billion—rising in a symphony, and she threw herself off the building, the Phoenix diving to earth, and she reached out her hands and caught Jeff's limp empty body, caught him just yards from hitting the packed crowds, and she cradled him in flame and returned to the roof, and began calling for Maguire.

Rogue saw Jean fly off the roof. She raced to the edge of the building, running so fast she caught her foot and skidded hard until she hit the low barrier wall. Tears streamed down her face; she scrambled to her knees to peer over the building's edge and saw a tiny figure hurtling toward the ground. She forgot that she had no powers because the urge to jump after her friend was so great she almost followed. A hand touched her back; Kurt, looking at her with a question in his eyes. She sagged against him.

And then Rogue felt heat and she turned to see wings of fire stretch bright around Jean's impostor. The woman threw herself off the building, streaking toward earth to catch that tiny body before it hit the ground, and Rogue watched, breathless, as they returned to the rooftop.

Kurt said, "Do you think it is possible?"

"I don't know," she said, but the Phoenix alighted beside them and lay down Jeff's body, and Rogue looked into the woman's face and saw something more familiar than simple flesh: a softness in the mouth that did not reach the eyes, those blazing radiant eyes that held a farseeing gaze, the same that had peered out of a man's face for almost a week now. Rogue heard an equally radiant voice, familiar and strong, call out to Maguire. She looked and finally saw him; he stood on the other side of the mini-jet.

Jean went after him. *Their* Jean, back inside her body. Rogue knew it. She touched Kurt's hand and gazed out across the rooftop. She did not like what she saw. Logan was down on the ground, holding his side while trying to dodge the fast strikes of bright claws. Scott's left arm had scorch marks all over it. Cyclops had thrown him off and the distance between them was dangerous; the man danced away, his hand on the visor like it was a lifeline.

Rogue ran to help him. Halfway there, clouds of smoke surrounded her and two strong arms engulfed her waist. She heard Kurt yell out and then the world disappeared—

—and reappeared a quarter of a mile over the city.

"I'm tired of playing games," Nightcrawler said.

He dropped her and disappeared.

She fell to earth, screaming.

Jonas Maguire had one of the most powerful minds Jean had ever encountered. He was not, she thought, a particularly strong telepath in the most basic sense, but the things he could do, his capacity for holding vast amounts of information, staggered her. She peered into Maguire's mind and saw that Renny had returned, but that he was fighting to break free of the trappings that contained him. Renny had tasted Jean's power. He remembered, and he wanted more.

"Return them to their bodies," Jean said, and it was her voice again, her body, and oh what a feeling to come home to familiar flesh, that beautiful shell that was hers and hers alone. "Do it."

"I won't," Maguire said, backing away from her.

"Then I'll force you," she said, and burned past his mental shields. She caught glimpses of his life: a woman stretched beside him on a bed of grass with a baby sleeping between and the sun so soft and warm on their lovely faces, and again, his wife, his Maria, dancing in the kitchen to sweet lullabies as the baby crooned, and later, hugging a teddy bear, and later making love on a quilt, and later, dropping them off for a day of shopping while he went to the hospital, suffering terrible nausea at lunch, awful doom, looking out his office window to see smoke rising and oh, he tried, but he could not take just any body, not that mother over there with her own child, not that man, not that one, or that one, and Maria slipped away into the darkness, the darkness singing to her baby and then he was gone, too, gone from that life until Maguire became something new, something darker, something—

"Stop," he croaked, tears running down his face. "Please."

"Fix them," she said, and still he hesitated. Jean returned to his mind and found the tendrils leading to Mindy who was in Rogue, Rogue who was in Jane, and forced his mind upon the task and watched him make the switch.

Someone caught Rogue before she hit the ground. Dazed, heart thundering, she stared into green eyes and found herself, that shy face that was so familiar. Relieved, she hugged the girl and forgot—she of all people, forgot—and her skin brushed skin, and suddenly she knew what it was like to die from her touch, that black hole made of skin as Rogue fed on Rogue. A sucking sensation, as though every pore in her body pushed outward and shriveled. She imagined what the impostor must be feeling—power and memory, a disparate personality folding over her mind, trying to take control.

The impostor cried out, eyes rolling green into white, and suddenly Rogue was in the air again, free-falling. She saw herself, the woman she had been, floating in the air above with her hands on her head, and all her good will disappeared as she thought, *I hope I drown you.*

And then, abruptly, she was that woman. She was herself in that body that only seconds before had seemed so far away. Rogue hovered in the air and the transition was so seamless that at first she did not realize, did not believe; only, this floating sensation was her still falling, hallucinating.

But she looked down and saw Jane rushing away from her, flailing in the air. Rogue moved on instinct, dropping like a stone, and it was beautiful to have a body that obeyed her when she wanted to defy gravity.

She caught Jane, but the woman barely breathed. Rogue remembered her dying self, caught in the web of her skin. It was not a good memory. She returned to the rooftop.

Mindy now waited inside Maguire's brain, but she and Renny both were burst from the seams of their confinement, flooding into that place where Maguire kept his own sacred space, and Jean could not stop the flow of their spirits, or how they overwhelmed. She tried to help him, but—

—Logan was next.

It was always a lie when people said they were prepared to meet their end. Logan had told that lie once or twice, and he was telling it to himself again. He was bleeding pretty bad. Not that it was getting his spirits down or anything.

He staggered to his feet and managed to dodge a direct blow to his stomach. Those claws sank into his lungs instead. He tasted blood, and gazed into his own smirking face—

—and then he found himself on the other side of the claws and his body felt good and strong, and oh—oh, poor kid, that poor girl—and he sheathed his claws and caught Patty as she fell to the ground, dead. The teddy bear stuck in the back of her belt looked especially mournful.

Jane did not want to leave Wolverine's body. She fought viciously and nothing Jean did could hold her. She wanted blood and she went after the sweet spot inside Maguire's mind, tearing out a chunk. Jonas screamed.

Jean tried not to listen. She found Kurt and—

—his counterpart enjoyed this joke a little too much, dropping people off in the middle of the sky and then dashing away to parts unknown. Kurt thought it was especially rude, and especially terrifying to be free-falling through the sky, but he saw Rogue fly toward him and he trusted her to catch him—

—and she did, but Kurt watched her do it from a distance and he looked down at his hands, his lovely blue hands with their thick nails and oh! His tail. Oh, how very wonderful to be home again.

Patty was harder. Not as bad as Jane, but she whined a lot more and at this point Maguire was no longer building barriers. Patty flowed like a snake from Nightcrawler into the corners of Maguire's mind, writhing on a round white belly, but Jean had no more time for these people because Scott was the only one left, and she did this one special, with a light touch—

—a very light touch on his mind, and he knew it was Jean the moment she entered his thoughts, because though she had flown off the roof, the Phoenix always rose: his Jean, his lovely wife with her beautiful heart, and she carried him from that burning, hurting place— his borrowed body seared, skin cracked and black and peeling, his lungs full of fire—and with a sharp kick she knocked the malevolent stranger out of his real body.

She placed his soul inside the flesh, settled him sweet, and with a kiss and a touch unwound a golden thread, pinning it to his heart, pinning it to hers.

And then he opened his eyes and the world was red again and Jean stood in front of him, radiant in that red, and he leaned forward and hugged her.

21

THEY DID NOT ATTEND THE MUTANT-RIGHTS MARCH.
Jean used her telekinesis to gather up the bodies. Careful,
quick, because Logan heard helicopters coming: news re-
porters or the police, who had probably noticed some
commotion on the rooftop. A beautiful thing, being able
to hear them coming.

He thought it was another beautiful thing to see their
impostors, those lost men and women, float through the
air to the mini-jet. Beautiful, because Jean was back to
her old self, powers intact. And yet, he felt an odd sadness
in his heart when he looked at the woman he had lived
in. Patty, dead. He even felt sorry for Mindy, whose heart
had stopped soon after Scott left her body.

The rest of them stared unblinking, unmoving. Logan
studied their faces, trying not to be distracted by the
smells and sounds rushing through him, or the familiar
weight of his skeleton, grounding him to earth. He
rubbed his knuckles and felt a good sharpness just beneath his skin.

The X-Men piled into the mini-jet. Maguire sat up-
right in the back, eyes open but unseeing, restrained only
by the force of Jean's mind. Drool dripped down his chin.

Scott spared him a quick glance before powering the jet engines.

"Well," he said, quiet. "At least we're home."

It was good to be home again. Little comforts, like the luxury of hot coffee in the morning, a shower, actual toilets. Beds, washers and dryers, a closet full of clothes, not going hungry because forty dollars might have to last five people on a trip across America.

And yet, Rogue would not give up those memories for anything.

Maybe one I would. If I could, I would change that, at least.

A man dead. Rogue thought about calling the administrator at Belldonne to wheedle out the name she had wanted so badly. She knew what Logan would say: that she was a glutton for punishment, better to leave well enough alone.

She stood in the doorway of the infirmary and watched Logan sit on the edge of Jubilee's bed. The girl was still asleep.

Remy was not. He lay very still in the next bed with only his eyes moving, glittering in the light. He looked terrible; the left side of his body was one large bruise and his lips were cracked. He said nothing to her, simply waiting. Rogue remembered what it was like without her powers—her fear and insecurity—how she had been uncomfortable touching even when she could.

You need to grow up, she told herself. *Or else stop complaining about the hand that's been given you. The only thing keeping you from being happy is yourself. It doesn't have anything to do with skin.*

No, nothing at all to do with that. Rogue reached into her pocket to finger the card that Suzy had given her. Nine of spades, dreams and illusion. Her skin was the illusion, her excuse. Untouchable body, untouchable heart: the perfect recipe for never getting hurt.

Rogue walked to Remy. She watched him take a deep breath. He did not say anything, just reached for her. Rogue fought her instincts and did not pull away as his fingers wrapped loose around her covered wrist. She sat down beside him and kissed the air above his head.

"I'm glad to see your eyes again," he murmured. "I missed that about you."

"That so?" she asked lightly. "I was here the entire time, sugah. I'm sure you saw plenty."

"No," he said, and his hand tightened. "Your body wasn't what I missed."

Heat spread through her face. She forgot how to speak.

Remy smiled.

Logan paid no attention to the lovebirds. A distant part of him was happy for Rogue, that she was there and touching and being touched. *About time,* he thought. Maybe the trip into someone else's body had been good for her, after all.

It certainly had not been good for Logan, nor Jubilee. He watched the girl's face, hurting for her, trying not to imagine what had happened but knowing exactly: each punch, each touch fueled by rage.

When she finally began to stir, to open her eyes, he felt a moment of panic.

This was a bad idea. What were you thinking, making yourself the first thing she sees? You'll scare the kid.

He stood, but before he could take a step he felt a small hand grab his fingers. Jubilee still had her eyes closed.

"Hey, Wolvie," she whispered.

Logan swallowed hard. "Hey. How're you feeling, darlin'?"

"Not bad," she said, and tugged on his hand. He sat, perching uncomfortably on the edge of the bed in case she freaked out and he needed to run. But she just smiled, and finally opened her eyes.

"I'm sorry," he said. He had not intended to apologize for anything, but the words slipped out, hoarse and broken.

"Wasn't you," she said. "I figured that out."

"But it was my body. I thought . . . I thought you would be afraid of me for that."

"Dude," she said, those fearless blue eyes still staring at him. "You're crazy."

A short gasp of laughter escaped him. Gentle, slow, he reached out and ruffled her hair.

"Yeah, kid," he whispered. "I suppose I am."

The rest of the team eventually trickled into the infirmary. They brought chairs with them, or perched on empty beds. It was good to be together. Home, again. Jean gazed around at all their faces, familiar as her own, and for a moment missed those worn human bodies that had carried them across the country, and which now lay in comas, kept alive by machines.

For a while no one said much, and then, slowly, with great detail and occasional laughter, they told their stories—the escape, the journey—or here at the Mansion, the unraveling mystery of the impostors.

"So that's how it goes," Jean said, when almost everything else had been told and all that was left was the how and why of their survival. "All those times I thought I felt Cerebro or my counterpart, it was really just the Phoenix."

"I still don't get it," Rogue said. Remy sat behind her with his arm draped over her shoulder, his hands occasionally playing with her hair. Rogue had a lot of color in her cheeks.

"The Phoenix force is separate from my mutant abilities, although it does add to and enhance them. When I was taken from my body, the Phoenix was left behind, but it . . . recognized the difference. It knew that I was gone—me, Jean Grey—and it went searching for me. I think it would have stayed, but Jeff's body wasn't compatible for what it wanted. When I got face-to-face with *my* body, though, the Phoenix . . . arranged things to its satisfaction."

"Meaning it switched you back?"

"Exactly."

"Nice," Logan said. Jubilee sat close beside him, not a sign of unease in her slim body. Jean thought Logan looked more rattled. She did not blame him; knowing that her body had been used to harm Remy . . . well, it did not get much worse than that. She still felt responsible.

"I called the hospital," Scott said, propping his feet up on a bed railing. "There's no change in Maguire. He's still a vegetable. Same with our . . . hosts."

"As far as Maguire goes, there isn't ever going to be a change," Jean said. "His identity got eaten alive by those five, and they're too lost in him to ever return to their own bodies. They are stuck there together until the day he dies." Not that Patty or Mindy ever had a choice in the matter. Their bodies had died in the fight; they were lost forever.

"He is a relatively young man," Kurt said, his voice heavy with meaning, and that was something Jean did not want to think about. Maguire's body was in the most terrible kind of prison, the darkest mirror for minds with nothing to do but reflect upon each other the worst of their madness. Jean had returned to Maguire's mind one more time before dropping him and the others off at a private hospital where Xavier had connections, the influence to buy quality care without any questions asked.

She did not want to enter his mind again. At least not for some time.

"We do bear some of the responsibility," Ororo said quietly, looking over Logan's shoulder at the teddy bear in his lap. "We killed his family."

"We killed a lot more than that," Scott said. "We have a lot to answer for."

"Even if it was just an accident?" Jubilee asked.

"Dead is dead," Rogue said, looking at her hands. "Doesn't matter if you kill by accident. There's always a price to pay."

"Perhaps we did not pay enough," Kurt mused.

Logan held up the teddy bear, its fur scruffy and worn and sweet.

"We're paying," he said quietly. "I think we'll keep paying, for a long time yet."

A low chime sounded through the room: the alarm. Scott ran to the wall monitor and patched in to the main computer.

"Trouble," he said. "The Brotherhood, maybe. Police reports are coming in from Atlanta."

They all looked at each other, silent and unmoving.

"We'll be careful this time," Jean said, but her voice wavered, uncertain.

"Yeah," Logan said, handing the teddy bear to Jubilee. He stared into the girl's broken face and said, "I guess we know the alternative."

Epilogue

SEVERAL WEEKS LATER, AN ENVELOPE FROM A LAW OF-fice in North Dakota arrived for Scott Summers, Jean Grey, Logan, Rogue, and Kurt Wagner. The envelope contained two letters and a key. The first letter was dated two days after their arrival home in New York.

"What's that?" Jean asked, peering over Scott's shoulder.

"It's James," Scott said. "He finally remembered where he heard the name. He's leaving his home and land in care of the school."

"Oh," she breathed. "Oh, my."

The second letter, from the attorney, said just a little more.

That afternoon the five of them flew out to North Dakota to bury James. They dug the hole with shovels and pickaxes, and laid him to rest beside his wife. They did not say any words, but sat beside his grave for a time, watching the sun cross the sky and the grass thrush in the wind. The lilac tree, though it had no blooms, looked especially pretty.

They left after the stars came out. Dog went with them.

About the Author

Marjorie M. Liu is an attorney who has worked and traveled throughout Asia. When not writing, she enjoys reading comic books, designing websites, and returning to old movie favorites, some of which involve light sabers, various applications of the Force, and small green men with pointy ears. To learn more, please visit her website at www.marjoriemliu.com.